THE INTERRUPTION

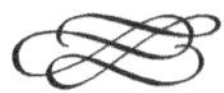

JACKI KELLY

OTHER BOOKS BY JACKI KELLY

THE SWEET ROAD SERIES
The Sweet Road Home
The Sweet Road To Love
The Sweet Road Back

DATING JUST GOT SERIOUS
Blind Date
One Date At A Time
Date Me
A Single Date
Speed Date
Done With Dating
Fear of Dating
Dating Just Got Serious – Box Set

OTHER BOOKS BY JACKI KELLY

THE BAPTISTE SERIES
Packed And Ready To Go
Going Backwards

THE SEBASTIAN ISLAND SERIES
Pictures From Paradise
Trouble In Paradise

THE RULES SERIES
Played By The Rules
Rules Don't Apply

OTHER BOOKS
A Season of Bliss
In Pursuit of Perfection

PLAYED BY THE RULES

Jacki Kelly

Copyright 2024 by Kelly, Jacki

ISBN: 978-1-942202-35-6

First Edition Electronic February 2024

Published by Yobachi Publishing, LLC

This is a book of fiction. Names, characters, places, and incidents either are the product of the author's imagination or are used fictitiously. Any resemblance to actual persons, living or dead, or events or locales is entirely coincidental.

All rights reserved. The reproduction or utilization of this work in any form or in any part by any means electronic, photocopying, or other means available now or in the future is forbidden without written permission. For permission, please contact JACKI KELLY at jackikellybooks@gmail.com.

NEWSLETTER SIGN-UP

Keep up with all Jacki Kelly book releases and projects. And, of course, there is always a giveaway. Don't miss out. Join her newsletter by clicking the link below. Don't worry. She won't spam you or flood your inbox.

https://jackikelly.com

This book is dedicated to all the women who pushed me to keep writing even when I thought my muse had moved on to more fertile ground. And also, to those who told me I'd stepped out of my box and charted new territory with this book.

S TRIKE ONE

Odessa

No matter how hard I tried, I couldn't erase the thoughts crawling through my head like worms eating through a corpse.

Every one of my grandmother's conversations about The Interruption played in my head like a kid with a new toy. According to her, sometimes, souls got stuck on the way to their final destination. She said there were lots of reasons why that happened, but none of them was good. Grandma always talked about folks she thought who got stuck and wreaked havoc on the living. She thought she and Grandpa lived all those years in that run-down shack sharecropping for awful folks because someone stuck in the Interruption had a vendetta against her ancestors.

That apparition who snatched me before I reached heaven must have thought I had unfinished business, too, and if I did, it had to be with Daniel. That old husband of mine was an evil man. Every one of his indiscretions was as new and raw as the day he'd inflicted them. I wasn't going to be satisfied until he was as dead as me.

I wiggled my swollen toes in the grass. A pair of shoes would have been nice, but I didn't need them where I was going. Daniel hadn't spent any of my insurance money on my burial, which was obvious from my faded house dress and no wig on my head. My good church wig was probably still sitting on the top shelf of my closet if Daniel hadn't thrown all my belongings away. I patted my hair. At least my cornrows were neat.

According to that apparition, I had a short time to correct all the wrongs I did before moving to the next portal.

The way I figured, in that time, I could best anyone who had ever wronged me, too. But only one person came to mind.

Daniel.

That bastard had made my life miserable. He'd woke up every morning looking for ways to rain on my sunshine. Sure, other people had crossed me, but not like him.

Nobody was as bad as him.

Nobody was as mean as him.

And nobody deserved a comeuppance more than him.

I stood and stretched my arms toward the source of my strength the way the Good Book says we should. Because if I walked in the house looking like myself—a ghost—he'd drop dead from a heart attack before I could lay a hand on him. And God knew I wanted to harm him like he'd done me all those years.

With my eyes closed, I envisioned myself taller, slimmer, younger, and without the missing teeth. I knew what kind of woman Daniel liked, and she didn't look—or act—like me.

Within seconds, my sagging, aged skin tightened and was as smooth as the yellow silk dress that now clad my body. My knotted, arthritic hands looked soft as a summer sky. Even my swollen toes fit into the heeled pumps that I spirited for my feet.

If I'd had this kind of power when I was living, I could have done and been so much more. Too bad this magic was only for dead folks.

The recently dead.

My grandma—who raised me because my momma was too busy hanging in the juke joint and laying about with men —used to talk about the Interruption. Her grandparents from Africa spoke about the place between Heaven and Hell where dead souls got stuck when they had debts with the living or the dead that remained unsettled. Of course, I thought it was all talk, but here I was, waiting on one of them angels to swoop down and carry me to glory.

I checked my appearance in a car's side mirror. The familiar folds in my mahogany skin were gone. The face staring back at me was as unknown to me as everything else. I wasn't asking any questions. I would use this power until it ran out.

I stood on the sidewalk and looked up at the house I bought with my money. I often wondered if Daniel had married me because of that house. In the beginning, I let him strut around like he was a king because I wanted him to feel comfortable. But it didn't take long for him to act like he used his money to buy the house. I shook my head as the thought made me sad.

I focused on the flower garden where my yellow snapdragons bloomed. The weeds had already taken over, but everything else about the house still made me proud. I imagined Daniel wouldn't keep it up. He'd live in it until it fell around him. He valued nothing.

I knocked on the door, forgetting the days when I struggled with the groceries and the key to get into my own house and Daniel was too lazy to get off his rear end to help me.

"Who is it?" Daniel's gruff voice hadn't changed. I guess I'd expected it to soften as he mourned my absence.

"Ruth." I used my grandmother's name. He wouldn't recognize it since he paid such little attention to me.

He opened the door. "Do I know you?" He studied my face while his barrel chest blocked the entrance.

"The church asked me to stop over to see if you needed any help. Since you lost your wife, the elders thought you might need assistance." I bustled by him, stood in the entrance hall for a moment, and then made my way to the kitchen. "Let me fix you some lunch. You probably haven't eaten yet today."

"Well, that sure was nice of the church. At least the congregation was considerate enough to send me a pretty thing." He followed behind me like a dog sniffing after a treat.

I opened the ice box and peered inside. "What do you know about First Baptist? I've never seen you at a service."

"I don't have time for that, but my wife used to go whenever the doors opened." He settled in the chair. The only time Daniel came into the kitchen while I labored over his meals was to bark orders.

"Why don't you go to the living room and enjoy your ball game while I fix this meal?" I picked up a spatula, and tried to shoo him away with it, but like a fly on shit, he wouldn't budge.

"I'll sit here and watch you. There's plenty of food here. Those church folks have been bringing food every day since Odessa passed."

"Do you miss your wife?" I didn't dare look at him, or I might get on with what I had planned instead of savoring every minute.

"I stopped missing her a long time ago, well before she died. Odessa was pretty when we first married, but she let herself go."

Heat marched up my back. The slow burn was as familiar to my dead soul as it was when I was living. "Taking care of a family is hard work. On the other hand, maybe she was doing her best."

"It doesn't matter now." He smacked his lips. "She's gone, and it's time for me to get on with my life. You married?"

As if that mattered to him. "No." I faced him, still holding the spatula before me. "What do you have planned? Now that you're all alone?"

"Odessa left me some insurance money. So I'm going to take a trip. A nice one. First-class all the way." He looked up like a film of his excursion played on the ceiling.

I may have looked different, but I didn't feel different. It took a few years for me to give up on my love for him. He'd mashed it down until the only thing left was contempt. Contempt sat on my chest, burning a hole in the remnant of my soul.

I busied myself fixing the steak. Daniel loved his red meat more than he ever loved me. I pulled seasonings from the cabinet, and Daniel never asked how I knew where to find the ingredients. Even when I put the frying pan on the stove, he was too busy gawking at my ass to notice I never turned on the flame. My legs in those heels were enough to keep him distracted from the sorcery whirling around the room. The drool gathering at the corner of his mouth threatened to roll down his chin and stain his shirt.

I imagined he wanted this version of me in his bed while he huffed and puffed for satisfaction and forgot about mine, as usual.

I held that russet potato in my hand and let the heat from my soul soften it enough to eat.

He inhaled a deep breath when I placed the plate in front of him. "Girl, this sure does look good. Aren't you going to eat, too?"

I slid into the seat across from him and positioned my chin in my palm. "This isn't about me. It's about you." I gazed at him like he was the god he thought he was.

He sliced the steak and shoved a massive piece in his mouth. I hoped he wouldn't choke on it before I had a chance at him.

With every bite, I searched his face, trying to remember what he'd done to make me follow behind him like one of those blind mice. Maybe he'd had a special power and had used it on me like I was getting ready to use mine on him.

He chewed with his mouth open. "How about we go out this weekend? I'm tired of eating at home."

I batted my eyes. "Your wife isn't even cold in her grave yet."

He laughed with a mouth full of food. "Odessa is gone, and even when she was here, it never stopped me. Sitting here, crying over her, won't bring her back. A man has got to keep living." He finished the last piece of his steak and rubbed his stomach like always.

"I'll think about it." I stood. "For now, go sit in the living room while I tidy up. I'll come right in."

He was out of the kitchen without offering to help me clean. That man wasn't ever going to change. I stretched my hands over my head to return the kitchen to its pristine state. Then I made my way to the living room. The back of Daniel's head rested on the chair while he stared at the television screen. His coarse hair had thinned since I last looked.

I never made a sound as I walked into that room. It wouldn't have mattered. With his belly full and his favorite team winning, he wouldn't have cared.

He moaned when I slipped my arms around his shoulders and rested my left hand over his heart. He thought he deserved the attention of a pretty young woman. His heart pounded against my palm. Daniel couldn't move. I made sure of it. Without removing my hand from over his heart, I made my way in front of Daniel.

He didn't flinch. Instead, he stared at my face. "What the hell?"

"Shh, don't talk. It will hurt less."

I closed my eyes long enough to return to Odessa. The silk dress loosened, fading back into my house dress. My skin gave way to gravity and wrinkled like a dried prune.

His eyes widened with the kind of fear I knew so well.

He needed to see me—the woman he'd mistreated instead of loved.

He needed to know I was the one that brought his demise.

He needed to see what he'd done to me.

I watched as our thirty-year marriage flashed before him. He winced with each vile word he'd spoken to me and gasped at each blow he'd inflicted. The way he squirmed under my hold and the fear that darkened his eyes satisfied me. I wanted him to see the torture I'd lived.

When the tableau ended, he tried to talk, but I wasn't listening to his sorries. With my hand, I penetrated his shirt, then dove into his flesh and grabbed hold of his pulsing heart. I yanked it free from his chest without leaving a scar or spilling a single drop of blood.

I held his evil heart in the palm of my hand, pushing it close to his face. I clamped my other hand on his shoulder and held it firm when he tried to pull away.

I moved my face within inches of his. "You never had any heart while I was living, so you don't need it now."

His face locked in fear as he drew his last breath. A moment later, his heart evaporated.

I walked out of the house with a chuckle. The coroner wouldn't be able to explain what happened here.

STRIKE TWO

Willa

I used to be a strong woman who knew what she wanted and had the confidence to go after her dream. I haven't seen that version of myself in a long time. What children and an unfaithful husband can do to your mind is amazing. They zap the juice from you.

I reached under the kitchen sink, shoved the cleaners aside, and grabbed my bottle of vodka. Since I was the only person in the house capable of cleaning, my drink of choice was safe there.

I held the bottle high and scrutinized the contents. It was just enough to carry me through the early evening hours. I poured it into the glass of iced tea and took a swallow.

From upstairs, the raised voices of my teenagers bickering over whose turn it was to take the dog for a walk reached me. A few minutes before, they argued about the latest streaming video. If the two weren't quarreling, they ignored each other, and the house was as quiet as a mausoleum. Just like their father, they found lots of ways to ignore me. But I had what I needed in my vodka. It wasn't an even exchange, but life seldom gave me what I thought I deserved.

The dog strolled into the kitchen and settled next to me. Rex had been part of the family for seven years. And in all that time, the kids still hadn't figured out a schedule for taking him for some exercise.

They'd wanted a pet and promised me the sun and the moon if I let them have one. I was stupid enough to think they intended to brush him, feed him, clean up after him, and love him. But now he was my dog. I should have known they wouldn't keep their commitments. I added their broken promises to my list where all the other broken promises lived. But mothers always had hope and dreams. Otherwise, we wouldn't crawl out of bed in the morning.

No one was more gullible than a mother. Added to that, I was also a trusting wife. Well, no wonder I was such a sad sack, sneaking drinks every chance I got—hiding my liquor in my iced tea, orange juice, and coffee. I looked forward to the numbing sensation that took the edge off my days and dropped me into bed at night.

Rex glanced at me while I rinsed the last of the tomato sauce from a plate and stuck it in the dishwasher. His tail wagged faster with every minute it took me to get him outside.

Instead of shouting upstairs for Ava and BJ to shut up, I grabbed the leash off the hook and clamped it around Rex's neck. "I love you, doggy." I rubbed the top of his head and gazed into his soulful brown eyes. "I wish everyone in this house was as loving and patient as you."

I reached for my glass and drained the contents. If my husband, Burt, was home—like he had promised to be—I'm sure I wouldn't have had that third drink, but there are only so many broken promises a person can take without resorting to alternative methods to ease the pain.

At least I wasn't like my friend, Judy, who handled her divorce by running up her credit cards and then had to take a second job as a house cleaner to feed her three children and keep a roof over her head. Yeah, I was better than that.

Burt and I hadn't come to the point of discussing divorce. We had a beautiful home. I drove a brand-new Buick and never wanted for anything material. It was only the intangible stuff I couldn't get my hands on, like love, patience, and understanding. But I didn't want to be single or raise Ava and BJ alone. So, I drank away the unhappiness I couldn't shake.

"I'm going to take Rex to the park," I yelled upstairs and

waited for one of them to come dashing down to tell me they'd do it instead.

"Wait, Mom." Ava appeared on the landing.

My heart leaped. Could it be that one of my children would do what I asked hours ago?

"Don't forget we have to pick up my prom dress tomorrow. The store closes at three." Ava was all bright-eyed and excited. Her hair was shiny again, and the pale look of death had finally vanished from her face.

I should have been happy to have her back home and acting like an average teenager. When she returned from rehab this time, I thought Burt would be different, or we would be different. Neither Burt nor I wanted her to fall off the wagon again. That last bout was rough, with the stealing, the lying, and the days of not coming home while she binged in some drug house. Burt and I hadn't slept for weeks while we waited for news about her. I couldn't help thinking the police would knock on the door and tell me they'd found my beautiful daughter dead. But after her return and the long stint to get her clean, it hadn't taken Burt long to slip away again. This time, instead of begging him to love us all a bit more, I gave up.

I had to stop wanting more and more. Happiness was always in front of me until I stuck out my hand to grab it, and then it slipped through my fingers.

I blinked back my disappointment and focused on Ava's sweet face. "Yes, I know. I'll get it tomorrow when I'm running errands."

"That's what you said today." She threw her hands in the air. "And no dress."

"Ava, don't worry. I put a note on the refrigerator." Looking up at her made me dizzy, so I started for the garage.

"Mom, don't forget." She always had to get the last word,

as if it were her job to raise me instead of the other way around.

I picked up the empty vodka bottle and tucked it under my arm—no use leaving evidence behind.

In the garage, I secured Rex in the back seat of the car, then placed the bottle on the passenger side floor. I'd drop it in the waste bin in the park. My family didn't know I soothed my sadness with liquor. It was my secret, and I wanted to keep it that way. We had enough to worry about with Ava and BJ.

I wondered what little teenage secrets BJ hid from us. If I had to guess, I'd say it was an excessive masturbation based on his long showers, stained bedsheets, and the abundance of traits he claimed from his father.

With the key in the ignition, I started the engine and put the car in reverse. Glancing in the rearview mirror reminded me I hadn't opened the garage door. I pushed the button on the visor and waited for the door to rise.

I'd had a lot to drink tonight. As soon as I got home, I'd turn in. No use waiting on Burt to come home. If true to form, he'd climb into bed well after midnight, cozy up to me, and give me a quick finger job. Of course, he'd expect that to satisfy me—until he saved some of his sexual prowess to make love to me properly—and with me shit-faced, I'd be happy he'd even remembered I had a pussy that needed tweaking now and again.

Rex whined. He really needed to go. He would have been happy to do his business in the yard, but I needed to get away from the house for a few minutes, so I hoped he'd wait.

Even though the speed limit was twenty-five, I pressed my foot harder on the accelerator. I didn't want Rex to have an accident and erase my new car smell.

The deserted streets said everyone was where they needed to be for the night. The park was empty, so I didn't need to park properly. I pulled up near a cluster of trees, and grabbed the poop bag from the console and the empty bottle from the floor.

"Okay, Rex. It's your time."

He licked my face as I released him from the restraint, then dragged me into the park. It was my fault for making him wait so long.

In a short time, Rex raised his leg beside a tree and peed a small lake. After walking a few feet, he squatted again and did his stinky business.

After picking up his waste, we strolled a bit. Rex pulled me along while he sniffed every few feet. The walking and the tugging cleared my fog, making all my problems rush at me, fresh and unresolved.

The pain settled in my chest like a hot blade. I couldn't help wondering why I'd accepted so little. Burt didn't love me the way he used to, which made me think no one else would. Though I loved the kids with my whole heart, they were a disappointment. The cuddly babies that had brought me so much joy now only dished out pain. I know they were trying to find their way in the world. I didn't think it had to come with so much back talk, disrespect, and acting out. Was I so unlovable that everyone I cared about couldn't return an inkling of consideration?

I stopped to catch my breath and ease the load on my shoulders. Instead of the clear night sky buoying the weight, the stars appeared as lonely as me, each individually spaced as if it existed alone in the darkened night sky.

At the trash bin, I dropped the poop bag and bottle, pulled Rex back toward the car, and secured him.

As if I was fooling anyone, I headed toward the expressway to a liquor store across town. Having a shop owner become familiar with my habit was a line I didn't want to cross.

The moment I walked inside, my nerves settled. Being near my favorite brand of vodka was enough to calm me. I walked the aisle and looked at all the brands, fingering a few along the way. The varieties made my mouth water. I wanted to taste them all and wondered if the more expensive ones would numb me better than the others. Finally, I reached for the label I knew best. With one in each hand, I paid for my purchase and returned to the car.

Without locking the door or putting on my seatbelt, I opened the bottle, inhaled, and swallowed the saliva gathering in my mouth. Excitement rushed through my chest. The first sip coated my mouth and stung the back of my throat. By the third gulp, relief engulfed me, helping me forget all the sadness waiting at home.

Rex whined as if he needed a drink from my bottle.

I glanced at him, then settled back in the seat and waited for the edge to melt away. I took another swallow—a bigger one. With my head against the rest, the knots that had tied me up loosened. For several moments, warmth washed over me and buffed away the sharpness that shredded everything in my life. It felt like I was relaxing in a hot tub, my body soothed by the water.

When I couldn't put it off any longer, I shoved the half-empty bottle under the passenger seat and headed toward the expressway. With the windows open, the cool breeze blew my hair across my face. I had no idea what time Burt would make an appearance, but I wanted to shower and be in bed before he got home.

The vodka bottle rolled out, and I quickly reached down for it.

I looked back at the road.

Why was I in oncoming traffic?

By the time I saw the car, it was too late.

I jammed on the brakes.

The car spun sideways.

With stiff arms, I gripped the steering wheel, willing the car to stop.

It didn't slow fast enough.

The mouth of the young girl in the backseat of the other car formed a perfect 'O'.

She made no sound.

The adults in the front seat wore stunned expressions before impact.

Then my world went black.

STRIKE THREE

Ronita

Cato sat two rows behind me in the back row of the classroom. He slouched at his desk and stared at his dirty fingernails. Even from where I sat in the middle of the room, I detected his foul mood.

Every few minutes, I pretended to glance at the boards across the room so that I could sort out his expression and figure out what caused his bad mood.

He glanced up and nodded. Cato's gaze felt like a warm hug, making my skin tingle with excitement. But he was so absorbed in the stuff going on in his life that he doled attention in bite-size conversations as if pouring too much at one time might render him helpless.

I faced forward, satisfied with the sensation that we had a thing. It took me a long time to get him to notice I had a pulse. For months, I'd primped and preened to get his attention, but he was immune to my flirtations.

I wasn't particularly good at flirting since I'd never had a boyfriend or any male relationships, but I'd watched enough television to give me ideas.

My plan for Cato started at the beginning of the school year and had taken more time to implement than I'd imagined, but now we were here. Finally, we had a plan, and thinking about it kept my stomach in knots all day. But I wasn't going to graduate from high school without seeing it through.

And time was running out. Only ten days to finals week.

The teacher tapped his pointer on my desk. "Ronita, can you answer the question?"

"Uh … uh." I glanced down at my textbook. "No." I barely

heard my reply and willed myself not to pee in my pants at being caught unprepared.

"You've been distracted all morning." Mr. Moore's sounded firm. "Pay attention."

I nodded.

I didn't want him to make another call to my mother. She was already threatening to take away my phone. But History was the last thing I wanted to think about. Even so, I sat up straighter to satisfy Mr. Moore.

Cato cleared his throat, but I refused to look in his direction. I imagined he was pleased with himself for getting me in trouble. I couldn't explain why Cato drew my attention, but he was like a magnet. I knew the difference between right and wrong. I'd learned how far I could push my mother before she'd take my phone or ground me, but when it came to Cato, I was willing to risk everything to be in his company —for him to talk to me, smile at me, give me the tiniest bit of attention.

He was cool and smarter than he looked, but my mom would find something bad to say about him. According to her, nobody was good enough for me. If only she knew that I wasn't good enough for anybody.

I didn't want to pretend to be a good girl anymore.

It was boring, and it wasn't me.

On the inside, I was a different person. I often felt like I lived outside of my skin and watched a version of myself going through the day.

School boys wanted easy girls who made out behind the school or dropped to their knees to give head—girls who laughed and had friends.

Fun girls.

I was ready to be one of those girls, but Cato treated me like his kid sister, which had to end today.

If I waited another year, I was afraid I'd never break free, and one day, my fine veneer would chip and reveal the cheap tin of my life.

Since my father died, my mother hunted for a new husband to plug into our family mold. I was tired of the endless string of *uncles* who came and went from our house. Added to that was my growing fear of dying, too, which had me holding my breath without even knowing it several times a day.

The last one had gotten too handsy. That's when I decided losing my virginity would be on my terms, not those of my mother's passing boyfriends.

The school bell rang, ending class. I gathered my books, tucked them into my bag, and strapped it to my back. When I turned, Cato was already out of the room.

I strolled into the hall to find him leaning against the lockers, rolling his toothpick over his tongue. He wasn't very tall but made up for it with muscle.

"It's about time." He pushed off and stepped toward me. "I've been waiting forever."

"It was minutes." I shoved his shoulder. "I had to get my things."

He studied me for a moment. His eyes searched my face as if he wanted to say something meaningful, something special. He pulled me into his arms, pressed his lips against mine, and kissed me.

In front of everyone.

Like we were dating.

My stomach fluttered.

When he released me, I stepped back. "What was that?"

"That's what you wanted, isn't it?"

I batted my eyes while my tongue felt warm and thick. "Yes ... but ... I don't know. You never acted like ..." I don't know what I expected to feel, but this wasn't it.

Cato's hand slid down my waist and rested on my ass. He

massaged my butt through my jeans as if he didn't care who saw. That's what I liked about him the most. He didn't follow the rules or let anyone get in his head.

"Let's go." He kept his hand in place and squeezed my ass again.

"Okay." I led him out of the building. Once, we were in the parking lot. I focused on his eyes. "Are you sure you're okay with our plan today?"

He nodded.

"I'm ready. I swear I am." I wanted to sound firm. "I even have condoms in my backpack."

He nodded again.

"Are you okay? You're acting different."

"I'm better." He didn't sound convincing. "Any more problems with your mother's boyfriend?"

I stopped and stared at him. "Why?" Heat rolled down my back. I'd told him about *Uncle* Jack and those frequent brushes that seemed more sexual each time, but I wasn't sure Cato had been listening.

A smirk took over Cato's face as he nodded slowly. "'Cause I took care of him."

"Took care of him?" I puzzled his words. "What did you do?"

"He won't mess with you no more." Cato kicked a rock across the parking lot.

I didn't move. Cato's bruised knuckles caught my attention. "Why?" The word stuck in my throat. I was afraid to know too much, but I needed to learn more. Cato had a side I wouldn't want to cross. I couldn't wait until tonight to see if *Uncle* Jack would come by the house sporting his blue blazer and a bottle of single malt scotch, like usual, but I had enough anxiety churning in my stomach without adding more.

Cato shrugged. "Don't want to talk about it. You

shouldn't have to give up your virginity because you're worried about him, so I fixed it." He tugged me toward his car.

"That's not the only reason for my plan. I want to do this. It's not just because of him." I put my hand on Cato's arm, hoping he'd see I was serious.

He stopped. His mood darkened. "It's done. Let's go."

Suddenly, our arrangement didn't seem like a good idea. My thoughts buzzed with *Uncle* Jack and Cato's mood, taking away the joy I'd felt earlier.

I followed Cato toward the car. I'd seen this temperament before when he was mad at the world. "You can't keep pretending you're fine. You need to talk to someone for help."

He grabbed both my hands. "That's the gift you're giving me, right?" He kissed my cheek, then unlocked the car.

We climbed inside. We'd talked around the sex topic for several weeks. I didn't want to be a virgin anymore, and Cato was willing to participate in my plan. But now, instead of our lovemaking being the tender moment I wanted, it blurred with thoughts of the bruises on Cato's hands or a possible dead man.

Cato backed the car out of the lot and headed toward town. "I have a place I want to show you before we ... you know."

"Uh...do we have time?" I wrung my hands. "I need to be home before my mom, and you're not in the mood."

He patted my thigh. "Don't worry. I'll get you home in time." He gripped the steering wheel so tightly that the veins popped in his hand, and his clenched jaw made me nervous.

"Where are we going?"

He stared straight ahead. His seriousness deepened. "My favorite place in all the world."

"You haven't seen anything outside of town, so how do

you know this is your favorite?" I poked him in the ribs. I wanted him to laugh, to act happy, but it didn't work.

"Just because I haven't jet-setted all over the world like you and your mom doesn't mean I don't know what I like." He huffed. "Why does everybody think they know what's best for me?"

I drew in my arms. "I was kidding you." A knot tightened in my stomach. The day wasn't turning out as I'd hoped. We were supposed to be excited, but his attitude was as black as my boots.

We rode in silence. With the windows down, the wind whipped my curls. I was content to sit beside Cato with the sun on my face. Saltiness filled the air and stung my nose as we neared the coast.

Cato took the road to the cliffs, and the sound of loose rocks crunched under the tires, rocking the car. He slowed.

The wind picked up and made it impossible to talk without yelling. I rubbed my arms against the chill, wishing I had a jacket and the right words to put Cato in a better mood. He didn't need to solve my problem with *Uncle* Jack. I'd managed to dodge him this long. I could have figured it out. Besides, Cato had his issues at home with his relationship with his father, that included hitting and yelling and so much abuse.

Cato pulled the car to a stop and climbed out.

"Aren't you going to wait for me?" I jumped out to catch up with him.

He shielded his eyes against the sun as he glared at me over his shoulder. His eyes were darker than usual and made me stop where I stood.

I needed him to know he could count on me and that I'd always have his back. "I'm sorry about that comment. Okay?" I tried to make him believe me.

"Yeah. I know." Cato shrugged.

He resumed his pace, and I fell in step beside him. He kicked a few rocks as we made our way toward the overlook. His funk was thicker than the wind. I would suck it up and understand if we had to wait another day.

He settled on the edge of a rock overlooking the steep drop.

I sat beside him and refused to look out at the fall-off. Nothing put me closer to death. I held my breath with my arms wrapped around my waist, bracing against the wind. "Did something happen?"

He studied his hands, rubbing them together as if trying to calm himself. I saw tiny cuts on his knuckles that I hadn't noticed before. His shoulders heaved up and down as he struggled to breathe.

"Just my dad." He looked out at the horizon. "He's been on my case. Just when I think he'll let up, he starts all over again."

"Did he hit you, again?" I nodded toward his hands.

Cato snickered and gave me a sideways glance. "What do you think?"

His sarcasm made me draw back. I felt small for not understanding his circumstances. What did I know?

I thought anyone who had a father in their life was lucky. I'd often thought I'd take my father even if he hit me occasionally, but looking at the hurt on Cato's face, I packed those thoughts away for good.

I reached for his hand and squeezed it. He clasped my hand tighter but kept staring ahead. I couldn't think of the words to make him feel better, so I sat with him, even if it meant I'd get home late. Quiet with Cato was better than arguing with my mother.

After several minutes, Cato pulled his hand away and cupped my face between his palms. His touch was tender, and he held my eyes for a moment, then kissed me again.

Longer and slower this time. If he spoke, I was sure he would have said he loved me, and I was willing to have sex with him under the blue sky and the gust of winds.

My mind raced with everything we could do now that we were a couple.

"You need to stand up for yourself." He didn't look at me.

"I know." I lifted my brows. "It's not easy."

"Just in case I'm not around all the time."

I nodded. "I know," I repeated, not liking the tone of this conversation. "But you're always going to be around. Right?" I gave him a playful push.

He half-smiled. "See, I'm not as useless as my father thinks."

He stood and walked to the edge of the cliff. His straight-back made me think he had a lot on his mind. He shoved his hands in his pocket.

I gave him a moment, then joined him, even though he stood too close to the edge. But a girlfriend is supposed to support, and he needed me. I touched his back. "What do you want to do?"

"This. Stay here where it's peaceful."

Another car pulled up near the cliff, and two women climbed out with a poodle on a leash.

"Maybe we should go." I kept my eyes on the strangers.

Cato shook his head. "I'm not going back."

"Where will you go?" Fear pumped through my veins.

The height of the cliff.

Cato's distant behavior.

The cold.

I wanted to hit a reset button and return to history class. Maybe grab a jacket or suggest we get burgers. Anything had to be better than standing on a cliff, freezing my ass off.

Cato brushed my hand.

He took another step forward and tittered, then he raised

his arms level with his shoulders. "I'm going to meet my Maker."

I grabbed his shirt as he took a giant step.

But it was too late. He disappeared over the edge.

I screamed or tried to. I glanced over the brink at Cato's crumbled form below.

I screamed. The noise came from my gut, and I couldn't stop.

Tears blurred my vision.

This day was supposed to be different.

The rocks under my feet shifted, and like Cato, I sailed off the edge.

Broken Promises

Odessa

After what I did to Daniel, I high-tailed it back to where I belonged. By lifting my hands in the air, I was on the bench where I was supposed to wait for whatever came next.

I wasn't happy that I didn't go directly to heaven. That's what I had expected. All those hours spent in church should have given me an express ticket through the Pearly Gates.

Hoodwinked.

Again.

I settled on the bench between two other women who paid me no attention. I glanced around with my nose stuck up in the air. I ain't gonna trusting another soul again. Maybe, I'd give up trusting all together. It never got me nothing.

My current surroundings certainly didn't meet my expectations. I hadn't seen one angel or Saint Peter with his book of names. The descriptions I heard in Sunday school and church differed from what I saw. No matter how often I glanced over my shoulder or stared at the scenery, it didn't fit. Wasn't no use in believing anything anyone said, even the preacher.

The bench numbed my ass. Nobody would ever tell me what to do, where to go, or how to act again. But the only different from before, was Daniel, that evil man I married, wasn't standing over my shoulder yelling about his dinner or his nightly beer.

Daniel isn't yelling at nobody, now. I chuckled to myself. Satisfaction filled my chest.

My grandmother hadn't told me much about the Interruption, and most of the time, when she started talking about it, I'd play with the rocks in the dirt yard, thinking she was crazy jabbering again. But I knew enough. Probably more than the two sitting with me.

I crossed my arms.

Satisfied.

Daniel isn't my worry no more, and for that, I could have sung so loud the skies would've opened up. But then it dawned on me like a brick hitting my head. What if Daniel was in the Interruption now, looking for me?

"Oh, shit," I mumbled and looked over my shoulder.

"What?" The skinny brown girl sitting on one side of me glanced up.

"Nothing." I smoothed out the wrinkles in my dress.

The girl's curly hair was perfect in every way. She studied her hands like she expected them to free her from this spot. She done lived a good life. I could tell by the shade of lipstick stuck on her lips. That awful shade of orange matched the color on her fingernails. Someone took time with her for sure.

On my other side sat a middle-aged woman who hadn't stopped crying since we landed here. I waited for her to run out of tears because nobody could cry forever. And I knew that better than anyone. Daniel gave me reasons to bawl every day, but one day, I had no more tears, because I had no more love.

I cleared my throat and reached for the young girl. She looked like she needed me more than the crybaby.

I patted her back. "Honey. It's going to be okay. Don't look so sad."

She looked none too friendly, so I quickly pulled my hand back.

Her head jerked up, and she narrowed them dark brown eyes on me like she meant to harm me. "You don't know anything about me." She shifted away. "Leave me alone, old woman."

"At least I lived to be an old woman." I snorted. "Young'uns aren't taught manners no more. In my day, I wouldn't fix my mouth to say such a thing to my elder."

"And look at us now." She looked down her nose at me, the way Daniel used to do. "With all that teaching, you're no better off than I am."

"What's your name anyway?" I didn't expect her to answer. The anger coming off her was as real as the grass under my bare feet.

She shifted to face me. "If I tell you my name, will you leave me alone?"

I raised my brow. "I ain't promising nobody nothin' ever again." My tone was as nasty as hers. Used to be someone who talked to me like that, and I'd hunch my shoulders and shuffle away with my head down, but now things were different. I'd decided to claim all the riches promised to me for turning the other cheek and following the good word.

She sucked her tongue and glanced at my ashy feet. "Ronita."

"I'm Odessa. Ain't no use telling you my last name, 'cause I ain't wit that man no more and don't want nothin' of his." I glanced at the crybaby on the other side, who was only sniffling now and seemed interested in what Ronita and I talked about.

"I'm Willa." She dried her eyes on the sleeve of what had to be her best church dress.

I nodded. "Odessa."

A darkness that would never go away lay under Willa's eyes. Daniel had had that look, too. It came from too much alcohol and not enough water.

I shook my head and held back a chuckle. "Ain't we a

bunch of misfits?" My grandmom used to say if you wanted to make God laugh, make plans. Boy, she sure was right."

"Don't care. I don't want to talk anymore." Ronita stood and stepped away.

"No need for you to be so hateful." I stretched out my arm to reach the sleeve of her fancy gown, but she sauntered off like a two-year-old. "Don't go too far."

Ronita's sleeping gown ballooned in the wind. She looked like she should be napping, not running in this field. At least her family put her away in style. All I had was an old house dress that wasn't good enough to wear to church.

She paid no more attention to me than Daniel when I told him not to eat that pie at the church picnic, and he gobbled it up anyway. I'm the one who cleaned up the sheets when his bowels went loose in the middle of the night.

I rolled my eyes and watched Ronita run off.

I turned to Willa, who looked like she had found another fountain of tears.

"I ain't looking after nobody but my damn self. We was told to sit and wait, and that's what I plan to do. I needs to get my Glory." This next step was important, but I wasn't fixin' to tell that to a snoot nose young'un with no respect. I huffed and tightened my arms around my ample stomach.

I sure didn't want the ghost of Daniel to find me sitting here waiting for him to do what I did to him, so I hoped the next step would happen soon.

Fresh tears rolled down Willa's face. "What makes you think Glory is what's coming next?"

"'Cause I know." I wiggled my swollen toes in the thick grass and tried to figure out why I wasn't wearing shoes. I bet Daniel didn't put shoes on my feet out of spite. He had a mean streak big enough to make the Devil smile. Daniel probably mad I left before cutting the grass and washing his drawls.

With another shrug, I inhaled the sweet scent of honeysuckle that thickened in the air. It reminded me of my mother when she dressed up and headed out for the night. She used to have time for everything and everyone except for me. Thank goodness for my grandmother.

I tapped my foot to the imaginary music that played in my head. Sitting in this meadow was the most peace I'd had in years. The grove was better than all the places I left behind. The sky was a blue I'd only seen in crayon boxes. The lush grass sparkled like emeralds. If this wasn't heaven, it was mighty close. I wiggled my ass on that bench, anxious, thinking heaven was so close.

My knees that used to ache and hinder my steps, making me sit when I wanted to stand, didn't bother me no more. Back then, being uncomfortable was as familiar to me as my wide nose. It was going to take some getting used to this new me, without all the aches.

Wherever I was going next, I'd handle it like I did everything else—with my head up and gaze focused.

"Odessa," Ronita's loud voice shattered the peaceful silence. "Maybe we're in the wrong place."

I think I liked her better when she wasn't speaking to me. Who did she think she was, questioning the directions. Questioning anything.

The way she walked with her shoulders hunched like she was carrying a heavy weight pulled at my heart. But I had my problems, and she had hers. So I didn't need to ask questions and get mixed up in whatever dragged her down.

"Someone picked this place for us," I snapped. "We ain't got no right to question that guidance." My days of tending to the needs of others should have prepared me for this moment. But nothing in life prepared me for death.

I sure didn't expect to be stuck with a snobby teenager and a grown crybaby. I expected the folks to be old like me.

Good church-going folks like me. Except for that one thing I did to Daniel, I was good as could be. Never harmed a soul.

Ronita had her hands on her hips. "What will happen if we don't wait?"

"Our deciding is done. We don't have to worry about nothing, no more." I sat back with satisfaction. According to the Good Book, all I had to do now was wait. Wait on the promises I was due.

Willa sniffed. "How can you be so calm?"

"Because I'm a believer. We need to stay together and wait, the way we was told." I talked loud enough for Ronita to hear me. I wasn't in the mood for none of her foolishness. Nobody or nothing was going to stop me from finding out why I was expecting big puffy clouds, streets paved in gold, large thin wings, and pearly gates that glistened like pure sunshine, and I got something that looked like a fancy park instead.

Whenever Grandma talked about the Interruption, she lowered her voice and glanced over her shoulders as if she expected to see ghosts. She said it was full of trickery, creatures, and challenges. So if these two didn't follow instructions soon enough, they'd come running to me to pull their asses out of danger.

Messages From Whom

Ronita

Odessa called out, but that old woman couldn't tell me what to do. And Willa didn't have much to say. She looked as stunned as me.

Maybe Willa could teach Odessa to mind her business. I stomped in the opposite direction of the bench, looking for an escape. There had to be a way out.

My unhappiness started at my feet and spread through my body like the blood that used to fill my veins. I thought death was supposed to end all emotions, but I had no relief. Visions of Cato going over the cliff haunted me. I'd convinced myself that, with the right words, I could have stopped him. Cato was my friend, the happy spot in my school day. Existing in any form was impossible without him, which made this place another form of torture.

A giant black bird buzzed my ear. I ducked and swatted it away. It screeched loudly, then made another swipe at me. With its tiny black eyes staring at me, it pecked my ear and captured my earring.

"Ahhhhh," I wailed and ran my hands over my hair. Disease-ridden birds scared me more than bees. I touched my ear and felt a speck of blood. "Why is this bird attacking me?" I shook my head, hoping it hadn't pooped in my curls.

"I'm not supposed to be here," I yelled at the sky. "Someone made a mistake. I've got to go home." I march further ahead. Anger fueled my steps.

Every time I closed my eyes, I saw Cato stepping off that cliff. And every time, a little bit of me died again. Why would he want me to witness such an awful thing? Why did he do that to me? I thought he liked me. It's his fault I ended up here, and for that, I would never forgive him. As if that mattered in this place.

I needed to get to my mother. My ears filled with the sound of her crying. I tried to end it by covering my ears, but it didn't help. I had to let her know I was okay. And I wanted to know why she let anyone dress me in something so pompous. I'm not a pink girl. She knew my favorite color was black, and if I had worn black jeans, I would have been happier in death.

Habit had me reach for a nonexistent pocket to retrieve my cell phone. Not having it tucked into a pocket, like always, was foreign.

This jacked situation had me thinking someone played a prank on me. If so, they'd done an excellent job because I'd always dreamed I'd live forever. People my age didn't die.

The hem of my gown tangled under my fancy slippers and slowed me. I looked down at the unfamiliar garment. The crinoline itched like fire ants. The minute I scratched in one place, a new irritation started in another. I'd rather be naked, but I needed a better understanding of where I was first.

I stopped, grabbed the hem, and ripped the delicate fabric until I exposed my knees. It was the only satisfaction I'd had since arriving. I would have kicked off the shoes, but I might need them. I had no idea where I was, but I might need them to return to my mother.

I glanced back at Odessa, who sat on that bench like she thought all her prayers were getting answered. Didn't she know there weren't any happy endings anywhere? If anyone deserved one, it was Cato. Besides, Odessa was old and didn't have much to look forward to anyway. From the appearance of her dress and gnarled toes, she had been dumped in a potters' field and left by city officials to rot.

Odessa and Willa could sit until vines wrapped them like

mummies because I wasn't expecting the yellow brick road the way they were. Even though I hadn't paid much attention to catechism—because I couldn't stop texting Cato—I still knew suicide was the ultimate sin. Even though that's not what happened, I didn't think I'd get a redo because of a technicality.

The end of my journey had no pretty bow with beaming ancestors ready to welcome me into eternity.

But before I got that final decision from some red-horned mutant, there were people I needed to see and ease their pain. Some in a good way. Others, not so much.

I let the torn fabric slip through my fingers and watched as the gentle breeze carried it into a blooming tree.

"Ronita, you better get back here." Odessa's voice carried to me like she was close and whispering in my ear. "You might be walking into trouble."

I turned around, thinking she had caught up to me, but she sat in the same place with that smug expression like she had all the answers.

Giving her one of the evil glances that I'd perfected on my mother didn't pause Odessa the way I wanted. She expected me to obey.

"I told you I didn't want to talk anymore! Besides, I'm dead. What's worse than that?" I spat out the foul-tasting words.

"You don't want to find out." She huffed and crossed her arms.

Even though her words chilled me, they couldn't stop me. Following rules wasn't my thing. That's how I ended up here in the first place. "You keep on sitting. I've got something to do."

I walked faster before Odessa decided she had more advice. She must have thought she could take my mom's place. I didn't have time to set her straight. The sooner I put some distance between myself and this fairytale place, the happier I'd feel.

No matter how far or how fast I walked, I couldn't put any distance between Odessa and me. I still saw her sitting with her hands in her lap. I picked up my pace, stretching my legs as far as they would extend almost running, and I went nowhere. She musta had a leash around my neck and kept pulling me back.

"What the hell, old woman. Why can't you let me be?"

She threw up her hands. "I ain't done nothing to you, and there ain't no need for you to use that kind of language with me." Her bloodshot eyes held disappointment.

"Then why can't I get away from here? Away from you?" I stomped, knowing it was childish, but frustration consumed me. I moved back toward them.

"Why don't you sit, Ronita."

Willa's calming voice almost convinced me to listen, but I snapped back. "Don't you start, too,"

Odessa gazed at me with her scary eyes. That weird smirk made me shudder. "I can't explain what's going on. You ought to sit down and find some patience. I'm sure we're going to get some answers soon." She patted the empty spot on the bench.

I gave up and returned to sit next to Odessa and pointed my finger at her. "Are you a witch?"

She jumped like I tried to poke her eye out. "Watch your mouth, girl. I'm no such thing. You don't know me well enough to talk to me any kinda way."

I expected steam to rise off her skin as her body became a knot.

The big black bird buzzed my head again. This time swooping so low, its feet tangled in my hair for a moment.

I swatted and ducked. "What the hell?" I tucked my head low and scanned the sky. "Why won't that bird leave me alone?" I sounded like a whiny brat instead of the raging teenager I was trying to portray, but that bird gave me the creeps.

And this wasn't an ordinary bird. From the branch above, it stared back at me and squawked every time I moved. I ran my fingers through my hair.

Odessa chuckled. "Looks like you made yourself a friend." She talked with her hands. "You know, my family was fond of birds."

"Yeah, yeah, yeah." I stood. "You all ate a lot of chicken. I don't think that counts." I spied the dirty creature from the corner of my eye, stepping side to side on the branch. "Birds are nasty. They carry germs. I want that one to leave me alone."

The winged beast came at me again and almost landed on my shoulder, but I ducked behind the bench.

I shot a glance at Willa and Odessa. "You both saw that, didn't you?" I pointed at the crow as it zoomed back to the same branch. From a distance, it looked friendly as it tilted its head right and left.

"Stay away from me," I screamed at the bird, the sky, and the world.

Odessa chuckled, and her chest jiggled. "You'd better be careful. That bird might be just what you need."

"What do you mean?" I sidled back beside her, hoping she'd forget how I'd spoken to her and protect me if needed.

She patted my knee. "Patience, child. Patience." Her expression told me to worry.

The Tale of Two Deaths

Willa

I dabbed at my eyes with the sleeve of my dress. Burt should have tucked a handkerchief in my bra. He knew I was a crier. The way I whimpered as we spoke our wedding vows should have been a big enough hint. We didn't celebrate birthdays, anniversaries, or family events without me breaking into tears. But this time was different. They flowed from me like a faucet someone forgot to turn off.

Something cold touched my neck. I half turned and swatted behind me, but only the trees swayed in the distance. Facing forward, I placed my hand on the cool spot left behind and drew a deep breath.

"Odessa, did you see anything?"

She rocked forward. "Anything like what? I see lots of things."

I wanted to strike her. "I felt something on my throat— like a hand." I peered around Odessa. "How about you, Ronita? Did you see anything?"

Ronita rubbed her arms and stared at the bird in the tree. "What? No. I'm keeping my eye on that damn creature."

Odessa's eyes narrowed, and her lips turned down, dismissing me.

"Never mind." I readjusted against the back of the bench. If I let my emotions run wild, I'd need something strong to drink, which was impossible in this place.

In the next instant, fingers wrapped around my neck again. This time, it was firmer and tighter. They choked off my breath with a swiftness I couldn't overcome. I clawed at my neck but felt nothing I could grasp. I tried to stand and kick my feet to escape, but the grip was too powerful, pressing on every bone in my throat. I flailed on the bench like a fish, unable to draw a breath.

Odessa drew away from me. "What's wrong with you, Willa?"

Just as quickly as it happened, it stopped.

I gasped and ran my fingers across my throat. "You had to see that." I croaked. "Something was choking me." The flesh on my neck still felt cold.

Ronita stood. "I need to get away from here. You two are crazy, and this place is creepy. It might look pretty, but so does a thunderstorm until lightning strikes.

Odessa studied me the way Burt did when I threw an accusation at him. "I ain't seen nothing. You sure you okay?"

"No. No, I'm not okay." I spun around and took a thorough survey of the surroundings. "I'm telling you something is here with us. Something bad."

"I suppose that's possible." Odessa crossed and recrossed her arms as if she was impatient for whatever was supposed to happen next, and Ronita stared at that bird, not letting it out of her sight.

"How can you be nonchalant after what I just told you?"

"Ain't nothing bothering me." Odessa rocked.

I looked her over like I would a used car. "Yeah. Nothing is bothering you. Why is that? A crazy bird is chasing Ronita. Something tried to strangle me, and you're untouched. How do you explain that?"

Ronita nodded. "Willa's right. Why is that?"

Odessa huffed. "I ain't got to explain nothing. Besides, how the hell would I know?" She drew herself up and stuck out her chin.

Every time I closed my eyes, I saw BJ and Ava. Their tender faces came to me as the babies they used to be, not the unruly teens they'd morphed into overnight.

Tears started again. If only I could turn back time and

have my innocent little ones back, the ones who needed me more than I needed them. The ones who kept me up all night with feedings and diaper changes instead of pushing their curfews and using illegal drugs.

Odessa side-eyed me again. She had grown weary with me, but I had as much right to cry as she had to huff, puff, and cross her arms every few minutes. I was heartbroken, but Odessa was downright mad. If she had answers about what we were waiting on, maybe I could butter her up and get them out of her.

I turned to her. "Why do you think we're waiting? Is some chariot supposed to drop down and carry us to heaven like that hymn says?"

Odessa snickered. "I don't rightly know. But I have been following rules all my life, so I will sit and wait. No use in stopping now."

I inched closer. "I hope you don't mind me asking, but how did you die?"

She shot me a frown and then looked out over the valley. "Just dropped dead while cooking Sunday dinner. I guess my heart had enough."

I exhaled through my mouth. She hadn't been in an accident like me and caused harm to others. Maybe this wasn't the bench for a one-way ticket to hell.

She turned back to me. "How 'bout you?"

I fumbled with the hem of my dress, wishing I had something to drink to lessen the intensity of her question. I couldn't tell her the truth, so I hunched my shoulders. "I don't know."

She smacked her knee, then settled her hands in her lap. "Liar." Her lips formed a thin line. "Everyone knows how they died. Maybe you died because you're a liar."

"And you're mean." I scooted away from her and sat quietly for a moment mulling over her statement. "What makes you think everyone knows how they die?"

She looked at me out of the corner of her eyes. "I know a lot more than you think."

"Tell me."

"Why should I share anything with you if all you're going to do is fill me with lies? I ain't got time for no foolishness. And I ain't gonna play no more games." She heaved as if talking to me exasperated her.

I looked down at my lap. "I have my reason for not telling you. It's nothing I'm proud of sharing."

"Well, say that. It's better than taking me for a fool. And being mean is better than being a liar. The Bible don't say anything about being mean, but it says plenty about telling lies." She turned her back to me.

None of us had arrived here without something burdening us. But I wasn't ready to share mine. I would have bet my load was twice as heavy as Odessa's and Ronita's combined. Odessa looked near eighty, so she had lived a long life. But judging by her wrinkles, it hadn't been all good or easy.

And Ronita was too young to have worries. She was about the same age as my Ava, and from the looks of her dress, her family must have cared about her fiercely. When I buried my mother, the funeral director tried to sell me that same expensive ensemble Ronita wore, but at two thousand dollars, I had better use for that money.

"You know, I wasn't always a liar," I muttered. "I used to be fun and full of life until I got married and found out my husband was only interested in a pair of breasts and a tight hole to insert his dick as long as it belonged to someone other than me. So instead of crying about his unfaithfulness or my daughter's addiction, I drowned my emotions in vodka. A half bottle at a time." I sucked in a deep breath.

Odessa's head didn't move much, but she acknowledged

my confession. "We all been there. Well, maybe not Ronita yet." She didn't look at me. "Life will chew you up and spit you out when it's done with you."

"Yeah, that's about right." I squeezed my hands together. Odessa's words summed up my predicament.

"So, you gonna tell me the truth?" Odessa squinted at the bright sun.

"I can't talk about it yet. I will one day."

If I stared straight ahead at the hills in the distance, I had an easier time managing my emotions. I'd never seen any place more scenic. There wasn't one dead leaf on any of the trees. It was more than I deserved and probably the preamble to something worse.

The tears built again, and I didn't try to stem them. They brought me comfort. They were the familiar thing that remained consistent. The way I figured, I'd have to cry a lifetime before I could ask for forgiveness.

Odessa shifted toward me. "What you think is wrong with that girl?" She nodded toward Ronita. "Why won't she follow the instructions?"

I shrugged. "I don't know, but teenagers carry a load we can't understand."

"What's hard to understand about sitting here and waiting?" Odessa smacked her thigh. The sound echoed.

"It's not like we're waiting on a train. I'm so scared of what might happen. next, I could shit my panties if I wore a pair." Odessa wanted me to agree but I needed to know what was supposed to happen next. I had knots in my stomach just thinking about the unknown.

Anxiety had grabbed hold of my legs, and there was nothing I could do to stop them from shaking. Finally, I pushed to the edge of the bench. Fear that made me want to run off like Ronita filled every pore.

Odessa reared up like she wanted to snag my arm and

hold me in place. "What you fixin' to do?" She narrowed her dull eyes at me.

"Whatever I please." I stood and walked in the opposite direction of Ronita. I had no idea which path to take to get to Tulsa, but I planned to keep going until I found a way to reach my family. All I needed was a phone and a credit card, and I'd steal them if I had to in order to get there.

The Creature Arrives

Odessa

Ronita and Willa were right. This place was beautiful *and* strange. Nothing my grandma told me prepared me for this experience. Sure, there was meaning in that bird chasing Ronita, and I don't doubt something had Willa by the neck, but I don't know what. And I couldn't help either of them. I needed to help myself and move on.

Ronita started towards the azaleas in the distance, and I pressed my back to the bench and inhaled the cleanest air I had ever smelled.

"I'm getting outta here," Ronita yelled over her shoulder. "I've got people to see."

"If you didn't get to say goodbye, it's too late now." I didn't even care if she heard. She wasn't gonna listen, no way.

The scent of honeysuckle tickled my nose. The only sound now was Willa, breathing like she was congested as she inched away from the bench.

On the horizon, a light glowed. It moved toward us at a steady pace, like a slow-moving freight train. An iridescent hue fell over the pasture in the most beautiful, saturated colors I'd ever seen. I didn't even see if Willa or Ronita recognized what was happening.

I took it in.

I couldn't move or avert my watery eyes.

A soothing calmness fell over me like everything was going to be alright. It was the first time I'd had that feeling since I closed my eyes in the emergency room.

In the distance, a tiny light appeared on the horizon and started to glow, stretching out like the star of Bethlehem on my grandma's Christmas tree. I couldn't look away from the blooming light. As it grew more prominent, it held me hypnotized. My body warmed as anticipation fluttered in my stomach. Hope and happiness filled my hollow places.

The iridescent hue settled over the park like a slow descending cloud. As it inched down, my anxiety inched up. I pushed off the bench, wanting to stick out my arthritic arm and touch what was happening before me. The pasture glimmered as if a rainbow started and ended in it. The trees shimmered as if someone had stroked each leaf with gold.

I stepped forward to see if this was the Rapture. Even though I knew better than to want too much, it could be the Devil, disguised as some grand adventure, just like my Daniel had looked like a savior but turned out to be Hell visiting Earth.

I froze. I couldn't move or avert my eyes as they filled with tears. The calmness that washed over me was a relief. It was the most peace I'd felt since the funeral director cramped me into that cheap, tight coffin.

I turned one way to look for Ronita and the other to see Willa. They headed in opposite directions like they were trying to sneak off. They might miss whatever was about to happen, but I didn't worry so much about them. I'd learned to look out for Odessa Eddiemae Jones, 'cause nobody else would, and I had plenty of evidence to show that was my truth.

Through the haze came a creature that looked like a giant eagle, in the shiniest shade of black I've ever seen, with enormous wings and tail. That animal had more life than the whole First Street Baptist choir. It didn't make a sound. Even with those sharp-clawed feet, it touched down a few feet from me without stirring a blade of grass.

I drew back. Fear thumped in my chest like it was knocking to get out. I should have been scared to death, but when you are already dead, you get a sense of freedom about everything. I didn't have much to fear anymore. The worst had already happened.

Atop the magnificent animal was another creature, and I called her that because nobody was that beautiful and human too. Where the bird creature looked wild and fierce, the rider was as angelic as those in fairytales. Instead of blond hair and blue eyes like described in most books, this one had raven-colored curls blowing in the wind like wild snakes, black eyes, and skin the same color as the bronze statue of Saint Peter that stood outside my church.

I knew it was a woman because her full, round, bare breasts hung heavy like she was getting ready to feed a baby. Each slender finger sparkled with bands of gold that matched the layers of necklaces around her neck.

With everything going on, I didn't have no fear. Iridescence glowed all around her and that creature she flew in on. Even my dry, wrinkled skin shined like a new copper penny in the light.

"Gather together, everyone. I am Princess Kenyata, the Goddess of Grace. The time has come, and I have a schedule to keep." Her voice sounded like a song.

I jumped forward and waved my arms. "I'm here and ready." I couldn't contain my joy or the feeling that, finally, something good was happening to me. I was moving on, even if it didn't look how I thought it would.

Princess Kenyata turned her gaze to me. "I must take you and your three companions. You were to stay together."

I couldn't move any further.

I shrugged my shoulders. Her words bounced off me. "Ronita is hiding in the bushes, and Willa is standing in the shadows." I pointed them out like we were playing tag. "I ain't seen nobody else."

Princess Kenyata smiled. "I know exactly where everyone

is, but I cannot force them to continue this journey, to walk toward me. Everyone must move forward with their free will. Welcome to the Interruption."

"I'm ready now." I rushed closer, hoping to get caught up and carried away with the two creatures. Instead, my boobs flopped around like they were free at last because that damn undertaker hadn't put my bra back on.

Princess Kenyata's laugh echoed against every tree in the valley. She showed teeth so white I had to squint. "I cannot take you alone. It's the four of you, together—or not at all."

"But I'm ready now." I stomped my foot like I thought I would get my way, even though it never worked for me.

"The four of you have been matched because your scales are equally uneven. You must work together to balance your inequities and move through the Interruption. I warn each of you that the longer you stay here, the greater your danger. You may not have the energy to complete your journey. And without enough energy, you will remain in limbo forever. Forces are working against you to keep you here. Good and evil forces aim to take what they no longer have from you. You won't always be able to tell them apart, so be alert, or you will end up in a realm of the Inferno, from which there is no escape."

I shook my head. "I don't understand. All my life, I've been a good Christian. Following the rules of the Good Book. It never said nothing about journeying with others or even named this place that you call the Interruption." My tone was firm because I wanted her to follow the rules. The ones the preacher drilled in my head since I was able to sit up.

Princess Kenyata smirked as if I was a naughty child who had disobeyed.

And she was right. She was right, but only that one time.

And I was already dead when I did that thing to Daniel, so it shouldn't count.

The princess continued. "Oh, Odessa, your slate isn't clean. You all are here because you have fallen short. Each of you has some atonement to complete, some virtue-building to do. But don't expect time to pass as it did when you were living. And be aware, there will be many deceptions in the Interruption just because it shines, doesn't mean it's gold."

I put my hand on my hip, ready to fuss at Princess Kenyata, but then thought better of it. So instead, I adjusted my stance to look humbler. "Why are you telling me all this stuff? If we need to continue together, they ought to know the rules too."

"They can hear me as clearly as you can. When the Goddess of Grace speaks, everyone who needs to hear me does. But, as I said, don't expect the Interruption to be like your previous life. Nothing is the same." She lifted her hand and brought it down slowly, pointing at me, and then in the directions of Ronita and Willa, before turning and doing the same thing in the distance.

I glanced at my dress. A gold pin glistened on my frayed collar. It looked like the creature Princess Kenyata rode on.

I fingered the pin. "What's this pin for?"

"That's not just a pin." She laughed softly. "It could be the difference you need to travel from one realm to the next. Don't take it off. Each of you has one. Together, these pins will help you identify good from evil and direct your path to the designated portals. But just like the four of you, the pins must work in unison. Together, they will see the good and the bad. Separately, they may only see one or the other. If you get separated, the pins will always bring you four back together."

"I only seen two others. Where's the other one?"

"Oh, he's here. Luis is over there, hiding in the bushes. I'll keep an eye on you. But remember, you must stay together. Now meet me in the next dimension at the designated time."

"What is the designated time, and where is this dimension? How will I know?" My voice shook along with my knees. I looked at my wrist. The only thing there was the tan line where my watch used to be.

I stepped closer to Princess Kenyata so Ronita and Willa couldn't hear what I had to say. "You must know what I did. What's going to happen to me? It can't be good. Right?"

"I don't judge. That's not what I'm here to do. My mission is to get you all from this portal to the next."

I raised my brows. "But there must be something you can tell me."

"No. But I will tell you to keep an eye over your shoulder. Your husband's path may cross yours now, and he might have a grudge to settle."

"You mean?"

"Just like you, he has the same opportunities." Princess Kenyata's hair and gown floated in the gentle breeze. "You can hope he takes another course of action."

I wrung my hands. "What can he do to me? I'm already dead."

She chuckled again. This time with more cynicism. "There are many things worse than death. Keep your pin near, so you won't discover what they are."

The light and aura that blanketed everything began to fade. As quickly as she had appeared, Princess Kenyata disappeared.

Evaporated.

Taking the glorious light with her.

With my knotted hands, I leaned into the wind, trying to touch the glow that was no longer there. Finally, when the vista returned to normal, I fell to my knees. "Look what you've done," I wailed. "Now she's gone, and we don't even know when or if she's coming back." The words tore from my throat with the same agony ripping at my heart. I was so close and couldn't cross over. It was like I was back in the emergency room, trying to hold on as my life slipped through my fingers. Someone wrote the story of my life in starts and stops, and I was damn tired of coming in last place.

Stepping Out

Luis

From my position behind the biggest Rhodaderium I had ever seen, I saw that older woman stretch and then disappear, and almost as quickly, she was back on that bench. As if that wasn't strange enough, two more women showed up. And like women tend to do, they started arguing, which made me content to continue hiding behind the bushes.

But things got weirder when that bird-like thing came through the cloud carrying that princess. I knew she was a princess before she said a word. You couldn't look that regal and not be one.

The princess told the others about me. I needed to step out of my hiding place and face them. But I wasn't in a hurry. I could have stayed right where I was so I didn't have to hear Janet's voice. Even in death, that woman haunted me.

"You always thought you were so special. Better than anyone else. Didn't you, Luis?"

I jumped back and landed on my backside. Janet found me again.

"It didn't take me long to figure out I couldn't count on you for a damn thing. You are the most selfish man I've ever known. And you will continue to pay for what you did to me."

I scrambled around on my hands and knees and got to my feet. Hiding from the three women near that bench was fine until Janet's voice joined me in my seclusion. I've been a loner all my life, taking in my surroundings before I made myself vulnerable. But the venom from my ex-girlfriend, Janet, made me vacate my hiding spot.

I straightened my back, settled into my charming persona, and walked toward the coveted bench. I'd rather deal with those three women than with Janet.

Living alone for nearly fifty years had been fine with me. I liked it. Now, I had to hang out with three women in eternity. I had pissed someone off.

Strolling toward them, I gave each one a good study now that Princess Kenyata had evaporated into the clouds. One mean, one young, and one that looked just right. The one named Odessa thought she was the boss.

I intertwined my fingers and gave them a good flex, then continued my stroll toward the bench where Odessa had been harping about everything since we arrived.

I'd planned to find out what was going on, fix my situation, balance my chakra, and then get on with the business of whatever this place intended next.

I didn't need to be around a bunch of yakking. I'd handle this blip, too.

I ran my hand across my throat, feeling the scar from the knife wound that had ended my life. I had no idea Janet would be so angry or filled with that kind of rage. I'd never promised her any more than a fun time. Something else always popped up when I thought I'd figured out women. They were as unpredictable as the weather.

I neared the three of them without frowning at the squinting older woman. I'd used as much charm as I needed to escape this situation. "Ladies."

"My name is Odessa, so don't come sashaying over here, talking smooth, like you ain't wrong. You late and done messed up everything." She smacked her knee and reminded me of a fussy old chicken with a head full of white cornrows.. If she didn't look so evil, I could forgive the scowl.

With her mouth open, the young one looked from Odessa to me. I focused on her. "And you're—?"

"That's Ronita." Odessa pointed at the young girl, then she turned and pointed in the other direction. "And that's Willa. And you must be Luis." She rolled her eyes.

I tipped my imaginary hat. "I could hear your conversations, so I know who you are. And I heard everything Princess Kenyata said. So we need a plan." I fingered the pin, now positioned on the lapel of my suit. "Maybe the answer we need is in this pin."

Odessa crossed her arms. "Ain't it just like a man to come in and take over." She sucked her teeth.

Willa stepped closer and stood next to the bench as if determining whose side she wanted to take. She tucked a lock of hair behind her ear and batted her eyes enough to resemble the women at the club when they wanted my attention.

My penis jerked to life, and my body warmed. Maybe this Interruption had an upside.

I inched toward Willa. She wore a band on her ring finger, but there weren't any rules in the middle of nowhere. I jiggled my pant leg, giving my erection room to stretch out.

"Oh, stop it, Odessa. At least Luis is trying." Willa turned to me with her hands out, palms up. "What happens now? She didn't tell us much."

"Yeah. Right. Well, she did tell us we have some balancing to do. The way I figure it, it must be from our previous lives." I chuckled.

"Of course, it is." Odessa kept her arms crossed.

Ronita raised her hand. "Other than a few catechism lessons, I don't know anything about the Afterlife, so I don't get what's happening."

"You ain't in school. You don't have to raise your hand." Odessa glanced at us and simultaneously managed to look down her nose. "What happened right here ain't got nothing to do with the church."

I shifted my weight to the other foot. "You have all the answers." I hope she didn't miss my sarcasm.

Odessa looked down at her bare feet. "Just 'cause I'm

wearing an old dress and no shoes don't mean I'm stupid. I've read books. I have some understanding of what the Interruption means."

She had my attention. "Are you going to sit on the information, or are you going to tell us how to get out of this park?"

"Oh, now you want something from me." She stood and waved her hands. "If you all had listened to me earlier, maybe we'd be halfway through this maze."

Willa moved closer to Odessa. "Okay. Okay. But we're here now. I need to get to my family. Home. I need to get home." Panic rose in her voice.

We stood in a circle, ready to form a huddle. I put a hand on Willa's shoulder. "Everything's going to be okay." I gave her the soothing voice I'd road-tested on over one hundred females. It was a blessing and a curse. But I kept that to myself.

Ronita jumped up. "If we get to go home, then why does she get to go first? If we must stick together, maybe we should vote." Her voice cracked, and I expected tears to follow.

"Calm down, everybody." I dropped my hand from Willa's shoulder and lowered my voice several octaves. "As I said earlier, all we need is a plan."

"Well, I sure don't want to go back home. Nothing's waiting for me there." Odessa rubbed her hands together without making eye contact. "But we've got to act like a team and do this together. No running off."

I held up my hand. "And nobody's the boss. We're all equals."

Ronita raised her hand again. "Even me."

"But what about my daughter's prom? There has got to be a way for me to let her know I'm still there for her. I was the one who convinced her she could go back to school and have fun. I don't want her to slip back into ..." Willa wrung her hands until her veins bulged.

The sun passed behind, gathering dark clouds. I waited to hear a roll of thunder or see a bolt of lightning pass between the trees. Instead, our shadows faded with each drop of the temperature. The wind blew hard, sounding far away as if gathering speed.

The tranquility faded. The wind echoed like a freight train. The sound was as threatening as the darkening sky.

A blast of air blew across the park, whipping their dresses and hairdos in a tug-of-war that the three couldn't win. I pulled my suit jacket tighter. A gentleman would have offered it to one of them, but I hadn't been a gentleman in years and couldn't start pretending now. Besides three women and one jacket, there was no way I could've won.

"Why is it getting so dark?" Ronita drew her arms together, and her eyes widened.

"I don't like the looks of this." Odessa craned her neck, glanced around then reached for Ronita's hand. "Ain't nothing good about to happen."

On the edge of a line of thorny bushes that I hadn't noticed before, a pair of glossy eyes stared in our direction.

Willa must have noticed the new company too because she moved closer. Even though she didn't touch me, there wasn't enough space between us for a leaf to get through. I would have been flattered if she drew near me because she thought I was brave and could protect her against a threat, but she would have been wrong. I knew how to look fearless because I had no heroic bones. I'd perfected the menacing stance to survive in the hard streets where I grew up.

I glanced over my shoulder, studying our changing surroundings and the pair of eyes glued on us.

Then, I noticed another oddity. "How can the wind blow so hard, and the trees remain still?" My voice flew away in what seemed like a cyclone, bearing down on us.

Then came a roar so loud it deadened every other sound. I'd never seen anything so strange.

Ronita used her free hand to rub her arm. "I've been trying to get away ever since we arrived. But, there's no way out." She looked drained, like she had to push her words out.

"She's right." Willa grabbed my hand and squeezed my fingers. "I tried, too. The same thing happened to me." She looked over her shoulder. "Suppose that thing wants to eat us." She nodded to the eyes that had inched closer.

Whatever stared at us was in no hurry, and it didn't make a sound. So while it stayed in the shadows, I had no idea if it wanted to watch or stalk us.

"If we're stuck in this field, then maybe we're meant to be food." Ronita's voice trembled.

I tried to loosen Willa's grip on my hand. "Nobody said anything about that. Princess Kenyata said creatures would want to take from us what they don't have. So if we were supposed to get eaten, she wouldn't have talked about meeting us in the next portal or realm or whatever. Right, Odessa?"

"I don't know," she snapped.

Willa turned to Odessa. "Take from us … that could be our life."

"We're dead." I didn't mean to shout at Willa, but if she was going to act empty-headed, someone had to check her.

Odessa held up her hands. "Maybe you couldn't leave because we weren't doing it together. Princess Kenyata said we had to stay together. Y'all don't listen."

A roar competed with the wind. Through the darkness came a four-legged creature half-walking, half-crawling. The face had nothing identifiable except jagged teeth that looked like they could rip the flesh off bones. Each one dripped with saliva.

I found my voice. "Run!"

Running For My Life

Odessa

Run?

Luis said *run,* and we took off like a pack of old wolves. Me, the slowest and the oldest. The last time I ran was when Daniel came home drunker than usual and swore I needed a beating because I looked at him wrong. So, to fend him off, I raced to the kitchen to grab a knife, but I fell. He punched me so long and so hard that I ached for days, and the bruises lasted for months. That's when I figured if I needed a weapon, I had better keep it in my pocket because I wasn't good at running. But he buried me with nothing. Not a bra and not with the box cutter I kept in my pocket.

Ronita was way out in front. She sprinted like an athlete. Whatever chased us wouldn't catch her. She had young legs, young lungs, and more fear than us.

I shuffled along like all I needed to do was catch the crosstown bus to church. My knees didn't hurt, but I wasn't a fast mover under any circumstances, and I couldn't do any better.

My heart pumped faster than my feet. I glanced over my shoulder and saw those eyes almost upon me, but I couldn't make out a face or a body.

I wanted to call out to the others to help me, but my tongue wouldn't work. The wind was choking my throat. To help me run faster, I tried pumping my arms back and forth.

Suddenly, my fingers tingled like ten thousand pins jabbed into my tips. "Ouch," I screamed between huffs and puffs. "Wait. Wait for me." I wanted to stop, but fear wouldn't let me. Even though I was dead, I didn't want nothing worse to happen. I grew up scared of the dark and still feared what I couldn't see.

Willa slowed and turned in my direction. "Hurry,

Odessa." She waved me forward as if that would help. "We have to stay together."

I heard panic in her voice.

"If we stop, that thing will get us," Ronita yelled over her shoulder without slowing her pace.

Luis grabbed for Ronita. "Willa's right." He stopped. "If we don't wait for Odessa, we won't get away."

Ronita let up and jerked her arms the way kids did when they didn't get their way.

The three came back for me as I hobbled instead of shuffling. My breathing was loud and labored. I wanted to rest, but I was too afraid to stop. My left hand tingled even more, but I couldn't stop to see why.

The darkness closed around me like a puffy cloud threatening to consume my flesh and soul. I couldn't help wondering what would happen if this thing caught me. Would I die again and awaken to a fate far worse?

Willa grabbed my hand, and Ronita held my arm. Luis held on to Willa. We connected like a chain; within an instant, my body grew lighter and easier to move. I broke through the restraints and moved faster. We raced across the field like antelopes. Our feet barely touched the earth. If I hadn't been so scared, I would have enjoyed the moment.

"Are we flying?" I yelled over the loud growl of the beast, who couldn't keep up with us. The further away we went, the louder he roared.

"I think so." A hint of laughter laced Ronita's voice.

I tightened my hold on Willa's hand, afraid if she let me go, I'd fall back to earth and into the snarling teeth of whatever chased us.

A flash of light blinded me. Blinded us all, based on the way the others squinted and dropped their heads.

Seconds later, we were in the middle of a dirt road. I released everyone's hands and spun around. The sky was clear and bright. The dark clouds were gone. I looked for the pair of eyes that had hunted us through the darkness. They were gone, too.

"What happened?" I swiped sweat from my brow. "Where are we?"

Luis coughed into his fist. "Don't know." He shoved his hands into his pants pocket, widened his stance, and glanced around like the rest of us. "But this place is different."

I took a few steps away from our group to look around. The street wasn't paved, and the sidewalks weren't defined. Instead, a well-worn rut marked a path. In the distance, a small cluster of wood and brick buildings huddled close together. "Why does this look familiar?" I scratched my head to figure out why nothing looked recognizable, but my soul told me I'd seen this before. I had a sense of intimacy with my surroundings.

Ronita's voice broke into my reflection.

"What happened to your hand?" Ronita pointed. "You're bleeding."

I followed her gaze. Blood dripped onto the dirt from the end of my arm—where my hand should have been.

My fingers were gone.

My hand was gone.

Jagged flesh hung from my stump like an old rag.

I stared with my mouth open and felt a tingle of pain or something unthinkable. I couldn't take my eyes off the area. Nothing this bad had ever happened, and I thought I'd lived worse. I had no idea how much time passed while I stared at the place where my hand used to be. My brain struggled to process what had happened. And maybe that was best. I had too much to handle.

My stomach lurched. "It got me." I dropped to my knees, tears welling in my eyes. "I don't have a hand." The words tore through me, ripping out the anger and resentment of a thousand unhappy lives. All that I'd lived in the past sixty years. Hadn't I been through enough? Bitterness churned in my stomach and rose in my throat, hardening what little remained of my heart. That thing wasn't nothing but Daniel. He ate my hand, but I'd bet anything he was aiming for my heart. I would have stood toe to toe with him for once if I had known it was him. The next time he came for me, I planned to be ready.

In my head, I traveled to the day I met Daniel. He wasn't mean back then. I had no hint that a monster lived in his soul. He was a gentleman—opening doors, asking my opinion, and even massaging my shoulders some nights. I can't pinpoint when he changed, but he faded away so gradually I never even noticed until one day the man I loved was gone. I imagine that's the way it always happens. Otherwise, no one would be in a bad relationship.

Willa had her fingers over her mouth. At least she still had her hands. "That thing took your hand." Her eyes widened. "That could have been any of us."

I narrowed my attention on her, wanting to strike her down. "But it happened to me because you all left me. Princess Kenyata told us to stick together, and if we had, this wouldn't have happened," I yelled so loud my throat ached.

I wanted to hurt them. "Your selfishness cost me more than it did any of you. And you're looking at me like I'm disgusting, old, and useless. Well, you better hope that when you need me, I come through for you." I narrowed my eyes at each of them, hoping they felt my venom.

"Maybe you need to do something with that. Bandage it or see a doctor."

The way Ronita scrunched her face made me draw back. "I'm dead." My flat voice could have been a slap. "I can't go to a hospital and tell a doctor to fix me up. I'm not even sure anyone can see us." I waved my handless arm at her.

Ronita jumped back. "Stop it. Don't touch me with that thing, that's gross.,"

My ears rang from the volume of her yell. I swatted at her to hush up.

"Okay. Stop yelling." Luis settled next to me. "You've stopped bleeding." He pulled a handkerchief from his breast pocket. "We don't have any bandages, but this will do." He wrapped my stump. "This won't happen again. We know better now." He stood and offered to help me up.

"Oh, now you want to help me?" I smacked away his hand and rose to my knees. "Princess Kenyata said creatures would take from us whatever they didn't have." I pointed my ragged arm at each of them. "I don't plan to give up no more, so you could be next."

They kept their eyes on me as if they expected another horror to befall me. I turned my back to them.

After a long silence, Willa touched my shoulder. "We're sorry, Odessa."

I bit my tongue and examined my bandaged arm. If I had to be minus a hand, at least it was my left one. As best I could, I shoved it into the pocket of my dress and started toward a cluster of stores in the distance.

It didn't take long for the others to fall in beside me.

"Where do you think we are?" Willa talked in my ear, all friendly now.

I wasn't no fool. I didn't trust her no further than I could throw her. She was secretive, and I hadn't figured out if what she was hiding would help or harm me. Given our predicament, she probably didn't mean me no good. None of them did.

I stopped and ran my good hand across my lower back. "I'm not sure. It reminds me of the town where my grandma grew up."

"And where was that?" Luis asked.

I kept walking. "My people didn't talk about it much, and I only visited once or twice. It was in Texas somewhere. That's all I knew. Some little country town."

Ronita stepped in front of me but walked backward. "Do you think that's where we are?"

Willa touched my shoulder again. "Texas is a long way from my family. That's where I want to go."

I took a breath to calm my nerves. "God knows what done chased me and ate my hand, and you gonna tell me what you want right now? I don't give a rat's ass." I pulled my stump from my pocket and pointed it at her. "We here, and this is where we gonna stay until I figure out why, so stop your whining." I kept walking. According to my grandma, everything in the Interruption had a reason, so I needed to figure out this riddle.

Ronita raced ahead. "Maybe we can join hands again and run to a new place."

"While I was running, I was thinking about my grandmother. I remember her telling me about running for her life when she was young. Kinda like what I went through back there. So maybe that's why we're here."

Luis snapped his fingers. "Maybe we need to do something while we're in this place. Maybe this is our unfinished business."

Looking like he'd just solved a complex puzzle and had all the answers, he strutted like a peacock.

He didn't know what I knew. But I kept my knowledge about those ghost tales to myself. Halfway believing and halfway scared my grandma could be right about all that could happen when souls got stuck between heaven and hell.

We stopped in front of a general store.

"Is this real?" Ronita tilted her head. "It looks like a movie set."

"Don't know." I looked around for something else familiar.

"Do you think anyone can see us?" Willa waved her hands in front of her face.

"Don't know." If their yammering stopped, I could collect my thoughts.

A woman came out of the general store. She held a small package close to her chest. I looked into eyes and skin the color of mine.

I gasped. It was my grandma, Ruth. A younger version of her that I hadn't known.

Even though she looked more youthful than I remembered, I knew that face. From the swell of her belly, she was gonna have a baby any day now.

If I wasn't dead with no heartbeat, I imagined it would have sped up or pounded harder.

The four of us stood inches from her. I nodded, but she didn't acknowledge me. Instead, she looked in our direction, stepped off the store stoop, and headed in the opposite direction.

Luis dusted his hands together. "Well, that answers your question, Willa. She certainly didn't see us."

I knew a way for us to be seen, but there wasn't no use in telling them. Not a one of them was trustworthy. As unruly as they'd been, with a little more knowledge, they'd act like a herd of cats and run in every direction. I smelled the need to stray coming off them as foul as sewage.

I started to follow my grandma.

"Where are you going, now?" Ronita caught up to me.

"That lady is my grandma, Ruth, and I'm following her. She must be the reason we're here."

Fools and Folly

Willa

Anger climbed up my spine. I threw my hands up. "This is madness." I stomped after Odessa. "Your grandmother?" I shrieked like a mad woman, then turned to Luis expecting him to chime in with me. He said nothing. Maybe fear of Odessa had glued his mouth shut.

She didn't slow her pace.

"Guys, say something." I hoped the sad look on my face would convince the others, but Luis only held out his palms, and Ronita gave me the infamous teenager shrug.

"We kinda owe her." Ronita lowered her voice. "She lost her hand."

"That's no reason to go along with something crazy like this." I used the same tone with her that I'd used when Ava or BJ did something stupid.

"Let's follow this through." Luis inched forward. "We can always turn back."

"But, I want to see my family, too. What about me?" I thumped my chest. "And how does it make sense that it's her grandmother? Her grandmother would have to be well over one hundred years old. Think about it."

Luis grabbed my arm. "Does any of this make sense? Look around, we're dead, but we're not in a box six feet under." He held my gaze.

"I can hear you, you know?" Odessa called out without slowing.

I had no good reply.

"Then follow her." Luis nudged me forward.

Odessa had set off as if she knew where to go, what she was doing, and why. I found no comfort in this situation. In some ways, I wish this so-called Interruption didn't exist. I wish I had closed my eyes and turned to dust like I'd imagined those before me had done.

I'd messed up. I should be sitting in my house, watching one of my reality shows and listening to Ava and BJ argue over walking the dog. I'd thought their arguing drove me mad. Then, I ended up in an absolute nightmare.

I trailed behind Odessa along with Ronita and Luis. Luis kept brushing my hand as if he meant to soothe me. Even though I pretended not to notice, I liked the gesture. Maybe he could be my buddy on this venture. I needed one.

Luis wore his handsomeness like a much younger man. Only his gray hair gave away his age. He didn't have the wear and tear of a man with family worries like children, bills, and spouses. His suit wasn't as expensive as Burt's, but it wasn't cheap. If I had to choose a movie star look-alike for him, I'd pick George Clooney—Luis had the same strong jaw. I let my hand rest against his but stared straight ahead.

Once I caught up with Odessa, I matched her stride. She swung her good arm and kept the mangled one in her pocket. I wished some of her confidence could rub off on me. She never hesitated or second-guessed this situation. My steps torched with trepidation. "Odessa, do you know what you're doing?"

"Nope." She didn't look at me.

"We're in this together. Suppose you're wrong. We all could suffer." I hoped she didn't detect my alarm. "Princess Kenyata said we didn't have much time—that we'd start getting weak."

Instead of seeing fear on her face, her dark eyes held defiance. I wouldn't have sought relief in vodka if I had determination like her.

I nudged closer to Odessa. "Do you know what year this is?"

"My guess, based on the age of my grandma ..." She tilted

her chin toward the woman. "I'm guessing early 1930 or maybe the late 1920s."

I grabbed Odessa's arm, stopping her. "Are you kidding me? We time traveled?"

"I'm not sure what you call it in the Interruption, but we back in time." Odessa sounded sure.

The clip-clop sound of the Old West came up behind us. A horse pulled up to Ruth and kicked up dust. I stepped aside as it passed, forgetting no one could see us.

Ruth walked in the grass but picked up her pace, glancing over her shoulder every few steps. Her eyes grew larger, and beads of sweat peppered her forehead. The weight of her belly her movements were awkward.

"Hey, gal." The horseman wore a yellow-stained shirt and spat a wad of tobacco at Ruth's feet. "You give your husband my message?"

"Yes, sir." Ruth's expression was defiant. "He said don't talk to you." She stepped into the field and lifted her knees, stomping the weeds under her feet as she kept moving.

"I aim to have that piece of land." He spat again. "You betta make sure he knows that. We can do this the easy way or the hard way."

Ruth kept her gaze straight ahead. Even though she showed no fear, I had enough for both of us. With that package clutched to her chest, she marched through the tall grass with determination.

With her good hand resting on her hip, Odessa stared at the scene in front of us. "Uh-huh." She talked through her teeth. Hatefulness scored her face. "See, we got work to do here." Odessa jumped in front of the horse, threw her arms in the air, and yelled louder than I thought she could.

The horse reared on his hind legs. His front legs circled like he was riding a bicycle as he tore at the reins. The rider held on for a moment.

"This is interesting." Luis rubbed his hands together. "Now we know animals can see us—or at least sense us— even if people can't." Amusement danced in his eyes, accompanying his raucous laughter.

The horse reared again—this time with more power. The rider sailed through the air, landing in the ditch with a solid thump that had to hurt every bone in his body. For a moment, he didn't move.

I stretched my arms toward the limp figure. "Should we help him?"

"I ain't helping nobody who threatened my grandparents." Odessa stuck her nose up and folded her arms.

Ruth never slowed down. She was almost running.

Odessa picked up her pace to catch up.

"Y'all better come on. I ain't hanging around to see how that man makes out. I don't rightly care."

I tugged Odessa's right arm but jumped back when I looked down at her bandage.

"What?" Odessa barked at me, flinging spit onto my face.

"What are you thinking? You can't change history; even if you could, your grandmother can't see or hear us."

Luis jumped to my side. "She's right."

It felt good having him support me because Burt never did.

Odessa rolled her shoulders and appeared to stand two feet taller. "Well, ain't this something? You two trying to tell me what I can and can't do." The smirk on her face frightened me. "Ronita, do you have two cents to add? 'Cause if you do, say it now, so we can be clear on who gonna boss me and who ain't."

"No. I don't care." Ronita kicked a rock into the field.

"Well, watch this." Odessa stretched her hands toward the sky, even the mangled one. Her flab folded into layers as she jiggled her one good hand, and then Odessa was gone.

Standing in her place was a woman forty years younger, with bronze skin, gray hair, and wearing a nicer but simple dress. The breeze picked up, flapping the hem of her dress around her strong legs.

Luis held out his arms, keeping Ronita and me behind the sorcery. "What the hell is going on here? What did you do to Odessa?"

She smiled before winking at us with a twinkle as bright as a diamond in her eyes. "I am Odessa."

The satisfied look on her face had me clutching my chest.

I glanced at Luis, but he looked more stunned than me. His mouth hung open, exposing his thick tongue.

Ronita pushed Luis's arm aside. With her child-like innocence, she touched Odessa's right arm, then let her hand trail down to the now perfectly formed hand. "How did you do that? You must be a witch."

The softness in Odessa's face drew me closer too, but not as close as Ronita, because something about Odessa still held me at a distance. She knew more than she told.

"No. No witch. But I know something about the Interruption, and I plan to use it to help my grandma."

"Teach me too?" Ronita held her palms together.

I moved in closer. I'd missed out on enough in life and didn't want to make the same mistake in death. "I want to know, too. Can we do the same thing?" I stretched my hands above my head and waited for a transformation. I flexed my hands and wiggled my fingers, but when I dropped them, I was still Willa, with a hint of vodka rolling off my stomach.

"Wait a minute." Luis rushed forward. "If you had this ability, why are you just now using it? You could have saved yourself and your hand. You aren't being truthful." He shoved Odessa's shoulder.

Luis probably could have gotten away with pushing Odessa because she was an older woman, but he'd messed up with this woman. The anger behind Odessa's eyes could have set Luis's suit ablaze. I expected him to turn to dust.

Instead, she grabbed him by the shoulder and shoved him into the dirt with a solid thud.

"Don't ever lay a hand on me again. I just soon pull your eyes out as look at you." Her razor-thin voice matched her eyes, which were so narrow I couldn't distinguish the whites.

Luis jumped to his feet and brushed the dust from his suit without looking at us. "If you know something, you ought to share."

"I ain't ought to do nothin'." Odessa her long, graceful strides showing no evidence of old age started in the direction of her grandmother.

Ronita glanced at Luis and me, then caught up to Odessa, falling into step beside her.

"How did Odessa do that?" I held onto Luis's arm, steadying my legs. He continued to knock the dust from his pants. His embarrassment must have made it hard to look at me.

"I don't know." He straightened. "But if we want to find out, we'll have to be much nicer to her. And I'm not above licking her boots if that's what it'll take." He walked after Odessa, leaving me scratching my head and wondering how to get that power from her.

Odessa The Teacher

Ronita

Odessa took long strides, and I matched her pace. This younger, agile woman was more likable than the older one. We weren't that much closer in age, but I thought we could become friends.

Now that she had two hands, she didn't look as scary either.

"How did you do that?" I kept my voice low, even though Willa and Luis could hear everything I said.

Odessa wore a smug look, leading me to believe she enjoyed her secret and didn't plan on sharing the details.

"If you tell me, I promise I'll listen to everything you say and do whatever you want." I hoped I could keep my promise, but I was better at breaking them than sticking to them.

"Child, you ain't proved yourself to be trustworthy. And I been fooled so many times, I don't trust a soul."

"But won't it be better for all of us if we can do what you just did?"

She stopped walking but kept her eyes on Ruth. "I'll think on it."

I had to say a lot more to change Odessa's mind, but I never got what I wanted by begging grownups. "How can we help your grandmother?"

Odessa ignored my question as if I were a pest she wanted to go away. She looked different, but she was still the same person after all.

"Did you hear me?"

"Don't know yet. I'll figure it out." Her breathing grew heavier.

A bird screeched, making me jerk around. "Oh, God. That

bird came here with us." I hunched my shoulders. "How did it follow us?"

"How do I know?" Odessa blinked. "If that bird is meant to be with you, maybe it can follow you anywhere."

I wish someone had answers. Living grownups pretended they had figured out everything. They were always dishing out advice like they had extra to give away. So why did dead ones become so ignorant?

I raised my shoulders to protect my neck, then glanced around as I tried to keep up with Odessa. Unfortunately, the bird circled overhead and cried like it wanted attention.

Odessa glanced up and shielded her eyes. "Maybe that bird is trying to talk to you."

"A talking bird?" I would have laughed if my heartbeat wasn't so fast. After what we'd just been through and then watching Odessa morph into a younger version of herself, it wouldn't surprise me if the bird started talking.

Odessa ignored my question, but I could see she had more to say by how her eyes narrowed and her head bobbed. "How did you die, Ronita?" Odessa slowed her pace long enough to make eye contact. Then she started marching again.

I took a breath. I didn't have many secrets, but this is one I wanted to keep. I sounded like a simpleton if I said I slipped off a cliff while watching my boyfriend jump. But if I opened up to Odessa, she might do the same. I could use a friend in this place for sure.

I inhaled and told her my story.

She never broke stride.

"Aren't you going to say something about how silly it was?"

"Child, if you ended up in the Interruption, I knew it wasn't something peaceful like you died in your sleep. Think about what Princess Kenyata said. We all got work to do."

"What do you think my work is?" I braced for her response.

"I don't know. Maybe you got more than one thing. But I'm willing to bet it's got something to do with that bird since he seems stuck on you."

I wanted to cry but didn't want Odessa to think less of me, so I drew my shoulders back, trying to be tough like her.

The bird dropped lower but didn't make a pitch for me.

"I hope you're wrong. Why couldn't it be a cat or a dog? Something cuddly."

"One thing about the Interruption ain't nothing easy or cuddly." Odessa nodded. "Instead of yelling at that bird, try talking to it."

Ruth neared a house that looked no better than a shack. The faded wood hardly seemed capable of keeping out the rain. If I looked really close in certain places, I was sure I could see inside. The one front window had a layer of thick dust. I'd seen pictures like this in my history books, but seeing it in person sent a tremor through my soul.

Odessa slowed her pace. She tilted her head from side to side as Ruth pushed open a rickety door and stepped inside.

"Do you know this house?" I glanced at Odessa. "Why would that man want it?"

"You got a lot to learn, little girl." She studied the house. "Do you know your history?" Her voice was full of criticism, pointing out my ignorance of something she clearly thought I should have known. I think she forgot I was only seventeen and had so much more to learn about everything.

I looked away. My thoughts went to Cato and our last class together. "Just tell me."

Willa caught up to us. "Tell you what?"

Luis shoved his hands into his tight pants pockets. "So this is it?"

"Yep." Odessa nodded without taking her focus off the

house. "I remember hearing stories about how my family used to own land, but Grandma talked about a lot of things, so I didn't pay much attention."

I wanted Odessa to trust me, to know I cared. So I stepped beside her. "Did they lose this place?"

"I don't rightly know. I think I've seen it, but this ain't where I lived with Grandma."

Willa walked around to stand in front of Odessa. "So why are we here? How long do we have to stay?" Her tone demanded an answer.

A bead of sweat rolled from Odessa's forehead to her cheek. I thought she would reach for Willa's neck, but she only shifted from one foot to the next. "We're here because this is where I brought us. And if you keep harping on why, I'll see how long I can make us hang around."

Willa balled up her fist. But I knew she wouldn't hit Odessa. None of us knew what Odessa was capable of. And I'm sure Willa didn't want to find out. Luis still had dirt on his knees from messing with her.

Odessa turned away from Willa and glanced toward the back of the house. "That's a cotton field." Odessa pointed at the prickly bushes topped with puffs of white. "I ain't never been this close to one." Even though she'd made herself young, the sadness hadn't left her eyes. "Those acres are worth a lot of money and caused my people a lot of pain."

I followed her gaze, wishing I knew more about what was going on so I could help her. Instead, I nodded my simple understanding.

Odessa started toward the house, swinging her arms like she finally had a mission she could win. "You guys stay here." Halfway to the house, she stopped and pointed at me. "You talk to that bird." A hint of concern in her voice warmed me and made me feel almost cared about. I wanted to make her happy, but she'd asked for too much.

I put my hands on my hips. "I will not." I yelled back "I want it to stay away from me. Far, far away."

Odessa tipped her head toward my feet.

My gaze followed to see the bird standing next to me without making a sound.

"Ahhhh." I jumped away from it. My knees almost gave out.

Odessa disappeared inside the shack.

I looked to Willa and Luis for help, but they stared at each other the way Uncle Jack stared at me when my mother wasn't around.

I kept my hands tucked close to my body and took another step away. "I'll make a deal with you, birdie." I talked the same way my Aunt Jean spoke to her dog. "If you stay away from me, I promise I won't try to kill you."

The bird looked up at me and tilted its head one way and then the other. It stared at me in a friendly way. Not as threatening as before. It didn't look like it wanted to peck out my eyeballs. I relaxed my shoulders.

"What is it with you? Go bother the grownups." I kicked dust at the bird. Instead of flying away, it flew up and batted its wings at my eye level. I should have been afraid, but maybe he'd worn me down. If I continued to be frightened of everything, I'd be a nub before we made it to the portal.

I headed toward Luis and Willa. The two of them had found a way of coping in this wilderness but not me. Not yet.

Getting away from this place and this bird couldn't happen quickly enough. I rubbed my hands over my arms, wanting to feel something. Anything would have been better than the strangeness we had stumbled into.

"What do you think Odessa is doing in there?" I asked in general as I squinted at the house.

"Who knows?" The veins in Luis's neck stuck out. "That woman is stuck on power. She should have told us how she did that thing with her arms by now instead of lording it over us." He stuck his arms in the air and drew them down slowly. He looked disappointed when nothing changed.

"I'm going to see if I can hear what's going on in there." Willa walked away, but Luis grabbed her arm.

"Don't make her angry." He released her. "Let's just wait. Maybe we can get out of here soon."

Willa relaxed against his touch. "So, is this how it's going to be? Us circling Odessa and doing whatever she says."

"Just until we know what's going on." Luis put his arm around Willa and drew her close. It was more than a move of assurance. I couldn't help feeling left out.

I blinked without looking at how his arm rested on her shoulder. "Princess Kenyata said we all had work to do. We'll get our chance." I convinced myself this was true. It gave me something to hold on to.

From how he tried to soothe Willa and how she relied on him, I knew they had each other's back. I had nobody because Odessa certainly wouldn't trust me after I ruined her chances on the bench. And Odessa didn't need anyone, least of all a teenager.

The bird circled above my head and then settled on my shoulder. Maybe this was my buddy. Without running him off, I swallowed the fear in my throat, reached up with my index finger, and stroked his head.

Why Not

Willa

The way Luis draped his hand over my shoulder emphasized what I lacked in my life. I couldn't remember the last time Burt made such a casual gesture. I wish I could say Burt was the source of all my problems—my drinking. But if it weren't for his lack of affection, plenty of other shortcomings in my life would have led me down the same path.

Luis pressed his lips against my neck. The moment was tender and gentle. I hadn't realized how deprived I was until a stranger offered me an ounce of attention. My feelings weren't dead. I sure felt warmth spreading between my legs.

I'd never cheated on Burt, but with all certainty, he demonstrated his unfaithfulness numerous times. Sometimes, I smelled other women on him, sometimes, he called me by their names, and sometimes he gave me their infections. And each time, I was too hollow to do anything but cry and drink.

How I managed to be so pathetic and still breathe was a miracle. I wanted to strike back at Burt. He may not have been the whole problem, but he was the root of much of it.

Ronita focused her attention on her pet bird. The two of them had wandered closer to the house.

I slipped my hand into Luis's. "Walk with me," I whispered in his ear.

His eyes grew wider. He took a moment to catch my meaning. "Do you think we should? What will Odessa say?"

"Odessa isn't our boss, and we're grown." My voice dropped to a pitch I hadn't used in years. There was no one to talk sexy to back home.

It was my suggestion, but Luis led the way to the field. I let him hold onto my sweating hand. If Burt could have sex with anyone he chooses, I could, too. I shook the thought away. Even in death, I needed to justify my behavior.

We neared the cotton field, and he stopped. "We can't do anything in a cotton field." He changed direction, pulling me toward a small garden surrounded by marigolds with a large oak tree in the center.

"Here." I tugged him toward the garden. The tree shielded my view of the house and Ronita, so I assumed they couldn't see me either.

Luis pressed my back against the tree.

I cupped his face and kissed him like I wish Burt had kissed me. The only way I could explain my urgency was revenge. Even though Burt would never know what I'd done, it did my heart good to take a stab at him. He screwed everyone he wanted. He'd cheated so many times, and I kept believing he'd change, that each time he apologized, he'd meant it.

Well, it was my turn to satisfy my lust. Luis didn't seem to mind that I barely knew his name or that he didn't know a thing about me. So when he slipped his hand under my dress and between my moist folds, I decided this act of hedonism was good enough for me. Luis let our tongues tangle. Kissing someone other than Burt was as strange as this place.

It was dangerous and exciting.

It was everything I wanted.

I rushed to unbutton Luis's pants before he realized the ridiculousness of our situation. I knew why I wanted him but had no idea why he rushed to have me. And in this place where no rules existed, it didn't matter.

His pants dropped around his knees, just enough to allow him to move unrestricted. He pushed my dress up to my waist and slipped his hardened penis into me with the ease of a warm knife through soft butter. He eased into me as if we had forever. As if we weren't moving on borrowed time. His kissing my neck told me he knew how to please a woman. Luis took his time. No matter how fast I rotated my hips, his pace never changed. I wanted to hurry. He slowed me down. While I may have thought I controlled this situation, Luis made it clear that he was the conductor with each thrust.

"That feels good, doesn't it," he spoke in my ear.

"Shhh. Everyone can hear us. Remember?" So much lust coated my words I didn't recognize the sound of my voice.

"I can't help it."

"Try."

I forgot about Burt and revenge and let Luis coax an orgasm out of me that must have reached back twenty years, gathering all the pleasures I'd missed and allowing them to flow through my veins and pores and quake every vessel in my body.

I settled on the ground when Luis released me, not caring who heard or saw us. My ragged breathing left me without the ability to close my gapped legs or to talk. And what would I have said?

Guardian of the Past

Odessa

The inside of my grandparent's house didn't look the way I imagined. The barren exterior hadn't penetrated the inside. Touches of a well-kept home were everywhere—in the homemade quilt on the thick-cushioned sofa and the curtains blowing in the breeze. Maybe my family had done better than most people. I didn't have no way of comparing.

Ruth stood by the stove, stirring a pot that smelled like beans and pork. The person I guessed was my grandpa sat at a small table. He rubbed his forehead like it would solve the misery on his face.

I saw my features scattered in each of them—eyes here, a jaw there, a dimpled chin.

The bloodshot eyes on grandpa were worse than the deep grooves carved in his face from the sun. "If I don't get what he owes me, we gonna lose everything." The timbre of his voice carried his burden.

Ruth put her spoon down and sat in the chair next to him. She reached for his weathered hand. "We seen hard times before. Us not having enough money, ain't no different."

He smacked the table. "Yeah, it is, Ruth. You know that red neck Thomas been eying this piece of land since the crop came in. If I miss one payment, he gonna grab it up."

"Tell Bonny the kinda mess we in—he'll git the money to you. He our friend and don't mean us no harm."

Grandpa pushed away from the table, stood, and rubbed his lower back. "I done talked to Bonny till my tongue ready to fall out. He got the money, but he ain't 'tending to give it to me." He stared straight through me and looked out the window.

I put my hand on his back. Touching him was as surreal as me standing in the past. As me standing in this house. As me being a ghost. The tension in his muscles pulsed against my palm.

He spun around. "Did you touch me, Ruth? How'd you get back to the table so fast?"

I jumped back, scared I'd stepped over some unknown line.

"What 'cha talking about, Ernest? I ain't moved from this seat. But it's mighty cold in here all of a sudden. I feel like someone walking on my grave."

He brushed his back where my hand had been. "Don't start talking like that. You ain't dead and in no grave. Ain't no such thing as ghosts."

She shook her finger at him. "Don't talk about things you ain't sure about. There are ghosts and spirits and haunts. Some of them is good, and some of them is bad. If I'm feeling one, I just hope it's good, 'cause we already have enough hardness in our lives, with this baby coming and money short." She rubbed her belly.

"Keep your mind on the problem facing us right now."

Grandma picked a scab on her hand. "I don't know what the world is coming to if one colored man can't trust another colored man."

"It ain't like that, Ruth. You know, Becca is expecting, too. I think Bonny is scared that if he pays me and his crop don't come in like he hopin', then Thomas gonna come after him next."

"But he ought to pay us what he owes us." She continued to rub her belly. The motion relaxed the tension in her face.

"You'd think Thomas would have enough money by now. He just a greedy old man. The more he gits, the more he wants." He brushed his back again. "I hear talk in town that he got money under the floorboards in his house, stocking it up like it's wood for winter."

"Then we ought to go git us some. My grandpappy worked for him a bunch of years and never got paid his due."

Grandpa shook his head. "We ain't thieves. Ain't nothing going to turn us to stealing."

She leaned back against the chair. "You, right. I'm just wishing it didn't have to be so hard all the time."

He patted her hand. "I got a few more days. I'll keep thinking on it."

Ruth looked around the room. "I don't want to lose this place. We got nowhere to go. We can't go back to my mama's house. Ain't no room there for you, me, and a baby."

He laid his hand on her leg. "Don't git worked up. I'm thinkin' on it."

She pushed away from the table. "Something ain't right in this house. I need to burn sage."

"Oh, woman, don't go heaping on more worry."

"It can't hurt nothing." Ruth gazed around the room, rubbing her hands along her arms. "I'm telling you something is in here with us." She moved to the kitchen and started opening drawers.

I didn't know what sage would do to me. Besides, I'd heard enough. I slipped outside.

I could help them. I didn't know how, but I had power. And if I did a nice thing for them, then Princess Kenyata might be happy and let me get on with this journey. I hurried, purpose fueling my steps.

Ronita rushed to me with that bird perched on her shoulder like a pirate. She needed to figure out who that bird was and what it wanted. At least she had started.

Luis and Willa stepped forward, looking like they stole something. "What's going on?" He stood taller than usual.

I gave him my best evil stare. "I ain't forgot you grabbed

me. Forgiving ain't something I do real easy. I learned that the hard way."

"Sorry about that, Odessa. I got caught up in the moment. I didn't mean no harm."

He sounded sincere, but that don't mean I trusted him. I planned to keep my eye on him.

I spread my arms. "They need money, or they gonna lose all this."

Willa held out her palms. "We don't have money."

Everyone was quiet for a moment. I looked at each of them. "We gonna have to come up with the money to save this farm for them, or we ain't going nowhere." I stomped my foot. If I couldn't help them, then nothing else mattered.

Willa inched closer, like whatever she had to say was important. "We shouldn't try to change history. If your family lost this land, you can't reverse that now. What about the ripple effect on everything that comes afterwards?"

I pushed my chest into her face. "You think I care about history?" I pointed to the ground with my index finger. "My grandparents need help, and I'm aiming to do just that."

"But if you change what's supposed to happen here, then maybe you don't get born in the future," Willa argued.

"She's right, Odessa." Luis rubbed his shoulder against Willa's. "This could impact a lot of people."

I shifted my feet. "I don't care." I talked through my teeth.

"How much money do they need?" Ronita's soft voice broke some of the tension.

"I don't know. But ain't no use in giving them a couple hundred dollars because the same thing could happen next year or the year after."

"We don't have any money, and now you want even more than that." Willa slapped her palm against her temple. "This is crazy."

Ronita tapped the bird's head. "Can we steal the money?

Since no one can see us, we should be able to get the money from almost any where."

Willa shook her head. "Yeah. Like that's an idea. I'm sure Princess Kenyata wants the four of us to start breaking the law. Stealing is illegal, you know? That's a sure way to keep us from getting to the next portal." She huffed like she was out of steam.

I didn't want to admit it, but Willa was right. I already had a blemish in the book. No use piling on more. "Taking the money would be the fastest and easiest thing to do, but that's not the way." I scratched my head.

Luis stuck his nose in the air and sniffed like an old hound dog. "I might have an answer. A good one."

With my hand on my hip, my ears perked up. "Well, don't just stand there looking pretty. What is it?"

He waggled a finger at me. "Not so fast." A sly smile slid across his face like he had me cornered.

The King Falleth

Luis

I couldn't help sticking my chest out just a little now that I had something Odessa wanted. I rubbed my hands together. My spine tingled.

Odessa scratched her forehead. "I'm tired. If you got something worth saying, come sit with me on the step." She turned around and made her way back to the house. Her pace was slower. By the time she settled on the bottom stair, her faded dress was back, and so was her gray hair and missing hand. The sudden transition brought me up short.

Willa tugged my sleeve. "Did she turn back on purpose?" she whispered.

"Ain't no use in gossiping behind my back," Odessa yelled. "We can hear everything each other says."

Still sucking up to Odessa, Ronita sat next to her. With the bird roosting on her shoulder, Ronita looked ridiculous, but at least she wasn't running around swatting her hands, and the bird had stopped squawking.

Odessa waved me over. "Well, what you got to say?"

Willa gave me an encouraging nod.

I shoved my hands in my pocket. "How do I know I can trust you?"

Odessa huffed. "How do I know I can trust you?" She threw her words fists. "I don't know you from Ronita's bird. You ain't end up here because you a good Christian man, that's for sure."

"You're the one with the power and didn't share when we were in danger. You're the one we shouldn't trust." I inched closer with my nose pointed up. I sniffed the air and hoped I was right.

"What you want, Luis?" Odessa spat.

"I want to do what you did—when you changed yourself."

I kept my tone level. There was no room for bargaining. When I was with Willa over there behind the tree, I heard Janet whispering again. She continued to linger out of sight. I needed to be able to fight her off.

Willa cleared her throat. "Did you turn back on purpose, Odessa?"

"Yeah," Odessa sighed. "It takes too much energy to stay that way. Nothing in the Interruption lasts forever, or at least I ain't figured out a way."

"Can you do it again?" Willa's face glowed with curiosity.

Odessa hunched her shoulder. "I reckon I could." She drew a deep breath. "Let me gather my wits a minute, won't you?"

We were quiet for a moment, listening to Odessa breathe so heavily that if she weren't already dead, I'd have thought she was dying.

"I ought to find a way to tell them Luis is a fraud. A big old coward."

The voice was back. I stiffened and glanced over my shoulder.

"Yeah, he's strutting around like he's willing to help someone. But I know he's so selfish he'd take from his own mother. He won't do a damn thing for anybody unless he gets something from it. I can't count the number of promises he broke. That's why I couldn't take it anymore."

I jerked around, looking for the source of the voice. "Did you hear that?"

"Hear what?" Ronita straightened. "I heard nothing."

Odessa flipped her hand at me. "Maybe you got your own demons, Luis." Her eyes narrowed. "What they saying?"

I shook my head. "Never mind." I tried to make light of it so the questions would go away. Nobody needed to know what the women in my past thought of me. I wasn't the same person now. "Look, Odessa, your family needs help, and I think I can help them in a big way."

Odessa placed her elbows on her knees. Her cloudy eyes pierced mine. "Say what you got to say."

Willa glanced from Odessa and then back to me. "Odessa, we all want to know how you got your power. We want to know if we can do it, too."

"What's in it for me, for telling you?"

Ronita touched Odessa's forearm. "Odessa, if we all have the same power, it will make us stronger, and maybe whatever ate your hand won't be able to harm us. Any of us. Maybe we can get to the next place faster."

Odessa took her time studying each of us as if she expected to read our intentions from our foreheads. "I'll think on it."

I folded my arms. "Don't take too long. If what I'm thinking is true, it's going to take some time, and who's to say we won't get chased away before we get it done." I eased away, still sniffing the air with great satisfaction.

"Okay, Luis," Odessa called to me. "I want to know what you got to say, but how we gonna do this?"

I nodded to her. "You go first. Then I'll tell you what will help your family."

Her eyes darkened, and I imagined her brain churned, looking for a way to shift things in her favor.

"That's the only way we can do this." It felt good standing my ground.

She pointed her finger at me. "We'll do it your way, but if you cross me, I'll find a way to hurt you good."

"Fair," I said.

The tension raised the hairs on my back. The air crackled.

Odessa took a deep breath and stood. She wore reluctance on her face. "Don't make me sorry for sharing."

"We have to trust each other." I looked at all three women. "Isn't that what Princess Kenyata told us?"

Odessa shook her head. "No, that ain't what she said. But come on, let's go stand in the clearing."

The three of us trotted behind Odessa like baby ducklings. My heart pounded against my ribs—excited about the knowledge she would impart. I already imagined all the things I might do with this new power.

We faced Odessa. She wasn't in a hurry and kept her hand clasped below her stomach. I wanted to hurry the process, but pressing her would make her slow down—or back out.

"First thing you got to do," she paused and cut her eyes toward me as if sharing what she knew would diminish her. "You got to think about what you want to be, what you want to do, where you want to go."

"Can we all do it?" Ronita's voice sounded more timid than usual.

"We gonna do Luis first." She enjoyed being bossy. I could tell by the way she doled out her knowledge. She used it as power. "Let's get on with this." She directed her attention to me. "What do you want, Luis?"

I looked at Willa, and her eyes begged me for something I couldn't give her. Not yet.

"I want to be alive again." It was a selfish wish, but it's what I wanted. If I'd been a little more careful, I wouldn't be on this side. I should have known Janet was crazy enough to slit my throat and hers. I'd seen the wild look in her eyes whenever she thought I'd spent too much time looking at or talking to another woman.

Odessa rolled her eyes at me. "Don't be foolish, man. Once you die, you're dead." The way she rolled her eyes said her patience had thinned.

"Okay, okay." I held up my palm while trying to develop a better idea. "I don't know yet."

"Then why is it so important for you to know how to do this?" Odessa shook her stump at me. "You only taking up space." She headed back to the step.

She sounded like other women in my life. The ones who didn't get me, who didn't have time to find out I had more profound thoughts, but it took me time to share them.

"Okay." I waved her back to the clearing. "I want to be seen. If I'm going to help your family, they'll need to see me. Can you do that?"

Ronita stepped toward Odessa as she entered the clearing. "I want to be seen, too. I want to see my mom and for her to see me."

"Me too," Willa added. "I want to see my children."

Odessa gave each of us a thoughtful look. "I don't know if it's a good idea for the living to see folks they done buried. But we can talk about that later. First, Luis, you got to concentrate on what you want. Then, when you've got a clear vision, close your eyes, and lift your hands above your head with your palms facing." She demonstrated. "You got to do this with your eyes closed. And I have to tell you, you'll be vulnerable during the transition."

"What does that mean?"

"It means anything can happen to you, and it may not be good."

She was trying to scare me, but I wasn't falling for it. "Nothing happened to you when you changed."

"It was a chance I was willing to take." Her voice dropped. "Are you willing to take that chance?"

"Yeah. I think I've got it." I took a deep breath.

"You won't do it right." Janet's voice was in my ear. "No matter what you do or where you go, I'm going to be there, making you as miserable as you made me."

I closed my eyes and wished myself taller, with broader

shoulders and a hint of a mustache. With Janet's voice in my head, I struggled to hold on to the vision.

When I lowered my arms, I took my time opening my eyes. The smirk on Odessa's face and Ronita's snicker made me look down. I wore plaid pants and a shirt but in different patterns. I'd shrunk three feet. Instead of standing six feet tall, I was so close to the ground that I could touch the anthill without bending. I ran my hand over my head, which was now bald. My thick black hair was gone.

"You couldn't have wished for that." Ronita laughed behind her fingers.

Odessa put her good hand on her hip. "I don't see how that get-up can save my family."

"What went wrong?" I yelled, flinging spit at Odessa.

She shrugged. "Don't know. But if my grandparents see you looking like that, they gonna think you in town with the circus."

"Can I try again?"

"Oh, you can keep trying, but you won't do any better, especially if I have anything to do with it. When you're the most vulnerable, I will snatch you down here with me, where you belong." Janet cackled.

The sound of her voice grated my teeth.

"I think you better." Odessa batted her eyes like she thought I was stupid.

Ronita raised her hand. "Let me try."

"No," Odessa snapped. "If you and Luis become visible and my grandpa sees you standing out here, he gonna pull out his shotgun. Now, Luis, you got to concentrate. This ain't no time for joking."

"I think … " I shook my head. "Maybe I'll try later. I can't focus right now."

"We had a deal."

I turned my back on Odessa. "I can't do it. I can't concentrate with y'all staring at me." I didn't want to face any of them. If I could have seen Janet, I would have grabbed her neck and swung her around like a piñata.

I spun around with my arms straight out, feeling for Janet.

"Are you trying to find me, Luis?" She placed her hands around my much smaller head and squeezed tight. Then she ran her fingers down my face, gathering my skin under her nails.

I couldn't tell if she read my thoughts or if we were connected. A slick of sweat dampened my shirt. Then Janet knocked me on my back, grabbed my leg, and dragged me away.

I flailed my arms, but it was useless. This small, I couldn't match Janet's strength or her anger.

"Help me." I stretched my arms toward Willa, Odessa, and Ronita. The words came out mangled because I was breathing so hard. I didn't know what Janet wanted with me. She'd already killed me, but her tormented mind wanted more. She probably wanted to pick the flesh off my bones like a vulture.

"What's happening, Luis?" Willa didn't move toward me. Fear marred her face, and she froze.

From my helpless vantage on the ground, Janet dragged me toward a swirling cloud of darkness. Once upon a time, she was calm and gentle. She never even raised her voice. Had I turned her into this irrational being?

I dug my nails into the earth.

Janet was stronger. Her determination must have given her Herculean strength.

I grabbed grass, weeds, and sticks, but they slipped through my finger.

Terror gripped my throat and chest, squeezing me like a vise.

I had seconds to save myself.

I closed my eyes and envisioned my former self, refusing to allow other thoughts to skew my concentration. I had to free myself because if Janet was successful, fear told me I'd spend eternity doing any God-awful thing she commanded.

I, Too, Will Slip Away

Willa

I couldn't tell what was going on. The shrunken-down Luis yelled and struggled and groped the ground like a lunatic fighting with himself. His body twisted and turned as if he couldn't control his limbs. Did he need my help or not? I was afraid to step forward. I was afraid of everything in this place, so I wavered, and before I could decide—

He disappeared.

He was gone. Really gone. Gone gone.

Even though he knew we were supposed to stay together, he vanished. I closed my eyes to calm my nerves. If only I had a better understanding of what this place required from me, I'd give it immediately just for some peace of mind.

I opened my eyes as heat engulfed my neck and intensified, burning me like a branding iron. I rubbed my forehead in exasperation. This little episode proved that none of the others cared about Luis enough to help him. At least I'd *thought* about helping. I bet they didn't care anymore about me or what I wanted or needed. My crisis was mine alone. Like any good mother, I had to put Ava's well-being in front of my own—in front of any threats the Interruption presented.

I ran my hands down the front of my dress, then fluffed my hair, trying to gather my resolve and courage.

Odessa had taken us back to the 1930s to change history. I couldn't think of anything more ridiculous than the concept of the Interruption. The idea of coming here was crazy and a waste of time when I could have helped my living daughter, who needed me now.

Today.

The urge to do what Luis had done left me struggling to breathe. What could Odessa do to me for trying? I was younger and certainly more robust than this version of her.

I took two small steps away from Odessa and Ronita. They were so engrossed in the trail Luis had left in the grass before his disappearance they never even noticed me.

I envisioned my family in my mind and with my heart. In my head I saw the stubble on Burt's face that appeared at the end of the day, and then there was a flash of the cowlick that BJ always slicked down with my styling gel. I smelled the candle that set on the kitchen table and filled the room with cotton and linen when lit. I heard the music drift from under Ava's bedroom door long after she was supposed to be asleep and saw the reoccurring pimple she covered with her bangs. My soul ached to touch each of them.

With no one looking, I closed my eyes and stretched my hands above my head. My mind filled with memories of my family and an image of my best friend since high school. I couldn't show up at home like myself and scare my family into an early grave. So, I transformed into Lisa. They'd welcome her. Lisa had been the prettiest girl in our graduating class and again at the sorority house in college. Back then, I had envied her long blond hair, unblemished skin, and carefree attitude. Nothing seemed to phase her or cause her to pull up short. I should have been more like her.

I heard Odessa scream, but when I opened my eyes, I stood in front of my house. My heart swelled with relief.

It worked.

I looked down at my dress and shoes, and I wore the same dress Lisa wore the last time we were together. A tailored rough silk black sheath, with three-inch patent-leather pumps. My hair rode my shoulders with lush curls.

I heaved a deep breath.

"I did it." I squealed, then straightened.

The house was almost the same, but Burt had painted it a shade of pale gray. Gone was the blue house trimmed in white that I'd left. Instead of mourning me, he'd been busy fixing up the house. Maybe he planned to sell it because memories of me were too hard to bear. I chuckled at the ridiculousness of my thought.

I walked to the door and rang the doorbell.

The jitters in my stomach went into overdrive while I waited. I should have thought of something to say, but my mind blanked.

A woman cracked the door. "Hello, Lisa." She knew me, but I had no clue as to her identity.

I opened my mouth, then closed it again. "Uh, I'm looking for Burt Marshall."

She turned around. "Honey, Lisa is here." She faced me and opened the door wider. "Come on in. You remember me, right? I'm Joan, Burt's wife." She tilted her head as if the movement would jog my memory.

My temperature rose several degrees, making my dress feel confining. I'd died only days ago, and another woman already lived in my house and called herself Burt's wife. This woman had made herself right at home. She didn't even wait until I was cold in my grave. Anger bubbled in my stomach like hot lava, preparing to erupt.

I stepped inside and brushed past her. In the foyer, I stopped short. Nothing looked the way I remembered. I whipped my gaze around the room, taking in the differences. How could these changes have happened so fast? The white painted walls and a gray sofa holding a mountain of gray and white throw pillows were all new. It looked like someone had thrown up muted colors everywhere.

Burt came around the corner from the kitchen. He was so handsome my mouth watered. He'd grown a mustache and a beard. The salt and pepper coloring made him more debonair. He appeared leaner, like he'd started using his gym membership to its fullest potential. His expression was too relaxed for a man who should be mourning his wife, even if he was only pretending.

"Lisa, I didn't know you were coming." He opened his arms and embraced me.

I inhaled his familiar scent and willed my knees not to buckle.

I pulled away. " I … I just wanted to stop by before I leave town. I still can't believe Willa is gone." The sentiment was genuine and carried in my tone.

The quizzical expression on his face deepened. "Leave town?"

"Yeah, you know from Willa's funeral." I studied him. Why was he being so evasive?

"Lisa, Willa's been gone two years. You were here for the funeral. Remember? You even came to our wedding last year."

Joan placed her hand on my arm. "Why don't you have a seat? I'll get you something to drink. You look like you've seen a ghost." She hurried off.

Burt led me into the drab living room that Joan must have decorated. I sat on the sofa, and he took the chair across from me. Worry etched his face.

Two years. I've been dead for two years. The thought whirled in my head with no place to land. Princess Kenyata said time was different, but she should have been more specific like she should have been about everything in that God-forsaken place.

"Since Willa … I've been a little off. I still can't believe she's gone." I held my hands in my lap. Two years. How could two years have passed when it seemed like I was scraping tomato sauce off the dinner plates only hours ago? "I'm okay.

Yes, I'm aware." I kept nodding my head, hoping he believed me.

Joan walked in carrying one of the crystal glasses Burt and I had received as a wedding gift. I'd been saving them for special occasions. I held back the laughter at how silly I'd been trying to preserve nice things for future use, and now I had no future.

Joan handed me the glass of water, then sat on the arm of Burt's chair and draped her arm around his shoulder.

If anyone had asked me to explain my feelings, I'd struggled for words. The only way I could keep my feet firmly planted on the hardwood floor was to inhale and exhale.

"How are the kids? Are they here?" I craned to see if I could hear them upstairs, bickering like old times.

Burt looked up at Joan, and something flashed between them. They had an intimacy I'd never shared with Burt.

"BJ is in New York. In college at NYU." Joan lifted her chest as if she had something to do with his success. "He's studying communications or filming or something like that." She laughed.

I waited for them to tell me about Ava. Burt rubbed his hands together and stared at the floor. My heartbeat slowed. I couldn't form the question that sat in my throat. If she wasn't here, it was my fault. I'd let her down. When she needed me to be there, I couldn't put the bottle down long enough to care for my baby girl.

"Ava," Burt paused. "Ava slipped up. I've tried to get her back in rehab, but she's pretty strung out. She's not listening." He shook his head.

A pang of sadness fell over the room and pressed onto my shoulders.

I caved into the mound of pillows. Tears stung my eyes and rolled down my cheeks. I might have gotten to Ava in time if Odessa hadn't withheld the knowledge. The bitter taste of revenge scarred my throat.

"How long?" I managed.

"Well, you know when she's like this, she doesn't tell the truth. But I expect it happened right after Willa died." Burt stared at his hands, and Joan rubbed his shoulder as if she could impart strength to him.

"Do you know where she is?" I glanced around for the pictures of my beloved children that had graced the mantle. They were gone.

Upstairs, a baby cried. Joan jumped off the chair arm. "Oh, Birdie is awake."

"Birdie?" I locked eyes with Burt for the answer.

He hesitated before saying. "We have a daughter. She's six months old and only sleeps an hour at a time."

"I've got to feed her." Joan dashed up the stairs.

Burt kept his eyes on the floor. I knew him well enough to know this wasn't a proud moment for him.

"A baby already. That was fast." The cynicism in my voice could have set the room on fire.

Without looking at me, he said, "We didn't plan it. It just happened."

"Oh, your penis just fell into her pussy when you were grieving your dead wife?"

"It wasn't like that." He stood and turned his back to me. "And why are you so upset? I know you're Willa's friend, but you have no idea what it was like before she died. We were going through a rough patch. She wasn't there for me, and I couldn't be there for her."

I nodded. That was the first thing he'd said that was true.

"How long are you in town?" He turned to me, wiping his eyes. "Where are your bags? You can stay here like you always did. It's late, and you know the spare bedroom is ready."

"The airline lost my suitcase. Hopefully, it will show up tomorrow." I hadn't given luggage a thought. I expected to walk in and see my family gathered around the table, sharing stories about fun times we'd had together and how much I did for the family. But other than Ava, no one had missed a beat.

Nobody still mourned me.

The Woman and the Child

Odessa

Before I could get to Willa to pull her arms down, she disappeared faster than Luis. I stared at the space where she'd stood and felt the blood drain to my feet. We was going from bad to worse.

"That's one selfish hussy." I spat out the words, then settled my stump on my hip and shook my head. I ain't bargained for this kinda nonsense. The three of them were as bad as the kids in the Sunday School, saying the proper thing on Sunday and acting like heathens on Monday.

I massaged my forehead and tried to get my head clear. Getting from here to heaven seemed like it was getting further and further and further away.

I sat in church every time the doors opened. I expected better.

"How can Luis and Willa leave like that? We need them." Ronita looked in the direction where Luis had slid out of sight. The Interruption was hard enough on her. She didn't need the only people she knew slipping away.

I sighed. I didn't need that any more than she did. Maybe I had to handle Ronita with a bit of extra care—to take her hand and hold on to let her so she'd know I wouldn't leave her stranded, too.

The bird on Ronita's shoulder brushed a wing against her ear. In all the turmoil, I never thought a stupid bird would bring her comfort, but the gesture calmed her. "What happens now?" Her shoulders slumped. That poor child looked around like she expected them to reappear.

I had no such expectations.

I knew they wouldn't. Nothing was ever that simple. If I could go back inside the house and ask my grandma for more information about the Interruption, maybe I could fix everything. When I was younger, she jabbered on about this stuff. I thought she was talking about conversations she'd heard growing up—passing along folklore or tall tales. I never thought that talk was real. But now I wished she could tell me what I needed to do because I was running out of ideas and patience.

Ronita interrupted my thoughts with that whiny voice. "If we don't stay together, what will Princess Kenyata do to us?" Her voice trembled, but she hadn't shed a tear.

"Don't look at me. I ain't got all the answers. And it ain't my fault Willa's gone. What I do know is this won't get us moving to that portal." I threw my good hand in the air. "Do you know where she was itching to get to?"

Ronita gave me a blank stare that made me wonder if she'd tell me if she knew. Instead, she shrugged a shoulder the way teenagers do, like that was an answer to my question.

I stared at her, hoping she'd have something to add. "We should've been doing more talking and less arguing, then we'd know something about each other."

She dropped her head like I had chastised her. But I wasn't just stating facts. Maybe I expected too much. In the Interruption, we were equal, so I had to stop thinking of Ronita as a little girl.

She gave me a look that made me pause. "I don't know anything about you, either."

I chuckled. "I guess you right. Ain't much to know." I searched my brain for something to tell her that wouldn't give too much of myself away. After a moment, I decided to keep my mouth shut and fix the problem facing us. "We can talk later." I motioned toward the house. "We got enough to deal with for now."

The sun set lower, and I wasn't happy to see night come.

With night came trouble or that terrible creature that chewed off my hand. I rubbed my stump with my good hand. No way was I gonna show up at the Pearly Gates with no arms and legs or more missing body parts. I was already unsure if anyone would recognize me without both hands, so we needed to handle our business and move on.

I sighed. "All we can do is finish what we came here to do, then find Willa and Luis."

The ground under my feet vibrated. In the distance, the pounding of horse hooves sounded in the air. It was a noise that took me back to my childhood when my grandmom and me watched those westerns she was so fond of seeing on television. That many horses coming that fast sent a sensation up my spine and warned me that this wasn't a casual visit.

I turned in the direction of the commotion. "Trouble's coming."

"What kind of trouble?" Ronita folded her arms around her waist and squeezed so tight her ragged gown rose above her knees.

"Human. I imagine. And if it's that man that threatened Ruth earlier, it will be ugly."

"Should we hide?" Her expression told me she had already tucked her tail and wanted to burrow into a hole like a mole.

"Well, they can't see us, so we don't need to do nothing. But it ain't gonna be the same for them." I nodded my head toward my grandparents' house. "We need to warn them."

Ronita's eyes got so big I thought they might pop out of her head. She touched my arm. "Will those coming hurt them?"

"For sure. Girl, you need to know your history. During Jim Crow, if a bunch of white folks was coming your way, it wasn't to say, "'Have a good day.'" I shook my head at her ignorance and tried to figure out why she was in the Interruption. She must've done something terrible to someone along the way because the way I see it falling off a cliff to save a friend should have gotten her a first-class ticket to heaven.

"We gotta warn them," I repeated it, firmer this time so she'd get some hustle. I looked around. "Go to that tree and grab the biggest branches you can. If we strike the house, grandpa will get his rifle and start looking for the trouble."

In the distance, a cloud of dust rose in the air as the riders grew closer.

Ronita didn't look too keen on my idea, but she followed my instructions. We started under the window at the front of the house, banging as hard as we could. Ronita reared back and swung with such force I thought she might break a hole in the wood.

From inside came the sound of running.

"What's that noise, Ernest?" The fear in my grandma's voice knotted my heart.

"Don't know, Ruth. But git low. Stay down till I say it's safe. You hear me?" He sounded solid and fierce like trouble wasn't new to him.

A moment later, he stepped out onto the porch with his rifle at arm level and peered into the darkening sky. He craned his head toward the sound of the arrivals.

I dropped my stick, stretched my back, and motioned Ronita closer. "We got to do more than this. It sounds like at least ten horses, and he can't fight off that many."

Ronita waved her branch in the air. "We only have sticks."

"We dead. We should be able to scare off the riders. We already know we can scare their horses."

"But they can't see us." Ronita rattled the window one more time before dropping her stick.

"That's our advantage. If they can't see us, they can't stop us. We can do whatever we want. Let's grab that clothesline and string it across the road. Those riders won't see it if they are coming so fast. Hurry."

Ronita raced and tore the clothesline from the trees. "If we wrap this rope tight enough around the trees we can knock some riders off their horses." Her eyes gleamed with delight.

I winked, and together we made our way down the long, narrow lane leading to the house. The sound of the approaching horses grew louder. I didn't think my heart had much tick left, but it was pounding now.

My grandpa had his gun ready, but streams of sweat ran down his face.

I hoped what Ronita and I planned would be enough.

Dead Doesn't Mean Defeated

Ronita

I tried to tug my gown below my knees, biding my time until I could ditch it for something suitable for me, then followed Odessa. We got into position, one on either side of the road, with the clotheslines tied tight to trees on both sides of the road.

Across from me the sour-tempered Odessa showed no expression. I needed to learn whatever she did to stay calm because my insides were raw. This place, the Interruption was creepy, and nothing made sense. "Odessa, what about Willa and Luis? Do you think they're okay?"

She shook her head. "Let's just do what we decided. We can't worry about Luis and Willa right now. After we get this done, we'll find them—or we won't."

I pushed my tongue into my cheek. The words rolling out of her mouth made it sound so easy as if we had all the time we needed and all the answers. I couldn't share her ease. The same fear that had gripped me when Cato stepped off the cliff settled on my chest again. "How can we find them? Do you know how to do that?"

"We'll figure it out. Now make sure your rope is high and taunt. It will stop some horses."

I glanced down the road where the riders were coming into view. "They're here." I sounded like someone strangled me. There had to be at least ten men on horseback. It was hard to tell because they rode close together, and the dust kicked by the ones in front hid those in the back. They rode angry. The house was only a few hundred feet away, so if we didn't stop them here, then Odessa's grandfather would be in real trouble.

I looked across the road, and Odessa gave me a slow,

encouraging nod that made me believe this plan would work. I tightened my hold on the rope and squinted toward the riders. Holding my breath was useless, but I did it anyway. My bird flew off and sat on a nearby branch, but with his eyes on me, it gave me assurance that I was doing the right thing.

They came fast, riding three across. The animals looked enormous from our vantage point near the ground. I couldn't help wondering if we'd get trampled if the horses came our way, then held back my snicker because we were already dead. Dying—the thing I'd constantly worried about—no longer existed.

The first three riders barreled toward us. Their horses tripped on the clothesline, tossing their riders off like bags of rocks. The other riders pulled hard on the reins, and the gang stopped.

More horses bucked and whinnied at the sight of us. They tossed several more riders, and then the animals spun around and galloped in the opposite direction leaving their riders stranded. I couldn't look away from the animals' colors and glossy coats.

As the lead men scrambled to their feet, they squinted and pointed at the house as if Odessa's grandfather had been behind the mayhem.

"Why ya'll on my property?" Odessa's grandfather yelled. He had his rifle trained down the lane, but the hitch in his voice said he wasn't as brave as he appeared.

A rider picked up his big cowboy hat, dusted his pants, and stepped forward. His horse had already trotted away. "We don't want no trouble with you, Ernest. We come for Ruth." The rider spoke as if it was a regular occurrence for ten white men to come for one black woman.

"What you need with Ruth, Mr. Brody?" Ernest's voice was deeper, and he pitched his shoulders back, standing taller. Maybe the mention of his wife's name toughened him.

"Now, Ernest. Don't go getting crazy. Why don't you put the rifle down?" Mr. Brody held his hands out at his side. "I ain't got no gun pointed at you."

"State your business, Mr. Brody."

Mr. Brody glanced down at his boots and pushed his toe in the dirt. "She killed Thomas Archer."

Ernest's eyes narrowed, and he hefted the gun higher. "No." He shook his head. "Ruth is with child. Ain't no way she could'a killed nobody." His words hung between them, filled with fear and anger and dread.

My stomach knotted. There was no way this would end the way Odessa had hoped. She craned her neck, looking from her grandfather and back to the men. Several of them had strayed toward the cotton field.

"He's lying, Odessa. What should we do now?" I whispered even though they couldn't hear us.

She dismissed me with her hand. "Give me a minute to think, child. We can do almost anything we want, but we got to be careful, so the blame don't fall on my grandparents."

Mr. Brody started toward Ernest. His pace was slow and measured, but hand stayed perched on his holster. "As I said, put your gun down. We can talk this thing over. I'm sure we can figure out what happened."

"Naw, I ain't aiming to do that." He took a step forward. "How you claiming Ruth done this thing?"

The curtain at the window shifted, and I saw the top half of Ruth's face. Her eyes were wide and filled with panic.

"She pulled him off his horse and hit him on the head."

Odessa shook her head and moaned like hearing that explanation caused her great pain. "Now they gotta know that don't make no sense. They gonna come up with anything to git their hands on this land."

Ernest shook his head. "Ain't no way you gonna tell me my Ruth pulled a man off a horse, hit him, and killed him. My Ruth is a tiny thing, all she got is a belly full of baby. You can't make me believe you finding truth in that story. Now why don't you go away from here and bother someone else?"

"Can Ruth come out and talk to me?"

Ernest glanced over his shoulder, then back to the talker. "You stay there and don't come a step farther." When the talker nodded, Ernest cracked the door and motioned for Ruth to come outside.

She poked her head out first before stepping on the porch. She stood inches behind Ernest with her hands on her stomach.

"Ruth." Mr. Brody spat tobacco into the dirt. "Tell us how you knocked Thomas off his horse."

"No, sir, Mr. Brody." She put her hand on Ernest's back. "I ain't touch Mr. Thomas. His horse got spooked and flipped him. That's what happened."

"Someone saw you talking to him." he shot back.

"No. He talked to me." Ruth kept her focus on her well-worn shoes.

Odessa walked across the lane towards me. "I had enough. This is bullshit, and they know it. This is just another way to railroad black folks."

She stepped in front of Mr. Brody, reached into his belt, and pulled out his gun, even though his hand still rested on it. She moved fast, it seemed like it happened in slow motion.

She pointed the gun at Brody's right foot and pulled the trigger.

He staggered, screamed, and then whirled on his left foot to face his posse. "Damn, which one of you jackasses shot me?"

The men gathered behind him backed up, shaking their heads. One of them pointed. "You shot your own damn yourself. Now stop pointing that gun at us. I tell you, something ain't right about this place." He looked at the men behind him for confirmation. "First, our horses get spooked, and you shoot yourself. Something ain't right." He shook his head.

Odessa pushed Brody's arm into the air and pulled the trigger several times. The group scattered like field mice.

Ernest rushed Ruth back into the house. He stood in the doorway a moment, then slammed the door, sealing himself and Ruth from the chaos.

Odessa kept firing until she emptied the gun.

I couldn't take my eyes off her and what she was doing.

The men still on their horses galloped away from the house, and the ones that had dismounted or been thrown off grabbed their animals, climbed on, and headed the way they'd come.

Boom!

A sound louder than anything I'd ever heard roared in my ears, knocking me to the ground scattering dirt, rocks, and tiny bits of cotton.

Boom!

And another.

I covered my head and tried to see Odessa through the falling debris. She was lying on the ground next to Mr. Brody, who struggled to his feet.

On my hands and knees, I rushed to Odessa's side, tearing the delicate fabric of my gown even more. I touched her shoulder. "Are you okay?"

She didn't move.

I shook harder. "Can you hear me, Odessa?"

She shrugged, then opened her eyes. "I'm fine." She glanced over her shoulder at the cotton field. "What the hell happened?"

Mr. Brody hobbled down the lane, away from the house.

The only noise now was his step-drag sound as he distanced himself from the shack.

Odessa and I remained seated. The blast still echoed in my ears, leaving me clutching for something familiar in such a foreign place.

"What now?" I rubbed dirt from my arm. "Your grandparents—what will happen now?"

Odessa rose to her feet, using her good arm. Her lips were tight, so I didn't expect an answer.

The door on the shack opened, and Ernest came out, still carrying his rifle.

"What was it, Ernest?" Ruth's timid voice came from inside.

"Stay put." He shouted back, and then he stared down the now empty. He eased down the crooked steps and started toward his field. After a few steps, he shaded his eyes against the sun and gazed over his land. He stepped back in shock, swiped his forehead with the sleeve of his shirt and shook his head.

Ruth came through the door, her face still taut with tension. She waddled down the steps and made her way toward her husband.

"Ernest, talk to me?"

"It's gone, Ruth. Our crop is gone. All gone. They blew it up."

"There's still some left, Ernest."

"What's left ain't enough to make us no money." He shook his head, and from where Odessa and I sat, his despair was tangible. "It's not enough."

Once A Cheater

Willa

I sat on the edge of the bed in the spare bedroom of the house I used to know so well. Burt's new wife Joan had wasted no time removing all touches of me and adding her flair. She was all brass, with muted colors and bare floors.

I'd spent the evening looking at Burt, trying to determine if he seemed happier or if he'd found what he'd searched for all those years. Bitter slime coated my tongue. I'd spent so much time wanting what would never happen. Why hadn't I left? If I had been strong enough to leave Burt when our relationship turned bad, maybe I wouldn't have looked to alcohol. Maybe my children would have been just fine. It was hard to imagine they could have turned out worse.

The price of our struggle was too high. It had cost us our daughter.

As Ava's mother, I used to tell her she was my heartbeat, so as a child, she fell asleep with her hand on her chest, saying she wanted to feel the *thump, thump, thump* of our hearts. So what was she feeling now? Since being stuck in the Interruption, I hadn't once placed my hand over my heart. Of course, I wasn't alive, but the thought that I no longer had that connection with my daughter dragged me like roadkill. There would be no rest for me, no moving on until I found Ava and saved her again.

I waited for the house to quiet, listening for Burt and Joan to fall asleep. When I heard no more murmurs or bare feet padding across the floor, I lifted my hands above my head and envisioned the crack house Ava used to frequent. The place where the foul smell of rotting food, unwashed bodies, and human excrement was once so powerful it made me want to puke.

I'd get my daughter out of there tonight if my powers were any good. Somehow, I had to make her believe she was worth more than anything else. Maybe I could help her more from this side.

When I lowered my arms and opened my eyes, I stood in front of a house that looked far worse than I remembered. I spun around and glanced across the street, then turned back. The boards on all the windows, the front door, and the darkened interior told me no one had been inside for years. Weeds covered the front yard and crawled up the dilapidated porch, making venturing any closer hazardous.

I'd come this far, so I needed to be sure she wasn't barricaded inside sleeping off her latest hit. I climbed the stairs and pried a loose board from a window. The inside seemed darker and more decimated. Debris covered the floor, so I was careful where I placed my feet. I rushed through the house, and only when satisfied she wasn't there did I push through the window and back onto the porch.

My anger with Burt perked to life, searing like a hot poker in my veins. If I had one wish, it would be that he could turn his attention outward just long enough to see his family and their needs. He was so busy with his new wife that he wasn't even aware Ava's old drug hang-out no longer existed. I couldn't stop staring at the vacant house. If my daughter wasn't here, where was she?

Unsure of where to go next, I dropped my shoulders. The meth clinics were closed, and she never went to shelters, so even with my power, I didn't have what I needed to find her.

A new set of tears streamed from my eyes. If Odessa saw me now, she'd start sucking her tongue and rolling her eyes. But crying was what I did. I had to get my sense of failure in the open where there was room for it to move around, or it would swallow me.

When my tears dried, I raised my hands and returned to the bedroom at Burt's house. I stripped down to my panties and propped against the headboard. Sleep was a million miles away. During my life, a bottle of vodka would have helped soothe me after news like this. But a drink wouldn't fix this mess.

Maybe I should have waited until we helped Odessa's family because I needed the help of my three new companions to put these pieces back together.

I closed my eyes, not because I was tired or wanted to sleep, but because I didn't want to see the life I'd left behind. It was too painful to bear.

A gentle knock on the door brought me back.

Burt opened the door without being invited in. "I saw the light on and thought I would see if you needed anything." He only wore a pair of athletic shorts. His bare chest and flat stomach made me long for the part of him I never had. Two years and my death hadn't worn him down. He looked vital, like the twenty-two-year-old man I'd fallen in love with so long ago.

He stepped further into the room. "Joan has been up with the baby, and the two of them just fell asleep."

I nodded, unable to take my eyes off him. It surprised me he still held such a large part of my heart. I couldn't help wondering if he still had some love for me.

I should have covered my breasts but was too weary to care.

"A new baby is a lot of work. I thought you'd had your fill with babies, bottles, and diapers." I paused. "That's what Willa told me."

He settled on the edge of the bed but couldn't hide the erection growing in his shorts. The way he stared at my breasts, I thought maybe he recognized the mole that sat left of my right nipple, but when I glanced down, it wasn't there.

My transformation into Lisa was so complete I didn't recognize this firm body.

He shrugged. "Joan is younger. She wanted children, and how could I say no? It meant so much to her."

Heat crept up my back and had to have turned my cheeks red. Was he ever that thoughtful when it came to me? I pushed those thoughts aside. It was useless to hold on to that resentment. It changed nothing, just like having sex with Luis had no impact on Burt. I wanted to get back at him, but nothing so simple would phase him.

"Do you miss Willa?" I held my breath waiting for him to answer.

"Every day." He didn't hesitate. "After she died, I had so much guilt—all the things I didn't do right. The way I treated her. She deserved more, but I couldn't get myself together. No matter how hard I tried, I was always fucking up." He shook his head. "I visit her grave every week and talk to her. Of course, Joan doesn't know, but it brings me a little peace."

The anger I held so tight melted, and I wanted to hold him in my arms. Many things would have been different if he could have said those words years ago. Maybe we could have saved Ava from her pain, too.

He inched toward me. "You always reminded me so much of Willa. Even more so now." He settled beside me on the bed and placed his hand on my thigh.

The warmth of his hand brought me back to life—waking up my body and sending warmth between my legs. I didn't think I could have those feelings for him, but I welcomed the sensation. I wanted him to make love to me, to show me the tenderness I'd missed all those years.

He nestled closer, and I knew what was coming. His familiar smell took me back to our beginning when I fell in love with him before our children arrived, before work, parenting, and stress changed us.

He cupped my face between his palms and stared into my eyes. "I can't explain my feelings, but I want you, Lisa. You never required a lot of talking or explaining." He parted my mouth with his tongue and pulled at my bottom lip with his teeth. I wondered where this Burt hid during our marriage.

I accepted his tongue and relished the dance we'd perfected over the years, wondering if any part of it was familiar to him. My breathing grew heavy but not as labored as his.

"It's been so long," he whispered between kisses. "Joan doesn't have time for me."

He'd probably said the same thing about me when he cheated when all I wanted was more attention from him.

I slipped my hand into his shorts and caressed his swollen penis. It pulsed with heat. His exposed body was the eye candy that would have kept me away from alcohol. I drank him in, letting my mind take pictures that might last me for wherever this journey ended.

He kissed every inch of my neck. Not the hurried kisses of a man doing his duty, but of a man hungry for me. He kneaded my breasts and teased my nipples with his teeth. I didn't know this, Burt, and didn't recognize my body. It tingled with pleasure I didn't know was possible. The moans starting in my throat, were filled with desire and need.

Burt raised his head. "Shhh. You'll wake Joan."

"I can't help it," I croaked and stroked his penis. As I spread my legs wider, I realized how much I'd missed during our marriage.

He slipped his fingers between my moist folds. His touch was slow, tender, and thoughtful. He kissed my belly button. Then his tongue ran circles around my navel as his finger slithered across my swollen clit. I swallowed the groan rising in my throat.

I shifted on the bed, dropping lower, and took his penis in

my mouth as he replaced his finger with his tongue. Maybe my mind should have been on getting back to Luis, Odessa, and Ronita, based on Princess Kenyata's advice, but Burt's tongue drove away my common sense and replaced it with the pleasure that had vanished from my life.

The way he lingered on my flesh felt like the apology I wanted and the appreciation I needed. My heart ached that we didn't share moments like this when we had the chance. Time had run out on us and left me wanting what I could never have.

I pushed those thoughts away and enjoyed the moment. My back arched off the bed as every vein swelled with blood.

The sounds coming from Burt let me know I had him right where I wanted. His body relaxed under my touch.

Burt eased my legs apart and slipped between them. With my eyes closed, I could pretend we were a twenty-something couple again and could orgasm with the right look or touch. My body gripped him and held on tight. I wrapped my arms around his shoulders and my legs around his waist. Our lovemaking wasn't the way I remembered. It was better.

As much as I tried to prolong the moment, I couldn't. The spasms that racked my body lifted my hips off the bed and left me spent in a way I hadn't felt since Burt walked away. Burt. He shuddered a moment later. His body stiffened, and then he collapsed against me.

In the silence that filled the room, I remembered why I'd come, and it wasn't to have sex with my husband.

"What about Joan?" I managed between whispered breaths.

"She's asleep and won't wake until the baby cries." He faced me and cupped my breast, massaging my nipple and stroking another fire in my core.

"No. I mean, you're cheating on her, too. Won't you feel guilty like you do with Willa?"

He stopped rubbing my breast and held my gaze. "What I want is Willa back. What I want is to put my family together again. I know this might not be fair to you, but I need you now. You are as close as I can get to Willa, and I need that tonight. Seeing you brought back all the pain, and I want to remember her for a while. I feel like I'm losing my mind." He paused. "Please, Lisa. Tonight reminds me of when you came to BJ's fifteenth birthday party. Remember, Willa passed out, and I pulled you into this very room."

My body cooled and turned rigid, loathing him with every vessel in my body. He had no moral compass and would never find what he sought because it didn't exist. Whoever said ignorance was bliss lied. My best friend. I should have known. Burt was always willing to put his penis in an available pussy.

Instead of slapping him, I removed his hand and clamped my thighs. "You should go back to your partner."

"Can't we get in one more for the road? Joan will be sleeping for a while."

I took a breath. "Burt, get some help, or you're going to mess around and lose this family, too. Haven't you caused enough damage?"

I shoved him out of the bed, but he landed on his feet. At the door, he turned toward me with pleading eyes.

"Go, Burt! Get out!"

Where, Oh, Where

Odessa

I'd made many mistakes in my lifetime, and I was woman enough to own each one. If I hadn't spooked that horse, maybe none of this would have happened. My grandparents had enough heartache. I didn't need to add more. The agony on their faces as they stared at their burning crop, felt like someone had reached into my chest and torn out my heart.

Now, they needed even more money.

I had the power to make their lives better and had done just the opposite.

Ruth held onto Ernest's arm as if she needed him for support. "Should we try to put the fire out?" she whispered as if afraid to speak.

He dragged his hand down his face. "What's the use? There is a big crater in the middle of the field. And there ain't much left to save." He pointed. "You can see the flames coming out that hole."

A tug on my dress drew my attention to Ronita.

"Can't you do something?" Her eyes begged me to help them. "Like make it rain to put the fire out?"

"I wish I knew what to do. That damn Luis said he had an answer. Then he disappeared from here." I swirled my stump above my head. "He probably never had nothing in mind. Just wanted to know how to use his power." I shook my head at how quickly I granted his wish when I knew better than to trust.

The two of us remained in the lane and stared at my grandparents. Emptied handed and no way to help them. But I ain't never quit nothing. Not even my worthless husband. And if I had to walk into a bank and take a pocket full of money, that's what I planned to do. So what could happen to me?

I suppressed a giggle.

My grandpa released Ruth's hand and stumbled toward the crater, where the flames flared.

"Ernest, come back here." Ruth reached for his arm, but he sidestepped her. "Don't go near that." The urgency in her voice drew me closer, wanting to save them from any more harm.

He settled onto his knees about ten feet from the burning hole, then crawled on his hands and knees.

"What you doin', Ernest? Please don't get hurt." Ruth rubbed her stomach with one hand and bit the nails on the other.

He looked back at her. "Calm down, Ruth. I ain't in no danger."

His assurance eased her worry. She nodded, then took a deep breath.

The love they shared was visible. It coursed through the air between them. If I'd had that kind of connection with my husband, my life could have been different. I wouldn't have had this rough exterior to protect my heart if I knew someone else was holding it, too.

Ernest continued crawling, then stopped and sat cross-legged.

I left Ruth's side and followed him. He poked his index finger in the dirt near the crater, then quickly snatched it back and swiped it on his pant leg. Then he blew on his finger like he was trying to blow out a candle. A wide grin spread across his face, slow and easy, like sap running down the side of a tree.

"My God, Ruth," he yelled so loud he sounded like a church choir that got happy on the first Sunday. "Don't that take the rag off the bush."

"What, Ernest? What?" Ruth took a timid step into the field.

He waved her to stop. "No, you stay there, Ruth. I don't want you to slip or fall."

She stomped her foot. "You come here right this minute and tell me what's going on?"

Ernest rose to his feet with two black palms and a wide grin that lifted the despair in my heart.

As he made his way to her, Ruth backed up. "Look at you. You're a mess. What's all that on your hands and those pants?" Her eyes narrowed. "I just stitched new patches to the knees last week, and you done ruined them already."

He placed his blackened palms on her face and pressed his lips to hers. She struggled to get away but couldn't.

She shrieked. "You're a mess. Now you're making me dirty, too."

"Woman, we ain't gonna have to worry about patches and dirt, no more." He held his hand out to her. "This is oil, Ruth. Whatever they set off in my field struck oil."

"Oil?" Ruth looked beyond Ernest like she needed to see it herself. She ran her hand across her cheek and studied her finger. "Oil?"

"Yes, woman." He picked her up and swung her around. "Do you know what this means?"

Her face crinkled. "I know what you think it means. But them white boys is gonna come back. And they gonna try even harder to take this land from us when they find out it's got oil on it."

"Don't you worry about nothin. For now, they running for the hills. After one of them done shot Brody, they gonna keep low for a while." He held her chin with his index finger and thumb and looked into her eyes. "You and me, we going into town right now to that new fancy colored lawyer, and he gonna tell us exactly what we need to do." He held her gaze. "You ain't gonna have to worry about nothin'. We might never come back to this place."

"What about my beans I been cooking all day?"

He dropped his hand to her shoulder and started her back toward the house. "We ain't eating beans tonight."

I watched the two of them stroll back to their shack with my hand over my heart. Maybe I didn't do so badly by them after all, and I didn't have to steal nothin' from nobody.

Ronita stood in the same place, looking around like she had lost something.

I waved her over. The grin on my face felt glued in place.

"Did you hear all that? They gonna be fine."

She shook her head. "I heard. So, what's next?" She glanced over her shoulder.

"What? Are you looking for that bird? I thought you'd be happy when it left you."

She sighed. "I was getting used to it." She shielded her eyes and stared into the nearby trees. "Maybe we can go see my mother now." She didn't sound as committed as before.

I had to be satisfied with the outcome for my grandparents, and as much as I wanted to hang around and see their joy in their new life, I knew I had to move on. We'd already disobeyed Princess Kenyata's warning and needed to get back on track. I just didn't know how.

The surrounding quiet intensified. Moments ago, the sound of horses, gunfire, and explosions tore at my eardrums, but now the hush made my tiny hairs stand up.

When the trees and the remaining cotton plants sparkled like glitter, I spun around, looking for the winged beast that Princess Kenyata would arrive on.

Ronita reached for my hand and squeezed. Unlike last time, she didn't scurry off to hide. "She's coming, right?" she whispered.

"Yes." The change in the atmosphere made my tone hushed, too.

Through the haze, the large wings of the griffin flapped, but nothing moved. The black creature was in bold contrast to the bits of cotton left behind.

Princess Kenyata swung off the creature in one fluid motion. Her colorful gown glowed like the surroundings.

Ronita stepped closer to me.

I draped my arm around her. "Ain't no need to be afraid."

"She told us to stay together, and we didn't." Ronita dropped her head and talked into her shoulder.

"Well, what have we here?" Princess Kenyata's voice was like music. She shook her head. "You haven't followed instructions."

"Wasn't 'cause we haven't tried." I had nothing to lose by speaking up. "You didn't tell me how to wrangle grown folks. I couldn't hold them in place, and I don't even know where they went."

Princess Kenyata came closer.

This time I got a better look at her grand features. I wanted to touch her smooth skin to see if it felt like mine. She was the prettiest woman I'd ever seen.

"It's not your duty to keep everyone together." She clasped her hands and studied us like two wayward children. "The four of you are equals and must treat each other as such."

"What are we supposed to do now?" Ronita squeaked like we weren't allowed to talk too loudly in the presence of the princess.

Princess Kenyata sighed as if she'd grown weary of us. She contemplated the two of us like naughty children and answered Ronita. "Rubbing your pins will always bring the four of you back together. And even though that sounds simple, it's far from easy. The caution is you might end up deeper in the realm than you wish. If that happens, reaching the portal will take longer, and the troubles ill be greater." She shook her head with what looked like despair. "My advice is to use your power with restraint. It can work to your advantage but also cause you more heartache. You open yourself to all the creatures in the realm every time you transition."

"What other options you got for us because it seems like you always give us two bad ones?" I batted my eyes, disgruntled with the Interruption and all its rules and regulations that did nothing but hold us hostage.

"If you'd talked *to* each other and not *at* each other, then you should know where they've gone. You can always go to them."

"But we don't know … " Ronita's face tightened. Going through the Interruption was too much for someone so young, making me think she had done mighty awful while living.

"Don't run out of time, ladies." Princess Kenyata stepped back.

Ronita reached her hand toward the princess. "Please, can't you help us? There must be more instructions or directions you can give us. The information you've provided so far is useless," she screamed.

To me, she sounded helpless.

Princess Kenyata reached out her slim fingers and pressed her palm against Ronita's pin. "You have everything you need. You're going to be okay."

Ronita flinched before pulling away.

I wrapped her into a tight hold because I knew how she felt. Unfortunately, there wasn't an easy way out.

Watching and Waiting

Willa

Burt gave me a pained look, and then closed the door. With a huff, I crossed my arms under my breasts. I didn't need sleep, so I sat on the edge of the bed and waited for morning. I'd arrived back home with vigor, but it all faded, drained by disappointment and the unknown fate of my daughter. I couldn't go from this place to another without knowing more about my sweet Ava.

I uncrossed my arms and pounded my fist into my thigh for being stupid and blind. I deserved the bloom of a big blue bruise on my legs for loving Burt so much that I couldn't see the real man. The one that tore his family apart one layer at a time.

Of course, Burt had slept with my best friend. He'd probably sleep with my mother if she were still alive. A disheartened chuckle sounded in my throat. I squared my shoulders and accepted my hand in this dysfunctional family structure.

Shame on me for not seeing what was before me and instead always wishing something would change.

From somewhere in the house, the baby cried. Which meant Joan would be up and starting her day.

I pulled on the same dress I had worn the day before and gave the room one last glance. Not much remained in the house as I'd left it, but Joan hadn't scrubbed all my touches from this bedroom. If she knew what Burt and I did about last night, I'm sure she'd move this room up on her list.

I glanced around for something familiar that would remind me of my life. And there, stuck behind several used scented candles, were class pictures and diplomas for BJ and Ava. At least, they'd graduated from high school. I lifted the framed photos and studied their smiles as tears stung my eyes. I'd never get enough of them in this world or any other. But tonight I'd gotten close to them for a moment.

I removed the pictures from the frame, tucked them in the pocket of my dress, and slipped from the room. I made my way downstairs, where Joan sat at the kitchen table, breastfeeding the baby, as a teakettle simmered on the back burner.

"Good morning, Lisa. You're up early. I hope the baby didn't wake you." Joan looked ready for a magazine cover—every hair was in place, her eyeliner drawn to perfection, and though she wore no lipstick, her pouting lips gleamed. I could burst her bubble if she thought her appearance would keep her husband from straying. He'd slept with middle-aged me, with love handles and frizzy hair.

"No. I'm an early riser." I looked around. "Where's Burt?" I didn't want to run into him.

"He woke up in a mood this morning, so he went to Willa's grave site." She batted her lashes, showing disapproval. "I'd thought by now he'd stop, but he says sometimes he runs into Ava. Talking about her last night made him want to see her." She shrugged. "Now that I'm a mother, I get it." She placed the baby on her shoulder and rubbed Birdie's back.

"I'd better get going, then." I started toward the door.

"Don't you want to stay for breakfast or tea?" She nodded to the stove.

"No." I shook my head. "I've already called a car. Take care of the baby." I was out of the house before she could think of another reason for me to stay. The moment I stepped on the porch, I closed my eyes, stretched my hands to the sky, and within seconds, I stood several feet from my headstone.

Seeing my full name engraved in granite sickened my

stomach, stopping me like a roadblock. Ice invaded my veins, and all I could do was shiver.

Burt kneeled in the damp grass, pulling weeds from the base of the stone. He looked haggard, with his shoulders hunched and tight. Sleeping around must have worn on his conscience and his soul.

I cleared my throat, and he turned toward me so fast that he lost his balance and ended up on his ass.

"Lisa?" He exhaled with what sounded like relief. "I wasn't expecting anyone." He glanced beyond me. "How did you get here?"

"I… um… I used a service." I towered over him. Looking down I noticed his hair had thinned. His age made him vulnerable.

He brushed bits of grass from his hands. "Are you still mad? I'm sorry. I didn't mean to." His jaws went slack, and his eyes were unfocused.

I'd seen that *'please forgive'* me look and heard his *I'm sorry* so many times, but now I saw it had no meaning, just empty words.

"Yes, I'm mad, and you're pathetic."

"It meant nothing… last night. I'm sorry."

"If I'm supposed to feel better because it meant nothing to you, I don't."

He kept his head down. "Then why did you come? You know we have this messed up history. I thought that's why you came."

"I came to see how the kids were doing." At least that part was true. "Not to have sex with my best friend's husband."

"That never stopped you before. You always said there was something extra kinky about getting in on with Willa so nearby. You could have stopped me at anytime last night."

I closed my eyes. "You're right. I should have. I'm just as guilty as you. I thought …"

My heart hardened even more against Burt and Lisa. I hoped they'd end up in the Interruption one day, and I could chase them through the darkness.

Maybe no one deserved my trust. I let my shoulders slump. I couldn't control the universe or those two. They deserved whatever they got. "I'm different now, Burt. Willa's death changed everything. Why didn't it change you?"

He stared at the headstone without acknowledging my question.

I bent lower to read what he'd inscribed in sprawling letters on the top of my headstone. *Loving wife and mother* sounded hollow, like something off a convenience store card. My stomach dropped. I'd expected more. Those words seemed too simple for all that I'd given.

Burt sat crossed-legged, and I settled beside him, studying his face. "I still can't believe she's gone." I wanted to hear him pour out some loving tribute to me—a testament to his love.

His facial expression remained neutral.

"Joan told me sometimes Ava comes here."

He nodded. "Yeah. Like me, she finds peace here." He plucked several blades of grass and tossed them in the air.

"What did she say the last time you saw her?"

He shrugged. "That she didn't need help." He mimicked Ava's voice. "She was just fine." He paused and pulled more blades of brass. "I try not to ask her too many questions. I don't want to push her away. Besides what else can I do? Willa and I tried everything."

"Giving up is not an option. If Willa were here, she'd keep trying." I sounded firmer than I wanted, but I'd rattle his brain in his skull if I thought it'd work.

He leveled his gaze at me, his eyes unblinking. "Ava is the reason Willa isn't here. She drove her mother to drink."

Even though his words held no animosity, I wanted to slap him for not taking any ownership of my unhappiness. But I was the only one to blame for my demise. Although I pushed Ava to get treatment, I should have sought some, too.

He pushed to his feet. "I'm heading home. Wanna ride?"

"No. I want to stay here for a while."

"Are you coming back to the house?" He shoved his hands in his pockets.

"No." I shook my head and picked at the grass the way Burt had done earlier. "That's not a good idea."

He looked away. "Have it your way."

I waved him off. The less of him I saw, the less guilt I felt. He didn't deserve my pity. Joan did.

I don't know how long I sat. Maybe it was good that time in the Interruption didn't tick by in hours and days because I was determined to sit there until Ava showed up.

The sun dropped below the horizon, and the temperature followed. The breeze picked up, and I used my hands to warm my arms. I couldn't help wondering if whatever tried to strangle me before could make another attempt in the cemetery. There was no better place for demons to show up.

I stood and walked around my headstone. When the sun peaked over the horizon, I still made circles, though they were tighter and more concentrated.

"Aunt Lisa, what are you doing here?"

I looked up to see Ava. I wouldn't have known my daughter's face if I didn't recognize her voice. She'd aged more than two years since I last saw her. Her once beautiful, full head of hair had disappeared, replaced with matted clumps barely covering her scalp. Her thin body couldn't stand against a strong breeze.

"I came for a visit." I wrapped her in my arms and held her so tight she stiffened.

Ava wrenched away, but her stench remained in the fibers of my dress.

Her eyes darted as if she expected to see someone else standing at the gravesite with me.

"I'm alone." I reached for her hand. "Sit with me for a while."

"No." She tried to pull away, but I couldn't let her disappear. She was the reason I was here and couldn't rest.

"Please." I held on firm to her hand. "Just for a little while." I crossed my legs and settled on the grass that felt damp with the early morning dew. "I miss your mom so much."

I wasn't sure Ava heard me. She looked at me, but her mind seemed to race, and her thoughts were elsewhere.

We sat in silence, which seemed to go on forever as questions percolated in my stomach.

I needed to think of the right words to get her talking, to tell me what she was feeling. "Your dad was here earlier."

Her head jerked up. "Today?"

I nodded, unable to draw my eyes away from the dark circles under her eyes and her rail-thin arms.

"That's impossible. I had breakfast with him this morning at the diner. He told me you came to visit a few weeks ago, and he didn't say you'd come back."

I wanted to smack my forehead. Why did I keep making time references? Even though nobody would believe me if I told them what was going on, I wanted them to take me seriously. Especially Ava.

"Yeah, right." I rolled my eyes toward the sky. "That's what I meant."

"Why are you back here already? Don't you have a job or family or something?" She contemplated me as if she knew I wasn't who I said I was.

"Can I be honest?"

She sucked in a deep breath. "Yes." She dragged the word out.

"I wanted to see you. I worry about you."

She left my comment hanging.

I reached out and touched her knee. "Would you believe me if I told you I keep having a recurring dream where your mother tells me I have to do everything I can to help you?"

With her shoulders hunched, she seemed to shrink into herself. "You don't have to worry. I'm doing better."

I gave her knee a little squeeze. "It's the dream. It's your mother." If I could have transferred some of my power to help her, I would have. "How about going back to rehab?"

She yanked away and struggled to stand.

I got to my feet before her, and the moment she straightened her legs, I pulled her into my arms.

It took several moments before I realized she was crying, and then my tears started, too.

"Talking to you is like talking to Mom. I miss her so much I'm numb all over. I treated her badly, thinking she would always be here."

My heart swelled like a balloon. Hearing these words made everything I was going through a wee bit better.

I massaged Ava's back, hoping she felt the love I tried to pour into her.

Icy fingers around my neck yanked me away from Ava.

"Lisa, are you okay?" Ava jumped back, looking at me with wide, terrified eyes.

I couldn't speak because the fingers dug into my windpipe, squeezing with so much force the only thing I could do was gasp and flail my arms. I rocked my head and tried to use my legs to pull away. The vision of Luis scrolled across my memory as he fought against himself, much like I was doing.

The look of terror on Ava's face scared me more than the unseen force fighting me. I wanted to tell her not to be afraid, but unfortunately, I couldn't find my voice. This was a battle I was going to lose, and as I looked at Ava with her hands in her hair, screaming for help, something sucked me away.

Come Back To Me

Ronita

Princess Kenyata vanished in a puffy cloud, lifting off on the griffin without addressing my question—my plea. I flopped on the ground, fighting to control my anger and disappointment as it consumed me.

Odessa placed her hand on my back but couldn't console me. This was the first time I had nowhere to turn. I couldn't go right or left. I couldn't crawl into bed, cover my head, turn up the music, and drown out the world. Screaming didn't help, and crying wouldn't help. Nothing would help. I was just stuck.

"Come on, Ronita. Stand up." Odessa's voice was soft, but it changed nothing.

"Why?" I pounded my fist in the dirt. "What's going to be different? We should sit here until Luis and Willa return so we can move on." I stared at the ground. Too exhausted to care.

Odessa's shadow fell over me. "I'd get down there with you but might not get up anytime soon." She patted my head like she wanted me to be an obedient child. "Well, we can't sit here. Ain't no telling how long before those two come back— or if they will."

I glanced up at her. "What do we have to do now, Odessa? I'm tired of all this. I want to go home. Or someplace where I can rest. I don't know what I did to deserve this."

"Girl, you don't know how far we got to go before we get to the end. Ain't no quitting in the Interruption. Now get up." Her voice was firmer, demanding I obey.

My bird settled on my shoulder with a squawk. I closed my eyes briefly, thankful that he'd returned. "Did all the noise scare you?" I stroked its head and looked up at Odessa again. "How can I find out why this bird befriended me? Maybe I should give him a name."

"You gonna make me sit in the dirt, aren't you?" Odessa settled on her knees, then plopped on her butt. "I don't have all the answers. God knows I wish I did. Then I would have solved all this stuff a long time ago." She circled me with her arms. Her stumped hand creeped me out, but I hid my expression from her so that she wouldn't let me go. "But let's give a few things a try."

She had my attention. She looked wearier than before. I hated to ask her for anything, but she'd given to Luis and Willa. Now was my turn, so I sat up straighter, and hoped whatever we did, didn't make matters worse.

Odessa pinched the bridge of her nose. "Close your eyes, raise your hand, and think about what you want from this bird. Do you want it to talk, to take you away, or to reveal his secrets? Whatever it is you want, focus on it. But you better not vanish, or I'll haunt you to hell."

"I won't." I puffed. She made it sound easy, but I wasn't a fantasy fan. Since my father's death, I've had to stay grounded in reality. With my mother dating everything in pants, I didn't have time to wish on stars or fairy godmothers. "Maybe I shouldn't waste this moment on a bird. Can I wish to change this?" I waved my hand behind me.

"I don't know, child." She sighed. "How about you keep it simple for now. I'm tired."

I nodded.

Odessa continued to stare at me as if she expected me to do something great. "Okay." I squeezed my eyes tight, raised my hands without touching my bird, and hoped this bird had answers, knew the path, and was something I could trust.

I drew my hands down but kept my eyes closed, afraid to see what I'd conjured. I reached up to touch my shoulder, but my bird was gone. My stomach lurched, and my knees weakened.

I turned my head toward my shoulder and took my time lifting my lids.

But my bird was really gone.

I panicked. "Odessa!" I called. When I turned to look at her, there in front of me, Cato sat in the dirt.

My Cato.

Whole.

As perfect as he was that day in class.

Without a scar.

With a big wide grin.

Cato.

I sucked in a breath, drawing away from him. He could have been real or my overworked imagination. Either way, my anger at him boiled in my chest. He was the reason I was stuck here. Like everyone else, his selfishness threw me into chaos.

I stuck out my hand but drew it back and held it to my chest. I looked to Odessa for confirmation. "What did I do?"

She raised her brows. "I don't know, child. What's happening right now is all about you. Is this your boyfriend?"

He blinked several times like his voice hadn't arrived with his body.

I scrambled to my feet. "I don't want to see him. Or talk to him."

"Well, you brought him here." Odessa shook her head like I was a disobedient dog who'd peed on the good carpet.

"How can I send him back?" My words were hot on my tongue.

Cato reached for me. "No, Ronita."

I jumped back. Hearing his voice sent me in a spiral that pulled me back to that last day at school. The day that was supposed to be magical and change my life. None of which happened. I moved further away. "Don't touch me."

He stood, then gave Odessa a hand as she struggled to stand.

I turned my back on him, torn between wanting to hug him and cracking his skull wide open like he did when he jumped.

Odessa came to stand next to me and rubbed my back. "You drew him here. Now find out why?" I'd never heard her speak with so much compassion. "The thing about the Interruption is you never know what's going to happen. Expect the worse."

I shrunk away from her touch. I didn't want to hear the reason. It was too painful. "I thought the bird might have been my father. He cared about me. He might help me understand what's happening here and keep me safe." I threw my arms in the air and then dropped them.

Cato walked up to stand beside me with his hands in his pockets. He had the same don't-care attitude that permitted him to throw his life away. "Look, Ronita, you got me." He shrugged. "I had to be the one. What happened that day … it wasn't supposed to go down like that. You were never, ever supposed to jump with me."

With my finger pointed at his face, I said, "I didn't jump, you asshole. I was trying to save you and slipped."

"I never asked you to do that." He barked at me. "I had a plan."

"Why did you even take me up there if that's what you planned to do? I didn't need to see that. My jacked-up life was enough already." I clenched my fists.

He tried to put his hand on my shoulder, but I wouldn't let him. If he touched me, I was sure I'd forgive his actions and everything that had happened. With all my anger, I still had feelings for him. My emotions were in two places, jumbled, just like everything else in this damned place. I couldn't separate one from the other.

I directed my attention to Odessa. "Can we get out of here now?"

"Wherever you go, Ro, I'm going with you." Cato sounded certain. Since arriving in the Interruption in the guise of my bird, he'd followed me everywhere.

I spun on him. Steam from my back rose through my flimsy dress. I held his gaze, refusing to allow him to look away. He needed to feel my wrath and understand how he devastated my life and landed me dead in seconds. He dropped his head and kicked a rock, ignoring my feelings like always. I dragged my eyes away and focused on Odessa. "What's next?"

She sighed. "I don't understand you, young people. But I guess I got my own issues." She scratched her head. "We were told to stay together, but if I rub this pin, we could be worse off. I'm not willing to rub it to see what happens next. We have enough troubles, and I'm not ready for it to get worse. I ain't caught my breath yet." She looked back at her grandparents' house.

"Princess Kenyata said it could happen, not that it would." I needed distance from the sight of the sad shack and everything that had happened here. "It might not happen."

Odessa held her gaze on me. "Are you willing to take that chance? You think we gonna end up at an all-you-can-eat chocolate factory?"

I wanted my bedroom, with the pink walls, pink stuffed animals, and the posters of Princess Tiana that I'd outgrown years ago but refused to take down. I wanted my mother to bake me brownies like she did that one time after my father died, and I thought we might be normal again.

"I think—"

"Cato, nobody wants to know what you think. You

shouldn't even be here." I shouted every word, and the release felt good.

He cringed but stepped back.

Clouds rolled across the sky. Big, gray clouds. Just like the last time. Odessa and I knew all too well what might happen next.

"That ain't a good sign." The fear in Odessa's eyes scared me too.

The sound of a train coming our way grew louder, and the cloud turned blacker with a fury I didn't want to see. I tugged Odessa's arm. "Which way should we go?"

Thunder rolled across the sky, but Odessa didn't budge. She stood as solid as a mountain.

"Odessa, something is coming for you again," I yelled louder. "We need to get out of here. Fast."

Captured By The Game

Luis

Time in the Interruption didn't have a comparison to anything in life. Day was night, and night was day. I didn't get hungry or sleepy, so determining time, much less my whereabouts was difficult.

I rubbed my eyes and sat up. The sheet covering me fell away, exposing my bare chest. I don't know what happened to the clown suit I'd been wearing, but I didn't miss it. I peeked under the sheet and stared at my naked body. With my eyes closed, I gathered myself trying to remember what had happened to me. Having nothing firm to hold me in place used to be a heady sensation, but now it had too many pitfalls to make me happy or carefree.

I couldn't tell if I was waking from a night of sleep or from being drugged or some wicked handiwork of Janet.

My head felt heavy. Everything I attempted was a struggle, even seeing in the darkened room, where the thick draping at the window gave me no hint of the time of day. On each side of the bed stood floor lamps with the lowest wattage possible.

I stretched out on the comfortable bed. It had the plushest linen I'd ever felt. I ran my hand over the white silk and smiled. Maybe this transition had nothing to do with Janet because I was sure it would have been brimstone, fire, and pitchforks with her.

The smell of something decadent reached my nose, and my mouth drooled. I swung my legs over the edge of the bed. At least I had transformed back into my usual self. When I'd raised my hands the way Odessa had instructed, that short version of me dressed in all plaid had startled me. I couldn't imagine where that previous persona had come from. Was it in my imagination, or did I also have Janet to thank for that?

The door opened like slowly parting curtains. I expected the worst, so I braced for what would happen next.

Janet came through the door carrying a tray laden with food. But the sizzling steak didn't draw my attention. She did. She looked like the girl I met in college. Years before, we became a couple, and she lost her damn mind.

"You're awake." Her youthful smile took me back to happier times. She settled the tray on the table and stood beside me at the foot of the bed. Her bare breasts were huge and round and spectacular. Few things about her excited me at the end of our relationship and my life, but her appearance woke up my body. She wore the tiniest panties I'd ever seen, showing off a pair of legs that could have won the Triple Crown.

"Janet, what's?" I couldn't find the words because I couldn't stop gawking.

"Isn't this better than where you were before?" She swung her arm as if revealing the room, and instead of the curt tone she had used to whisper in my ear, her voice was sweet, sultry, and sexy.

"Yes, it's nice, but— " I couldn't form a solid sentence. Like everything else, this was another moment that stunned me.

Janet strolled toward me and ran her index finger up my arm and across my shoulder. "Aren't you happy to be here with me?" Her touch was like warm honey trailing down my dick.

I tried to moisten my mouth. I'd be foolish to fall for anything she said, but I wasn't thinking with my big brain. The food smelled delicious, and a comfortable bed was better than hiding in the bushes or being with Odessa on that dusty farm.

I had to stop thinking with my little head and use the big one, or Janet would have me howling at the moon like a half-crazed banshee. "I don't know if I should be happy or cautious. You and I have some terrible history." I pointed to the scar that crossed from one side of my neck to the other. "Remember?"

"That was a long time ago. We should be different now." She leaned over and sniffed me, then wrinkled her nose. "I can smell that woman on you. Even here you're cheating on me."

"I'd hardly call us together. We are not a couple." My tone was as harsh as the way I jerked my index finger toward the scar on my neck, again.

"We have a second chance. Maybe this time you can be the man I wanted you to be back then." She tilted her head and batted her eyes.

She grabbed my erection and stroked it. "There's something about being here that you like."

"When you dragged me away, I thought you had something else in mind."

"I love you, Luis. I tried to prove that to you, but every time you saw another woman your head was on a swivel stick. There are fewer distractions now."

I had a hundred reasons to disagree with her. Being stuck was number one. But now, as I glanced around the room with its soothing colors, the aroma of a fine cut of beef, and a woman with enough curves to make me think I'd arrived in heaven, now wasn't the time to mess up this good thing.

She released me, then, with her fingertips, she pushed her breasts higher. She knew the sight of her breasts made my knees wobble.

Because I hadn't seen such a gorgeous sight in so long, I pulled her close and ran my tongue across each nipple. Then, leaving my dead man spirit behind, I pulled Janet into my arms and buried my head between the sun and the moon.

"We are good together, Luis," she purred, enjoying the moment as much as I did.

I didn't have to help her out of her skimpy panties. Instead, she tugged them off with one hand.

"Yeah. We had some good times and even better sex." I stood and took her in my arms.

"And here, we have no worries. I'll take care of you. I'm all you'll need."

Maybe I should have paid more attention to what she said, but who wanted to talk when I was this close to having sex?

I pick her up and carried her to the bed. She stretched out on the mattress with the happy-go-lucky giggle that had first attracted me. I crawled between her legs, wanting to take my time and show my romantic side and sexual prowess. The horny Luis showed up first. The sight and smell of Janet made me ravenous. My penis pulsed against her thigh while she held my face and planted kisses around my mouth. Then she plunged her tongue between my lips, and I stopped fighting the passion. I accepted her tongue like she was the love of my life instead of a cold-blooded killer.

I released her tongue, moved my lips across her chin, and then down to her neck. Her moans told me she loved the way my lips and tongue caressed her collarbone, so I slowed my pace, almost making her beg for more. The louder she became, the harder I got. Janet always wanted something more—more time, more caring, and more touching—and I had nothing but time. No one else waited for me.

Blood pooled in my loins like boiling molten lava. Pressure built. I slipped inside her and pushed aside the trouble this act could cause, just like I did when we were together. She was moist and warm and tight, and I wanted it all. Her hips bucked, lifting off the bed to meet each thrust. Sex was a pleasure where I could live forever, just not with Janet.

Three hours later, after multiple orgasms, Janet sprawled across the bed, finally spent. "Luis, nobody pleases me the way you do. That's why I couldn't let you go." She cooed with a sparkle in her eyes, and moisture gleamed between the mounds of her breasts.

I positioned my palms under my head and drew a deep breath, trying my darndest not to pant or pass out. Showing weakness to Janet was how I ended up in this never-ending nightmare.

The scent of the food still lingered from the nearby table. I raised and studied the platter of food Janet had carried into the room. I wasn't hungry, but if we ate, maybe that would slow her down and let me rest. "That steak sure smells good." I sat on the edge of the bed.

"Go ahead, have some. You'll need your stamina."

"Aren't you going to eat with me?" I picked up the plate, holding it at eye level for her to see.

"I'm not hungry. I'm horny."

I settled at the table and ate food I wasn't hungry for but needed time to sort out my thoughts. "So, what's your plan?"

Janet rolled onto her stomach. "Plan?"

I chewed a mouthful of meat. It didn't taste as good as it smelled, which didn't surprise me. Nothing was as it appeared. "You dragged me here, so you must have a plan. Don't you want to share it with me?"

"This is the plan. Now, hurry and finish."

I put down my fork. "You plan to screw for eternity? Don't you have some things you need to make right?"

"Like what?" She drew back and glared at me. She never enjoyed being challenged.

"Let's start with you killing me?" My voice spiked.

"You got what you deserved. You mistreated me every

day, and when you juggle people's hearts, you have to expect they might strike back. But I'm not mad at you anymore."

I nodded, dumbfounded by her answer. "Well, I'm still mad at you. You could have just dumped me." I ran my finger over my scar.

She jumped up and stood next to me. "But I love you. You're my soul mate. Now we'll be together forever."

"Haw." I didn't hold back my anger. There was no forgiveness for her.

I pushed from the table and took a quick breath to gain my composure. If I had to spend eternity in the confines of the darkened room, I might as well be in the bowels of hell.

Curiosity about my surroundings engulfed me. I rushed to the window and pushed the heavy curtains aside to see outside. I couldn't make out anything.

Not a light.

Not a star.

Not a glimmer of anything living.

I've never seen so much darkness, as if we existed in a void without connection. I turned to Janet. Her smirk mocked me. I made my way to the door. My heart pounded against my ribs, making it harder to breathe.

Janet continued to stare, her face expressionless.

With my hand on the doorknob, I snatched it open and stared into total blackness.

Standing Still

Odessa

I'd lived my whole life afraid to breathe the wrong way because Daniel's wrath would strike a blow that could take months to heal. Each time, I lost a piece of myself until the eyes staring back at me from a mirror were unrecognizable.

I doubted my power.

I doubted my intuition.

I even doubted my reason for living.

That was who I had become. I thought life meant me to be the dirt under my husband's feet, and that's how I felt most of the time.

So, the world and the afterlife had turned out differently than I'd imagined. I could let Daniel or this creature terrorize me through eternity or find a way to stand up for myself under any circumstances.

The expression on Ronita's face was enough to scare me shitless. And for a flash, I was ready to run like Ronita had suggested and continue being that shell of a person I'd lived for too many years.

The black clouds continued to roll our way with a darker streak right through the middle that had to carry bad news. The roar grew louder as it barreled toward us.

I faced Ronita. "I ain't spending all my time in the Interruption trying to outrun that thing." Above the noise, I yelled, "I did enough of bowing and scraping in my life, and I ain't doing it another moment. Whatever happens this time, so be it."

"But it took your hand." Ronita pointed at my stump. The horror on her face almost convinced me I didn't stand a chance.

"Ronita, I ain't running." I held my voice firmer than my

knees. "If that thing is coming for me, then I'm going to stand here and give it what for, too." Facing down Daniel was something I could never do. But now we were equal, and I was willing to try it.

"You think it wants just you?" She backed away, like she wanted no part of being near me.

Cato stepped forward. He was the saddest boy I'd ever seen. Was his sorrow because Ronita wouldn't meet his gaze? Or was his grief what caused him to end his life? His gaze swept between Ronita and me. "Yeah. Suppose that thing wants to harm all of us?"

I took a scant breath and gave them my attention because I wasn't used to answering to young folks. "The way I see it, we can spend all our time here running from things that chase us, or we can stand toe to toe."

Ronita considered what I'd said, then shook her head. "Odessa," she said my name quickly like she wanted to make sure I knew she was talking to me. "I don't know anything about the Interruption. This place is creepy." She stopped and looked at Cato. "I don't want to fight something that can take off my hand or my head."

I examined my stump. It wasn't the worst thing to happen to me, but I was old and done lived through so much. I wouldn't wish my hard life on Ronita or Cato, but this wasn't life. And they needed to toughen up. The sooner Cato stopped with those sad puppy eyes that Ronita ignored, the sooner they could adapt to what stared them in the face.

Cato stood taller. "What do you have in mind?"

My soul lifted, and I took a calm breath—finally, someone who was thinking like me. "I do not know. But if we ain't running, then nothing can chase us, right?"

He nodded slowly. "I guess. But are you willing to take a bite out of something if it comes for you? Because that is a beast, and talking won't work."

I straightened and tried to look confident. "Let's see what we got. Just be ready to pull anything we need."

Doubt marred Ronita's face. That child looked so afraid. I don't think she trusted her next breath. She sucked her tongue. "If I end up with one hand or one leg or one eye, I will make our time together miserable, Odessa. And I mean it."

"All I can say is protect any body part you aiming to keep." I couldn't coddle or promise to keep her safe with that thing coming at us like a fireball.

Cato glanced at his crotch, letting me know what part of his body he cherished. Then puffed out his chest. "He talked over the roar, then spread his arms in front of Ronita. "I'll protect you, Ronita. Stand behind me."

If the situation wasn't so dire, I might have found a chuckle.

She pushed his arms away and narrowed her eyes. "Yeah, like you protected me that other time."

Before we could do another thing, out of the darkness came the four-legged breast, whose eyes glowed like gold. We stood side by side, our shoulders almost touching. I hoped we represented a force to reckon with.

It slowed its pace but continued to advance.

Placing one paw in front of the other, it growled with each step.

I've never seen anything so ugly.

My heart thumped like a conga drum. If any of my bodily functions were still working, pee would have run down my leg. I should have been used to this kind of fear, 'cause I had experienced it often enough. I was ready to face those things that scared me. Even Daniel. Maybe this was what I needed to get on to the next realm.

With his eyes narrowed on me, as if I was standing alone, it kept coming. The way the wind blew, and the clouds gathered, I believed Nature had chosen sides, and I was all alone.

Ronita stepped close enough to brush my shoulder. "Odessa, this isn't a good idea." Her voice trembled.

"Don't show fear." I tried to sound fierce, but beneath my dress, my legs shook. I took a step away from the children. "If this thing wants me, ain't no use in putting you two in danger too."

I widened my stance and threw my arms out just as wide. I made a guttural sound that was so loud it scratched my throat. Then I yelled, "If you coming for me, you better give me your best shot." I summoned my nails into claws and my teeth into fangs as I tried to remember what tortured me the last time. I called on a gazelle's speed and an elephant's strength.

If Daniel knew what I had in store for him, he'd probably ask for more, too. So, I needed the wisdom of my forebears to make it through what he had in mind for me.

The creature slowed as my transformation materialized. Then, those glossy eyes widened. I couldn't tell if it was from determination or fear.

Cato or Ronita sucked in an awed breath from behind me, but I couldn't take my eyes off what was coming.

For a moment, the beast didn't move.

My heart pounded harder while my mind spun images of what could happen to me.

I had enough fear to defeat me before the battle began, but I stared back at that fear this time.

That thing sprung into the air from twenty feet away and then dived at my throat.

I'd never seen nothing so beautiful and so deadly. I brought my good hand down across the front of his face, catching one eyeball with the tip of my clawed hand.

It landed in front of me with a grunt and a thud. He didn't

move for a moment, but I was smart enough to know he had more to do. Then, with his good eye, he narrowed in on me with a look so vile I stepped back.

Before I could shake that eyeball loose from my nail, the beast rammed me in the stomach with the weight of its body, throwing me to the ground and knocking the air out of me. Daniel had no heart so if that's what he aimed to take from me, that's what I sought to protect. With my good arm covering my neck and chest and his eyeball still attached to my nail, I hammered him on the nose with my stump with the might of a thousand armies.

He whimpered as I shook the eye loose, and a white glob smashed against his snout.

He didn't back away. His jagged teeth were inches from my face, dripping saliva on my cheek. His foul breath smelled like hell, and shit met in a back alley.

We rolled in the dirt like two lions, clawing and scratching like wild animals. Dust and dirt clogged my nostrils and coated my throat, but I couldn't stop. I had to keep him from dominating me, or he would leave me worse off than ever. He raked his claws across my cheek, tearing away skin. I refused to use any of my strength to scream or cry from the pain. Pounding him with my fist was as useless as swatting a fly. He kept coming back, clamping his teeth into my arm as if it aimed to take my other limb. Finally, I shoved my stump between his teeth to pry his jaws loose.

Our strengths appeared equal, so I had to think faster and better. If he kept me on the ground, he'd surely kill me. I scrambled to my feet and planted them wide to stay balanced. I waited for him to charge.

He leaped into the air and came for my neck again, exposing his underbelly.

With my clawed hands, I grabbed him by the thick folds of his neck, piercing through skin and fur, and swung him around until I had enough momentum to slam him to the ground.

He hit the dirt so hard that the faint sound of breaking bones filled my ears. Even through his fur, I detected his backbone was no longer intact. Instead, the upper half went one way, his tail another.

Daniel didn't have the sense to ask for more power than he already had. He always thought I was dumb, but as he tried to gather his broken body, I stepped forward and pushed my foot into his neck, using the strength of my thick thigh.

"I might not be able to kill you again." I leaned lower and peered into an eye that I knew too well. "But I can make you wish you were dead again. It's over between us. You go your way, and I'mma go mine."

He whimpered under the weight of my body. A sound I'd never heard him make.

I grounded my foot harder to drive home my point, making sure he knew this was a new Odessa Eddiemae Jones. "Don't come for me again." I yanked his remaining eye from its socket.

Pride Before the Fall

Luis

I kept my back to Janet so she wouldn't see the fear in my eyes or detect the pounding of my heart. She thrived on fear, and I had enough to fuel her for decades.

If my shortcomings were in a race with Janet's, they'd tie for first place. I'd mistreated her and, on some level, maybe deserved everything she placed on me. I had no excuse for my thoughtless acts. Settling down and loving one woman was never my plan, and I should have told her that at every chance until she accepted our relationship status.

I never stood up to anyone. I'd rather run than fight. So, I had no best friend because the only person I could be loyal to was myself. In the blocks surrounding my childhood neighborhood between Grant and Sherman circles, there were too many gangs to fend off, so I didn't. I ran from them instead. It was easier for me to dodge confrontation than face it.

But I wouldn't get away from Janet by running in the opposite direction, slipping down a side street, and then sprinting to my front door. Playing for keeps was the only thing that worked in the Interruption.

"Come back to bed, Luis." Janet purred like a pampered pussy and patted the vacant space beside her on the bed.

Did she think I wouldn't care about the isolation she had planned or that she'd dragged me from where I needed to be to where she wanted me?

I faced her. "No. I'm not staying." My voice was level and firm.

Janet flipped onto her back. With her foot crossed over her thigh, exposing her woman parts for clear view, she snickered. "You don't know the way out." She studied her long nails.

Her nonchalant attitude angered me more.

"It's not as if you can take a car service back to that old woman and the others." She stared at me through the triangle formed by her legs.

"Where are we?"

She unfolded her legs, climbed off the bed, and came toward me. "This is our place. Here you have everything you need." She ran her index finger down my torso until she reached my penis. With a firm grip, she leaned toward me, pressing her lips against mine.

My body responded to her touch. As much as I wanted to remain limp, she knew every nerve, every pulse point on my simple body. She used them to please me and to punish me—and I'd let her. Even now, a part of me yearned to crawl back into bed and let her suck my penis until my mind went blank and my body withered.

I pulled away. "Stop, Janet."

"Aw, baby, you know you like it." She continued to stroke me. "It's not like you need to get up early tomorrow for work. All you have to do is let me do what I do best."

I dropped my head back, contemplating what she'd said. She made sense. It wouldn't be so bad if this is how I could spend eternity. Lots of sex because Janet never got enough. We had food and a comfortable bed. As long as we kept the drapes closed, I could pretend we were like honeymooners on some ritzy vacation. I was better at fantasizing than I was at living reality. Staying with the others had hidden dangers and even more bogeymen than Janet had planned.

I allowed her to coax me back to the bed. Janet pushed me flat on my back, then massaged my chest with one hand and my penis with the other. My body melted like butter into the sheets. Her warm tongue loosened my muscles. If I were under attack, I couldn't fight off a fly.

Keeping my defenses separated from the pure hedonism

of the moment was impossible. I closed my eyes and let her wrap her mouth around my thick shaft. She drew out my essence like a meandering stream. She didn't hurry, and I didn't rush her. When I couldn't hold back, my body jerked and gyrated before going still.

Hours later, I opened my eyes to find she'd secured me to the bed. "Aww, Janet." I tugged at the fabric, trying to release my arms and legs. "Why do you have to ruin a good thing by doing something stupid like this?"

"Who are you calling stupid?" Her eyes narrowed with the hatred that lingered between us. "We both know I can't trust you. Once you get what you want, you throw me aside and start looking for someone new. But I'm smarter this time."

I stopped resisting the restraints. She tied me up so tight it hurt just as much when I didn't pull on them. She looked as if she was waiting for me to respond. I'd never won an argument with her evil ass, and I wouldn't try now. In time, she'd want something from me, and then she'd hurry to free me to have her way.

I closed my eyes and remained still.

"Don't you have something to say?" She rocked the mattress.

I kept my eyes closed. "Nope."

She paced around the room, stomping like a child, demanding attention that I refused to give. I even pretended to snore.

After several minutes, the warmth of her body touched mine. "I'm sorry, Luis. You just make me so crazy."

I didn't move.

She placed her hand on my abdomen. "Wake up, baby, and talk to me."

The best way to handle Janet was to not give in to her bratty behavior. It took all the resolve I could muster.

She ran her fingernails down my chest, digging in with just enough pressure to open my eyes. "Did you hear me?"

"Until you untie me, I'm not talking to you, touching you, and I certainly not having sex with you." I drilled her with a look to let her know I was serious.

"Yes, you will."

Without changing my expression, I turned my head away and stared across the room at the blank wall. Hanging out here wasn't the great idea I'd first imagined. Janet was obsessed, not only with me, but with everything. She didn't buy one pair of shoes. She purchased a pair in every color. We didn't have one argument and end it. We'd several, piling them on top of each other until my head exploded. I had to stop thinking about sex and face the fact that in death, she'd find ways to kill me again and again.

Returning to Odessa, Ronita and Willa wouldn't be enough to rid my life of Janet. She'd pop up every chance she could.

The quiet dragged on for what seemed like hours. I didn't think Janet could be silent for so long. But waiting her out was the right thing to do.

She stretched out alongside me on the bed. "Luis," she said my name like a song. "You know I don't want to keep you tied up, but I can't trust you."

I kept my head turned.

"Okay." She sighed. "Promise if I let you go, you'll stay with me."

I continued to hold my tongue. I needed her to beg. It was the only way I could move from being the mouse into being the trap.

She sighed and took her time untying me.

To get away, I needed to use my smarts, so instead of jumping up, I forced myself to stay in the same position, but I gave her the attention she so wanted. "What do you know about the Interruption?" I didn't let on how much I wanted this information because then, of course, she wouldn't tell me.

"Not much. But I kinda like this plane. It's just you and me. I think we can hang out here for a while. Then we can move to another place and see if we find anything interesting."

"How?"

She reached across the bed, picked up my suit jacket from the floor, and dangled it in front of me.

I jerked upright. "How did you get my jacket? I had on plaid when I got here."

"When I grabbed you, you came back to your normal self. Clothes and all." She waved her hand as if this was trivial information. "Anyway, this pin." She pointed at the pin that Princess Kenyata had given the four of us. "This thing is like magic. It's how I keep up with you."

"Aren't you worried about the creatures that could be lurking out there?"

She gave my question some thought, then shook her head before she dropped my jacket. "No." She spoke with enough determination I had no reason to doubt her.

Across the room, I spotted her dress neatly folded on the chair. Her pin sparkled like sunshine. I quickly gave her my attention to ensure she didn't have a clue what I had in mind for her.

I turned over and cupped her breasts, one in each palm. She moaned the way I knew she would and continued as I rolled my tongue along the column of her neck. "Now, isn't this better than having me tied to the bed?"

"Yeah, baby." Her words were almost inaudible.

"Besides, you're the one who likes being tied up. Remember?"

With her eyes closed, the look of pleasure on her face let me know I had her. "But you never wanted to do it."

"Well, I will now. And it's going to be all about pleasing you."

Her eyes popped open. "You will?"

"I will." Making sure I didn't rush or give away my plan, I looped her hands together to one bedpost with the fabric she'd used to constrain me, ensuring she couldn't get her hands in a position to change her circumstances. I suckled her nipples, nipping at the tips the way she liked. She was so engrossed she didn't know what I'd done.

"Oh, baby. That's what I like."

I released her nipple. "I know." Then I trailed my tongue across her stomach and between her legs. With my tongue pressed against her core, I tied her ankles to the foot post. As I pleasured her, she didn't notice the double knots. She ground her hips into the sheets, letting me know I had her where I wanted. She moaned as if an electrical current flowed through her limbs. She squeezed her eyes tight and raised her hips as an orgasm controlled her body.

I moved off the bed.

"Oh, baby. Give me a minute, and you can do that again." She hadn't opened her eyes.

I slipped into my clothes, making sure my pin was in place.

"What are you doing?" Janet yanked her arms and struggled to sit up.

"I'm getting outta here." I kept my voice calm, but my heart pounded with anger. "We're done, Janet."

"You promised, Luis. You promised," she raged.

I didn't look away. I conveyed my hatred with my eyes. "No. This time, I promised you nothing." I picked up her dress and removed her pin.

"You can't take my pin." Her voice was so loud it cracked.

She jerked at the ties with so much force I feared they might give way and put us in a duel that neither of us could win. "I have to keep it. You bastard, give it to me—let me loose."

We locked gazes.

"Give me my pin and let me loose, and I'll tell you about your son." She spoke through her teeth.

I froze. "Son?" It was another lie. I wanted it to be another one of her ways to manipulate me. But the look in her eyes left me uncertain. Was this just another way to keep her claws in me?

I shoved her pin in my pants pocket, stretched my arms over my head, and vacated the hell she had planned for me.

Then everything went black.

Reckoning Time

Willa

With my eyes closed, the shock on Ava's face rolled behind my lids like a stuck reel, even though I had no control over whoever transported my body from the cemetery to this new place.

I hoped it wasn't some limb-eating critter like the one who snagged Odessa's hand.

I was slammed into a chair with so much force my head snapped back. The painful jolt made me open my eyes. I hoped to find something familiar that wouldn't scare the shit out of me. I wasn't disappointed.

I sat in a simple room, square, with four unadorned walls.

Nothing scary there.

A nondescript table made of sturdy wood sat in front of me.

Nothing scary there.

On the opposite side of the table sat two adults, one man and one woman. At first, I took them for detectives, but they didn't dress the part. Husband and wife, maybe? Sister and brother, perhaps? Or strangers? I couldn't tell.

They had cold, expressionless faces with thinned lips and dark penetrating eyes.

Scary.

I scrutinized them without leaning closer. Then, when I was sure I'd never seen them before, I tried to cross my arms under my breasts, but restraints made it impossible. My feet and waist were also restricted. I was strapped so tightly to the chair that breathing was almost impossible.

The people seated before me weren't here to welcome me to the Interruption.

Neither hurried to speak.

My fear increased tenfold. I had no way to defend myself.

"Who are you?" I yanked at the ties restraining my hands. "Where am I?"

The man nodded to the woman and then rose from the table. He walked toward me, and I shrank in my seat, hoping to take up less space or become invisible.

He circled the table and then returned to stand next to the woman.

I released my breath and took another long gulp of air as I prepared for the worst.

The woman looked up at him. "Should I go first, or do you want to start?" Her voice hitched. She was holding back tears.

"You go first, darling." The way he held her gaze, if they weren't husband and wife, then they had to be lovers. The tender way he looked at her and the way they spoke to each other made me think so.

She cleared her throat and looked across the table at me. "My name is Chloe Barron. I'm thirty years old. I died on my birthday." She gave a sarcastic chuckle. "The big 3-0. I'd been looking forward to it for months." She dropped her eyes to stare at her hands.

He placed his hands on her shoulders. His fingers tightened.

She lifted her head. "Our daughter, Ethel, was so excited about the little celebration we'd planned for my birthday." Chloe almost smiled. "Ethel was five years old. We were going to have cake with her then we were going to dinner. Just the two of us." She looked up at the man standing beside her, who I now guessed was her husband. "So, we were on our way to the store for ice cream. Ethel was in the back seat singing 'Happy Birthday' to me." Her voice caught, and she pinched her nose.

Before me sat the people—the family—who'd been in the

car I'd slammed. All that wishing and praying that I hadn't hurt anyone but myself disappeared, leaving me coated in layers of shame, guilt, and self-loathing. My brain released the fear and soaked in all my troubling thoughts about myself.

"I'm Payne Barron. I met Chloe in my senior year of college. The moment I saw her, I knew we'd get married, have a house full of kids, and live happily ever after." He bit his bottom lip.

I wiggled my arms as best as I could because they ached from the blood rushing to my fingers. The more they talked, the warmer I became. I wanted to look away from the pain now visible on their faces. I didn't know these people, but I'd caused them so much hurt that staring at them was unbearable.

"The night of Chloe's birthday, we weren't just going to dinner, as Chloe thought. After sharing the homemade cake that Ethel and I had made for Chloe's birthday, I planned to take her to a surprise party, where our friends and family would cheer her into her thirties. I started planning the event months ago and was as excited as Ethel that day."

"I had a surprise for Payne, too," Chloe spoke without looking across the table at me. She dropped her head, and for several seconds, her body shook without her making a sound.

With each shake, Payne huffed louder. The veins in his neck swelled.

Chloe composed herself, sniffed a few more times, and then continued, "Earlier that day, I'd taken a pregnancy test and discovered we would have another child. So I was going to tell him at dinner."

Payne winced.

I closed my eyes and bit down on my tongue. They filled me with their grief from that awful night. I hadn't just destroyed my family. I'd dismantled other innocent lives. Sitting across the table from them was one of the hardest things I'd ever done. It was more torturous than watching my daughter Ava spin out of control on drugs that first time when it all took me by surprise. I wanted to zap myself into another dimension.

I sat up straighter and accepted the throbbing in my arms. "I know saying I'm sorry is empty and useless now, but I am. There is no excuse I can give you for my actions." I looked from him to her, hoping something would change in their demeanor, but they gave me nothing. "If I could change what happened, I would. I had no ill intentions." The words tore from my throat, tears filled my eyes, and my nose started to run.

The three of us sat in silence for what seemed like an eternity. I was afraid to imagine what they had in mind for me. They brought me to this place for a purpose. Maybe they wanted to torture me, slowly and methodically, ripping me apart limb by limb, like what I'd done to their family. I'd accept their punishment because I'd earned it, then maybe I'd have peace.

Their grief saddened me, and I slumped back against the chair. My body was too heavy to hold up.

Payne rubbed his hands together, then reclaimed his seat next to his wife. He reached for her hand and held it.

I didn't feel worthy of looking at either of them. I wished I'd asked Odessa how painful it was when she lost her hand so I could gauge what to expect. I remembered reading books about the afterlife and knew purgatory could last forever. I willed my brain to stop fighting the inevitable.

Payne looked at his wife with an adoration that I didn't think existed. "Chloe, is there anything else you want to say?" Then, still holding her hand, he lifted it to his lips, kissed the back of her hand, then stood.

Chloe blinked several times. I got the impression that she was trying not to cry. "My baby. My Ethel will grow up without me. She probably won't even remember us. And nothing this woman says or does will change that." She glanced at her husband. "The only thing I ever wanted was a family with happy, healthy children. You stole our dream." She shook her head.

My anxiety ratcheted up. Here I was, blaming everything on Burt. If Burt hadn't done this, or if Burt had done that, but I'd turned out to be the bigger villain. He only screwed up his own family. I screwed up our family and brought another one down with me.

"Whatever you two have in mind for me, I more than deserve it." I sighed as tears spilled down my cheek. "I never meant for any of this to happen, but I was being selfish that night, feeling sorry for myself." I closed my eyes and saw their Ethel in the back seat. The perfect 'O' she made with her mouth, and the stab of pain in my chest felt like a red-hot poker, and all I could do was take it all in because I'd cause this grief. I needed to carry it.

Payne and Chloe locked eyes, communicating without talking.

My fear doubled because, until now, I hadn't thought they had a plan, but now it was apparent they wanted to harm me like I'd done them. But I was already dead. What could be worse?

Time dragged on while they stared at each other, and then I noticed the pins just above their heart. They each had one that resembled the one on my dress. I tried instinctively to touch my pin, but the ties cut into my flesh.

I leaned toward them and motioned to Payne's suit lapel. "How did you get your pin?"

The way he glared at me made me draw back.

Chloe released her hand from his. "Princess Nandi pinned us when we arrived."

"Did she tell you how they can help?" I pulled myself up and hated how anxious my voice sounded, but maybe what information they shared would help me and my others.

She glanced at her husband as if to get his permission to continue. "Look," she swallowed hard. "You've destroyed my family in a way I can't put into words, and in my mind, I'd like to do the same thing to you. Slowly. Over a long time." Her voice caught, and she held her hand up until she gathered herself.

I took a shallow breath so my existence wouldn't anger her more. Payne stared at me as if he wanted to peel away my flesh.

"In my heart..." Chloe started again.

I gave her my attention. She didn't display as much hatred toward me.

"...but in my heart, I know that's not the right thing to do, and it wouldn't change anything." She hunched her shoulders.

The hopelessness in her eyes held my attention.

There was so much I wanted to say, but I couldn't erase her pain.

"Chloe, are you sure this is how you want to handle her?" Payne's voice was more demanding than before.

"Payne," she talked without looking at him. "We discussed this." Her voice remained calm.

"But things are different here. There is no jail or laws or—"

"There is always right and wrong." She tried to convince him.

"I don't agree with Chloe." Payne's evil eyes penetrated my soul. "Just like you've destroyed my family, I will do the same to everyone you love. I know about your daughter and your son. They should join you soon in this hell where you've placed us."

Despair trapped my words in my throat.

I had no power to stop him.

Not tied up, not alone.

Chloe reached for his arm.

He jerked away, pushed away from the table and rushed toward me like a tidal wave aiming to consume the shore.

Revenge blazed in his eyes.

I screamed.

Then everything went black.

The Leader and The Followers

Ronita

Odessa had her foot on that beast's neck as if she had planted a flag on a new planet. Blood ran down her face and covered her dress, but she showed no fear. In fact, the slight tilt of her lips spelled satisfaction. Triumph.

If I had to be stuck with someone, she was the best.

The gouges on her face were deep and jagged. Seeing them, I touched my cheek to see if I detected deterioration in my skin. I still felt the same, which I hope meant we didn't need to worry about Princess Kenyata's warning about running out of strength. Yet. But I had no idea how much more time we had.

If Odessa had a beast and something chased Luis and Willa, I needed to watch over my shoulder to find out what awaited me.

I glanced at Cato as he observed Odessa, too. Maybe he was my beast.

I hadn't been an angel growing up. My mother had lots of stories about me worrying her bald, like when I climbed out the window to attend a party she had forbidden. Sure, I was sullen and stubborn and would rather scroll social media than talk to my mother, but chatting with her wasn't cool— all she wanted to talk about was *Uncle* Jack and how I needed to be nicer to him.

Maybe I'd landed here because I told Terra to stop being friends with Patty, and we set up that dating account for her. She kept getting whack messages from old men. But that was all in fun.

I shook my head. I had friends who'd done worse to people they disliked.

From the corner of my eye, Cato loomed like a shadow.

He kept his distance. He wasn't sure I wouldn't strike out against him.

He looked up. His mouth fixed like he wanted to speak but couldn't find the right words. I knew the relaxed Cato, and I'd seen the agitated one, too. But the guy standing near me now was unrecognizable. He wore the same clothes he'd worn when he went over the cliff. His family hadn't bothered dressing him in fancy clothes for a funeral like my mother had done. His family probably didn't have a memorial for him at all.

I couldn't help but want to know if he thought I was the same. I felt the same. But I wondered if the dead Ronita had a weird cast that he didn't find appealing. I shook that thought away. If I kept him over there, I'd be fine. In school, I'd spent so much time looking up to him that I never imagined I could get mad at him. Not this mad.

The beast under Odessa's foot vanished, but she kept looking down at the scorched spot where it had been.

"Is it gone for good?" I called out without getting too close.

"Don't know." Odessa rubbed her good hand down the front of her dress.

"Can we go now?" I hoped to get her focused on us and whatever we needed to do next. The idea of hanging out in one spot too long worried me. I wouldn't be happy until the four of us were back together.

Cato inched toward me as if I wouldn't notice.

But I kept him in view.

All the time.

Just in case.

I still held a place in my heart for him, but I didn't trust him. If he hadn't done that awful thing, then this dreadful existence wouldn't have happened. I'd never get over that day.

Never.

Cato touched my arm. "Are you going to pretend I don't exist?"

"Technically, you don't. You're dead." I stepped away from him.

"You know," he started with a chuckle. "I have the rest of eternity to get you to change your mind about me. I had no idea you were going to jump, too."

I snapped my head around and thumped my finger against his chest. "I didn't jump, you idiot. I fell."

"Whatever." He hunched his shoulders.

"Not whatever," I yelled. "You know I hated heights. You shouldn't have changed our plans that day." I spoke loud enough my voice pitched out.

Odessa hurried to me and grabbed hold of my arm. "Girl, what you screaming about? I thought you'd be happy your friend was here with you."

Her firm grip made me suppress my anger. I scowled at Odessa until she released my arm. "Happy to see him?" I spat out the words. "He's the reason I'm here."

Cato said, "I never meant for any of this to happen. I'd always protected her. So, I don't know why she's all mad at me."

"Cato," I said his name through my teeth.

"Well, child." Odessa nodded. "If you got a man in your life, you better be ready for turmoil. No matter how much we don't want to believe it, they never make us as happy like they say in them books."

She held my gaze until I nodded, forcing me to understand the meaning she conveyed.

Odessa turned back to the spot where she'd conquered the beast and clenched her jaw.

"You still worried about that thing?" I didn't want to see

her lose another hand and couldn't help but wonder if she had the same thought.

"Yep." She didn't hesitate. "I don't reckon I'm ever gonna be completely free of that beast. Maybe that's the cross I'm always gonna carry." She pulled her attention back to me. "But we can't worry about that now. We gots to keep moving." She turned to Cato with her good hand on her hip bone. "So, what you getting ready to do?"

Cato looked from her to me. "I was hoping I could stay with ya'll." He pointed to Odessa and me.

I'd seen that expression on his face before, it tugged on my heart. He tried to be tough and make others think he didn't have feelings, but I knew him better. He tucked his chin when he wanted to hide what he wanted to say.

Odessa's eyes widened. "I don't think that's how it works. What instructions was you given? Whatever they were, you need to follow them. There were only four of us, Ronita, Willa, and Luis,and me." Odessa counted us off with her fingers. "Who did you meet up with here?"

Cato hunched his shoulders and dropped his head. "I wasn't given any instructions."

I wanted to wrap my arms around him the way he used to do me whenever I came to him with a problem. But, as mad as I was at him, I didn't want to leave him alone in the Interruption. Nobody should have to go through this maze of unbelief alone.

"Then how did you get here? How did you find me?" I yelled again. For a person who had seldom raised her voice, it had become common now.

He was slow to respond. "I just wanted to see you so badly. I couldn't get you out of my head."

"Then why did you come to me as a bird? I don't like birds." I tried to see his eyes even though he kept his head down.

"I didn't know that either."

"Huh." Odessa huffed. "I ain't trying to keep up with five people. These three are already running around like they can't follow the rules."

Cato's head snapped up, and he stepped forward. "I won't be no trouble. Plus, I know a little about this place now. Maybe I can be some help."

"Suppose we don't want you." Even though I half meant it, a part of me was happy to see him again. A part of me rejoiced that I had someone who knew me and—until that forgettable day—had been the one that made me smile. But I wasn't ready to let him know any of that.

For the first time since meeting Odessa, she wore her doubt as visibly as her washed-out dress. She was a stickler for rules, and if Princess Kenyata didn't say it, then she wasn't willing to do it. I needed to do or say something before she declined Cato's offer.

"Maybe, he can be helpful," I chimed in.

"Helpful, how?" Odessa narrowed her eyes. "How he gonna help us, me?"

"I don't know." I wouldn't look her in the eye because she'd know my real reason. "But we can't just leave him here. Maybe Princess Kenyata will look at us favorably if we do something nice for him."

I made eye contact with Cato, and we could have been back in our history class because the tug on my heart was still there. I didn't know how long I could stay mad at him.

He gave me a half smile that revealed the dimple I seldom saw on his cheek.

Odessa nodded, liking the idea. Her mouth moved like she was chewing on the thought of pleasing the princess.

"I won't be no trouble." Cato stood taller, like his height might help convince Odessa.

"I guess," she started.

"So where do we go next? Are we going to try to find Willa and Luis?" I moved past the subject before Odessa changed her mind about Cato, then I almost saw Odessa switch gears. She touched her pin. "I don't think we should use these pins. We might end up in more trouble."

Hope surged in my chest. "How about visiting my mom?"

Odessa shook her head. "I think we need to regroup. Do what we can to get the five of us back together. Then we can move to the next portal and see what happens there." She snapped her finger. "I think this boy may be helpful. He's making more sense than visiting your momma."

I put my hands on my hips. "You brought us here to help your grandparents, so why is it a crazy idea for me to want to do the same thing?" It wasn't the first time I'd raised my voice to her, and her eyes widened.

"Well, it's two against one, and the instruction we got was to stay together, so we'd better." Odessa sounded so firm I couldn't think of an argument, and before I could object, Odessa rubbed her pin.

Then everything went black

Death Gets Worse

Odessa

When the world stopped swirling, I was afraid to open my eyes. Piercing screams drilled into my head like a hot poker. I covered my ear with my one good hand and shoved my stump across the other. It sounded like a choir singing loud, slow, and off-key, marching toward the gallows of hell.

With my eyes so tight, the cries seemed far away, yet right in my ear. They echoed and swirled around me like a hurricane.

Somebody had to be willing to do the hard stuff, and neither of those two children knew anything about difficulty or struggle. The hardest thing they probably ever did was refuse to eat their vegetables or go without their cell phones for a few hours. So, I had to rub that pin to bring us all back together, no matter the cost.

Ronita, with her hand on her hip, telling me she wanna see her momma like we gonna do that simply 'cause she had a yearning. The only reason I was standing in my grandparents' yard is 'cause I was testing out some of the things my grandmother passed on to me. Not because I knew it was possible.

So far, I'd spent all my days in the Interruption, wishing I had listened more and taken Grandma more seriously. I thought her talk was like Santa Claus and the Tooth Fairy. I nodded and wished she'd hurry it along so we could discuss something more interesting.

But I guess I can't be too mad at Ronita. She only wanted to do what Willa and Luis had done. They should have set a better example.

I rubbed that pin without giving the repercussions a thought. If it meant we could get on with this journey, then as far as I could tell, we didn't have no other choice. But when things went black, and the sensation of tumbling came over me, I had a moment of regret. Having my feet on solid ground was a benefit I'd taken for granted until then. Feeling like clothes tossed on high heat in a dryer wasn't no fun. I couldn't grab on to nothing, but at least nothing had a hold on me.

Yet.

I can't tell you what I expected to see or hear. I expected the worst, but when I opened my eyes, I hadn't come close to preparing.

The smell of rotten corpses singed my nose hair. And I knew the smell from growing up. Something was always dying in woods behind the house—a deer, a possum, a raccoon. So, I hoped it was only a dead animal left on the side of the road. But when I squinted just a sliver to look at my surroundings, it looked like I'd gotten into a worse situation.

Nothing was dead near me, nor was a mob screaming in my ears. I removed my hands from my ears since they weren't good at keeping the sound out.

I was seated on my big butt in soot. Cato had plopped in front of me in the same position, and Ronita sat next to him. We probably looked like those mice in the nursery rhymes but more miserable. At least we'd arrived with all our limbs, even though my hand hadn't returned.

The barren surroundings could have been a scene out of one of those scary movies I used to watch. If fire swept through these parts, the land still wasn't ready to bear fruit and wouldn't be for years to come. There was no sunshine or glow from the moon. Instead, a greenish glare lay broken over the land as if it went through a prism, and someone kept adjusting the position.

Beyond us was a stream of black sludge that resembled

tar. Items bobbed up and down, but I had no idea what they were and no interest in finding out. I wasn't even sure if we were still on earth. My arms peppered with goosebumps. I didn't know where we were, but I knew for sure, I didn't like it.

No place I knew resembled this charred, barren land.

We was worse off, and fear filled my pores. I tried to appear brave, and it should have been easy because I was already dead. What could be worse?

Something touched my arm and nearly scared the shit out of me. I thought it was Daniel, coming back for another round. But when I focused, I saw Willa. She looked like she done lost her bowels in her britches. And there was Luis, too, with relief in his eyes.

He stood first and dusted the soot off his pants. That man cared more about how he looked than he about anything else. "What the hell happened? And what is that noise?" He glanced at Ronita and Cato and then me as if I was the one who owed him an answer.

Willa was next on her feet. "Oh, my God! I thought he was going to strangle me. I didn't know what to do." Her voice rose above the groaning surrounding us. She rubbed her neck. "I'm still shaking."

I glanced at her little legs, and she was right. They vibrated like they had a motor. "Who was going to strangle you?"

She shook her head. Clearly, she'd said more than she wanted. "Never mind." She glanced over her shoulder, probably looking for her phantom ghost.

I got to my feet and didn't bother knocking the ash off my legs and dress. From the looks of things, it wouldn't have helped. We'd landed in a place that had burned out long ago, and the soot would continue to cling to us.

"And who is that?" Willa pointed to Cato, drawing back as if she thought he might do her harm.

"It's Ronita's bird."

"Her bird?" Willa asked warily.

"Well, boyfriend turned bird turned boyfriend." I flipped my handwith each word. It weren't my job to fill her in on what she missed. She'd have the answers she sought if she'd been where she was supposed to be.

Cato helped Ronita to her feet. She acted like she didn't want him to touch her, but she was only fooling herself. These old eyes can see things others can't. That girl's still carrying a torch for that boy, but I'd go along if she wanted to pretend. Besides, I reckon we had bigger things to worry about.

Ronita rushed to Willa. "Who was going to kill you?" Her eyes were large, like she thought we all might be in danger.

Willa stared at the girl, while contemplating how to answer or thinking up a lie. "Him." Willa stared over Ronita's shoulder with a distant gaze in her eyes. "Payne. The man who ..." She glanced at me, then clamped her lips together.

"How did we all get here?" Willa examined her rubbed raw wrists.

Luis came closer. "Yeah. What happened?"

The way he scrutinized me made me stiffen, just in case he thought he could touch me again. After fighting with Daniel, I was sure he'd be less of a problem.

"I brought us here." I kept my voice firm. I didn't need any of them challenging me. "I did what was best for all of us."

"How?" Luis demanded.

I wasn't sure I wanted to tell him because he liked to take advantage of things. But I guess this was different. "Princess Kenyata visited while you and Willa was gone. These pins ..." I touched the one on my chest. "will always bring us back together."

Ronita put her hands on her narrow hips. "Yeah, but she also said we could be worse off. Further from our final destination. And look at this." She swung her arms around, showing her displeasure at our current surroundings. "And this is a lot worse. Listen to that screaming. I'm not even sure that's human." The way she cut her eyes at Luis and Willa, at least she was ready to put the blame right where it belonged.

"So, what are we supposed to do now? How do we get out of this place?" Luis looked over his shoulder like he expected something to grab him again.

"We gonna have to figure that out." Cato spoke up, making me like him.

"This place doesn't look safe." Willa's voice wobbled.

I wanted to wrap my fingers around her neck and strangle her. "If you and Luis hadn't run off, none of this would have had to happen."

I pointed my finger at her and Luis. The two of them always manage to stand shoulder to shoulder. "Look." I swallowed hard. "You and Luis is the reason we in this situation. If I hadn't rubbed that pin and brought us all here, you two would still be out there somewhere, gallivanting around like you didn't care what happened to the rest of us. So why don't you two put your thick-ass heads together and figure out how to get us out."

Willa dropped her head.

Defiance marked Luis's face. "I didn't leave. Someone—something took me."

I batted my eyes at him. He was keeping something from us, too. Maybe we all had a secret that needed to come out.

The screaming grew louder as if a large angry mob headed our way. The sound grated on my ears like a dog overusing a squeaky toy.

Ronita turned to me. "Odessa, what's happening?" Her voice trembled.

I scratched my head, trying to remember if there was a tidbit my grandma may have mentioned, but I had nothing. No way my grandma or anyone she knew could have spoken about a place like this and lived to tell it. "I don't know. But based on where we are, it can't be good."

"Let's run." Panic had a good grip on Willa. She looked as if she was afraid to move and in flight all at the same time.

"Run where?" Luis looked over his shoulder.

"I have an idea." Cato glanced at each of us.

"What do you know?" Luis barked within inches of Cato's face. "You just got here."

Cato puffed out his chest. "I know more than you think." He paused, giving us time for his words to sink in. "I been through a lot since I got stuck here, and I know some ins and outs. That's how I found Ronita." He looked at her with a longing that tugged at my soul.

I patted him on the back. "What should we do?"

He looked at Luis and Willa, then cleared his throat. "We have to protect ourselves. Always. We've dropped a level or two, and more obstacles exist to fight."

"No shit!" Luis's sarcasm was as menacing as the look in his eyes.

Cato ignored him. "We need to stand with our backs to each other, facing out in every direction because they could come for us from almost anywhere. And they will."

The Unknown

Luis

This young punk showed up and wanted to tell the rest of us what to do. His attitude didn't sit right with me. At some point between life and death and all this bullshit, I wanted to call some shots.

If those screams hadn't irritated my nerves, maybe I could have thought of an escape for us. But I wasn't good at thinking up solutions so fast. If I had, perhaps I could have stopped Janice when she came at me with that crazed look in her eyes and waving that huge butcher knife.

I puffed my chest and straightened my stance. "Who is this kid? Why are we listening to him?" I didn't hide my venom. I didn't escape Janice to have someone else tell me what to do. If everyone in the Interruption were equal, nobody would get upper hand on me.

"Why can't we just raise our hands and get the hell out of here?" I looked at the four of them, daring them to challenge my simple solution.

Odessa placed her good hand on her hip and shot me a look that would have made me wither if I were still alive. "We can't do that, 'cause ain't no way we all going to think the same thing at the same time and end up in the same place." She pointed her index finger at her temple. "Think, man. Think."

Cato smirked. "So, as I said—" he shot me a look. "let's get in position. Those screams are getting closer."

I was the last one to get information. Cato and Odessa made me look like an idiot. They didn't know I had a vengeful side. The first opportunity I got, I'd get them back.

I stood between Willa and Ronita. I couldn't figure out

which one shook the most, but if we were supposed to fight off something, we were doomed.

A fly buzzed by my ear. I swatted it away, but the effort was useless because there were more.

Suddenly, there seemed to be hundreds of flies.

No, thousands.

No millions swarmed through the sky.

We tried to bat them away, but it was useless. They landed on our eyes and mouths and crawled up our noses. Ronita dropped her head to snort.

"What the hell is happening?" As soon as I smacked some to the ground, more came.

"I don't know." Willa must have thought ducking was more effective because she kept bobbing her head.

"Tighten up, everybody." Cato was the only one who seemed unperturbed by the pesky insects. "This is just the beginning."

"You've been here before?" I couldn't see Odessa since we had our backs to each other, but the way her voice wobbled, she was doing the same thing as the rest of us.

"I have." Cato stood stoically. "The smell is the worse."

"The smell?" I caught my breath. "It can't get worse than this stench, can it?"

"Oh, yes, it can." Ronita pinched her nose.

I was afraid to draw in a breath, but that only lasted a few seconds until I became lightheaded. The odor was thick and burned my nostrils. The fetid smell overwhelmed my senses making me double over.

That reaction made me recall my mother's nickname for me as *a cream puff*. I wanted to bury my head under my jacket. The odor coated my nostrils like smeared shit.

"Don't break formation. No matter what." Cato roared over the chaos.

Why wasn't this attack phasing him as much as the rest of

us? Maybe this kid knew more than he told. Perhaps he was behind this newfound hell.

Willa's body sagged against me.

"Stay strong," I whispered to her, barely parting my lips out of fear that smell or flies would enter my mouth.

The stink grew more pungent, reaching into my stomach and stirring up nausea. I wanted to tear away from the tightly knit foursome, throw up my hands, and escape. But showing such an outward act of cowardliness would expose what I've always wanted kept hidden.

"I don't know how much more I can take." Ronita started to pull away.

I grabbed her shoulder and pulled her back. "We can do this." I hoped I sounded encouraging because I wanted to run, too.

"I don't think I can." She bent forward and wrapped her arms around her stomach.

"It won't be much longer. Try to hold on. Lean on me if you have to." Cato's assurances encouraged me even though the smell and heat intensified.

"Look, there." Willa nodded her head.

I followed her gaze, and our tight knot shifted as the others tried to do the same.

Zombies was the only word I could find to describe what was coming toward us. I saw sharp teeth, blank eyes, and rail-thin beings who almost resembled humans. They weren't coming our way to welcome us to this new territory.

"What in the world?" Odessa broke away from the group and stared with disbelief. For the first time, she didn't look as confident. "What are we supposed to do?" Her voice trembled.

Cato reached for her arm and pulled her back. "Stay in formation."

"We can run," I yelled above the screams. "I don't think we

can fight them all. Look how many there are. Can we get on the other side of the pit? I don't see any way around it."

Everyone turned toward the pit just a few yards away. It was so dark and murky that crossing it seemed impossible without a boat; even then, I wasn't sure a ship would make it across.

"No," Cato spoke with authority. "Those creatures are going to that pit. We're just in their way.

"Well we can get out of their way, can't we?" Odessa yelled.

"No. There is nowhere to go. As I said, if we stand here and stay strong, it's our best chance." He picked up a hand full of rocks. His wind-up and delivery were perfect. He threw like a National League Baseball pitcher. The pebbles landed in the center of the pit and began to glow. Within seconds, the rocks turned to ash and disappeared. "Did you see that? That will happen to us if we don't prepare before going into that pit."

He quieted as if he expected one of us to answer.

No one did.

"Prepare how?" If there was another option, I wanted to hear it.

"No time to discuss that now. We have to do this. They won't put up much of a fight. We can do this. Once we get past this, then we can talk about options."

The determination in Cato's voice made me think we had a chance.

"I'd rather face them than get burned to a crisp." Anxiety tore through my chest.

Ronita and Odessa were slow to get back into their previous position. They kept glancing around like they wanted another option now.

"Come on." Cato herded us back together. "Hurry. We don't have another choice. It's this or nothing."

Even though I thought my idea could have worked if we thought it through, I returned to my position in our tight knot, between Willa and Ronita, with my back to Odessa. I couldn't let them look more fearless than me.

As the army of tortured souls grew near, the stench increased.

The screaming grew louder.

My heart pumped faster.

I didn't see a way to win this battle. Of course, the crew nearing us had nothing to lose, and as dead folks, maybe we didn't either.

From a few feet away, the screams became more audible. Before, I thought they were wailing in pain, but as they grew near, each one had a plea. The echoes of their voices mounted. Cries of 'help me,' 'I'm sorry', and 'save me' became discernible.

Maybe they were human at some point, just like the five of us, but churning through turmoil had left them less than human. They didn't seem to care that we stood in front of them. The masses came at us from all sides. Their limbs were long and bony. Their hands and teeth sharpened like claws.

Willa tensed beside me, and I felt her shrink as if she wanted to get on her knees.

I nudged her up. "Stand strong, Willa."

"I don't want to do this."

I could tell she was in tears, but I couldn't help her.

"We must. Now!" I yelled as a skeletal figure lashed out toward my face. I batted his hand away, and his arm fell to the ground. That encounter was too easy. I struck the other arm. With glazed-over eyes and sagging skin, the tortured soul bared his blackened teeth and moved away. As more approached, I held up my fist, ready for the next, and with each creature, the battle grew easier. One raked his clawed finger across my cheek before I could punch it away. I clamped my fists together and came down on top of its head. With a sound that pierced my soul, it fell to my feet and grabbed hold of my ankle. I pounded my doubled fists on its head, using all my strength until it slithered away like a snake on its belly.

From the corner of my eyes, Ronita kicked at something that may have once been a child. When it fell to the ground, she stomped on the bones like she wanted to mash it to be sure it wouldn't come for her again.

On the other hand, Willa only dipped and dodged everything that came at her. One creature almost took out Willa's eye, but I used my forearm to knock the claw away.

"Fight, Willa!" I yelled to her again, unsure if she even heard me over the noise.

I couldn't wait to see if she was willing to save herself. Another soul was on me with arms that looked like tree limbs. I grabbed one and snapped it in two.

The five of us kept our backs together, which was no way to fight a mob like this, but it worked. After that, some zombies lost interest in us and continued toward the pit.

As each new creature drew close, my courage increased. We weren't engaged in hand-to-hand combat. We only had to stand our ground, and the beasts continued their pace toward their destination.

There were so many of them the battle lasted for hours. I wanted to catch my breath, but I couldn't stop. The overpowering smell of rotten flesh weakened my knees, but for once, I didn't have the luxury of running from trouble. Instead, I faced the enemy and fought. With each soul that crumbled, I grew taller and more assertive.

When there were no more of them, the screaming didn't stop, nor did the awful smell disappear. I turned to face the pit, which glowed yellow and orange as the tar-like substance sucked up the souls.

Resting With Bones

Willa

I collapsed in the dirt. A puff of fine soil lifted around me, choking off what little air I'd inhaled.

The others gazed around as if they expected more creatures to come at us.

If that happened, I couldn't fend them off. Exhaustion had taken over every inch of my body. I struggled to breathe.

I hadn't had a moment to absorb the little time I'd spent with Ava. That had ended too soon. I had so many crucial things to say. My purpose for finding her was to help her, and seeing me evaporate probably traumatized her more.

With no idea if I'd get another opportunity, I wanted to cry, but my tears had dried up.

I tugged on the hem of Odessa's dress.

She glared at me with an evil eye. "What?"

"Is there any way to kill yourself in the Interruption?" I hadn't meant to get everyone's attention, but they all looked down at me like it was a weird request. "Oh, come on. I've had enough of this. Can't we get it over with?"

Cato shook his head. "Oh, no. You don't want to do that." His eyes widened. "If you think what you've been through is bad, believe me," he paused. "It can get way worse. I know what I'm talking about."

"So, what's next?" Luis nudged Cato. "Are we going to hang around until another wave of zombies attacks us, or will we use our power and get to a place that doesn't resemble hell?" He quivered.

Odessa plopped in the dirt beside me. "I'm tired. Why don't we sit for a spell before we decide?"

Ronita was the first to settle beside Odessa. "Good idea."

The two of them were best pals now. Cato didn't waste any time parking beside Ronita.

Luis stared at us. A thin trail of blood ran down his cheek. "Can't we find a better place to have a chit-chat?" He smoothed his hands down the front of his dirt-covered suit jacket. "I don't want to sit in this filth." His standoffish attitude drove me nuts. Who cared about his suit that now had scuffed knees?

I glanced at my dress, torn, soiled, and nowhere as pretty as it was the day the undertaker dressed me. We all had battle scars—scratches, cuts, and bruises, not to mention Odessa's missing hand.

When no one gave in to Luis, he sat beside me. He looked around. "What is so important that we had to sit and discuss it?" From the distant expression on his face, he wanted to be a million miles away. We all did.

Odessa cleared her throat and leveled her finger at each of us. "Princess Kenyata told us to stay together, and we didn't. She told us we needed to help each other get to the next portal, and we haven't. This..." She pointed behind her at the broken bones and filth. "This was the first time we stood together and helped each other. And it was a success."

"Yeah, yeah, yeah." Luis rolled his eyes.

Odessa put her good hand on her hip. "And Luis and Willa ran off like you didn't know no better. You know you wasn't supposed to do that."

"I didn't leave because I wanted."

His sharp tone made me look up.

"A creature like the one who took your hand dragged me out of here. I tried to fight it but didn't have enough strength in transition." He spat out the words as if they tasted foul in his mouth.

"And you, Missy." Odessa drilled me with a look. "I know you left of your own free will. So don't tell us no lies."

I placed my arms over my chest. "I had to see my daughter. She's vulnerable.". No one was going to make me feel bad about the choice I made. "She's back on drugs. And even though I'd thought I had only been gone a day or two, I discovered two years had passed." I held up two fingers. "Two years." The words tugged at my heart.

"There's that much difference?" Ronita looked perplexed. "Is it consistently two years' difference?"

I shrugged. "I don't know." I rubbed my chin. "I imagine it's not. I believe it's always different. I have no expectations of the Interruption anymore. It's easier that way."

Luis settled his hands on my raised knees. "So now, what do we do?"

"I need to go back and save my daughter." I didn't yell or show any emotion. If I sounded confident, maybe they would agree with me. But none of them had children. They couldn't fathom my depth of love.

"Why didn't you save her when you were there?" Odessa let her frustration with me show.

I squirmed. "Some force took me away. It was scary. I think they were going to do something bad to me." I looked down, hoping they didn't detect the sound of guilt in my voice.

"Now, do you both see what happens when you just run off and do whatever you want?" Odessa sucked her tongue.

"Well, you started it, Odessa. You were the one who took us to your grandparents' place. You never asked us for our opinion." I glared and dared her to say differently.

She drew back like she wanted to throw a punch. "I was thinking about my grandmother while I was running. I didn't know we'd end up back in time, so don't shift the blame. My actions were by mistake, and yours were on purpose."

Ronita held up her palm. "Okay. Can we stop arguing? We need to figure out where we're going from here."

"She's right." Cato inched closer to Ronita, but I don't think she noticed.

Luis rubbed his hands together. "I'm sorry I didn't get to help your grandparents. Things didn't work out the way I'd planned. I didn't know that demon Janet would come for me."

"It worked out fine." Odessa clapped. The excitement in her voice made me stare at her. How she found something worth clapping about in the Interruption was surprising.

Odessa continued. "They found oil on their land, and now they're millionaires. I don't think they could have a better outcome."

"Yes!" Luis removed his hand from my knee to smack his, and the hard sound boomed off the surroundings. "I was right. They found it."

"You knew?" Odessa scratched her chin and curiosity etched her face. "Don't pull my leg, Luis. I ain't mad at you for not helping."

"That's what I was going to tell you until I got sucked away." He closed his eyes for a moment like he was reliving something painful. "I'm glad it worked out."

Odessa nodded but, for once, didn't have a whole speech. "We need to get out of here." She glanced around and shivered. "If we use our pins, we could be worse off. And I don't want to think of anything worse than this." She swiped her face where a trail of blood had dried. "I don't know what to do next."

"I do." Cato raised his hand. "I've been here before." He gazed at Ronita as if he thought it might impress her.

She didn't look at him.

He stood. "We need to get on the other side of that stream."

Luis followed the direction of Cato's gaze. "How are we supposed to get on the other side of that muck? It's not water." He scrambled to his feet. "It's burning everything." His voice grew louder with each sentence. "We can't listen to this newcomer. What does he know? I'd rather take my chances with the pin."

I remained seated. "Luis might be right." I looked around for someone to agree with me.

Odessa folded her arms, looked back at the stream, and then at Cato. "Boy, ain't no way for us to get from here to there." She pointed her index finger at him. "How did you do it?"

"Like most things around here, you gotta believe you can. Each of us has to believe then we can make it across. If anyone has any doubt, it could cause us all to burn up in that pit."

Odessa shook her head and struggled to get to her feet. She tightened the handkerchief, hiding her stump when she straightened. "You must think we are like the Savior and can walk on water. I'm a believer in real life, but here ain't nothing the way it seems." She shook her head with ferocity. "Maybe Luis is right. We oughta just rub our pins."

"I agree with Odessa. That's ridiculous."

Ronita was the last to stand. "I'm not doing that. There must be another way. We need to think about it some more." She looked at Cato, then turned her back on him. "The last time I followed Cato, I ended up here. Don't trust him."

I shook my head in agreement. "Ronita makes a good point."

No Way

Ronita

They all stood and gave Cato reverence he didn't deserve. They didn't know him like I did. He talked a good game, but I wouldn't fall for it again. Believing him is what got me in this awful place. Now, he wanted to lead us across that stream that looked collected dead souls and gullible fools.

I pushed my foot into the soot. Finding my voice was easy if I used it to say something against Cato. "We can't listen to him. We all just saw what happened when those creatures walked into that pit. Not one made it to the other side."

The expression on Cato's face changed. He never looked happy, but my comment made him sadder, for sure.

He stood taller. "Ronita's saying that because she's mad at me." He jerked his hands as if he needed them to help make his point. "You must trust me. You all saw what happened. We can't stay here until another wave of those zombies starts their migration. We'll run out of energy sooner or later, and they'll drag us into that pit along with them. Look at Odessa. She already looks like she's run out of steam."

"I don't know, Cato." Odessa's skepticism had the others nodding in agreement. "If crossing that pit was possible, why didn't those zombies do it instead of burning to a crisp?" She kept her eyebrow raised while she waited for an answer.

Willa nodded. "I agree with Odessa and Ronita." She glanced around. "There must be another way out. Maybe Princess Kenyata will show up and lead us."

"She hasn't led us out of anything yet." Luis's stoic stance was another show of defiance. "We can't stay here hoping she'll come to our rescue."

"So, what do you suggest, Luis?" I challenged him the same way I'd done Cato.

"I don't know." He looked at his feet.

"Maybe we ought to rub our pins. We could end up better off." My voice shook with fear. "That pit is scarier than another realm."

Odessa shook her head. "You don't know that, child. In death, there can be some terrible things you can't even imagine."

I inhaled, hoping it would give me courage. "We've got two bad choices, and we must pick one."

Cato crossed his arms. His head bobbed back and forth, watching each of us as we talked. Finally, he directed his attention to me. "Ronita, trust me."

"No, I can't."

He sighed. "This is different. I wouldn't suggest it if I thought it wouldn't work." He was angry. I knew by the way his voice held no tone.

Luis tugged on his belt loops. "We have no choice. We can't keep sitting here." He looked over his shoulder like he expected another wave of the half-dead bodies to come for us.

We all dreaded the zombies. But I feared that pit more than I did the creatures. "We fought them once. We could do it again." Since everyone else was standing, I scrambled to my feet so they'd take me seriously.

Willa nodded to Cato. "Tell us how we're supposed to get across that pit."

Cato lifted his shoulders. "Like we do everything else. We have to do it together—holding hands, believing in one another, trusting that we stay focused on crossing and nothing more." He looked at me with a raised brow.

"Then we gonna be in trouble," I shook my head. "I don't trust you. How do I know you won't let me fall into the pit?" I shouted, not caring if he got angry.

Odessa stepped forward, holding up her hand and her

stump. "Wait a minute. This situation ain't about you two. This is about the five of us. Everything we do is about everybody." She made a wide circle with her good hand, indicating all of us. "We all been selfish, doing whatever we wanted, but we must stop. Our ability to get some peace depends on having faith in each other and working together. That shouldn't be so hard."

I folded my arms over my chest and tightened my lips. I was as mad now as when my father died. Back then, no one heard my cries or cared about my feelings. They all rushed to my mother like she was the only one hurting. Cato always wanted things his way. As far as I knew, this could be another one of his setups.

"So, what are we gonna do?" Willa stared only at me.

"Do you all believe Cato? Don't tell me you all believe him?" I gave Willa the same fierce look she gave me.

"We can't keep saying the same thing." Odessa motioned with her stump. "It's time for us to piss or get off the damn pot."

I raised my hand. "Maybe we can take a vote." I wasn't confident anyone would vote with me, but I couldn't follow behind Cato like the simpleton I used to be.

Luis sucked his teeth.

Willa rolled her eyes.

Odessa pursed her lips. "A vote. Girl, whenever I think you might be making a step forward, you go right back to being that schoolgirl. She paused. "But we gonna do it your way, just to get to the end of this. And the majority rules, just like in real life, so be prepared for the outcome." She gave me a firm look. "Who wants to do things Cato's way?"

It took a moment, and I thought my opinion had a chance, but then everyone raised their hand.

Odessa pressed her lips together. "You satisfied now, Ronita?"

I stomped my foot. "No." I sounded like a sullen child, but nobody cared.

Cato reached for my arm, but I jerked away. "This won't work unless we all work together." His sad eyes tried to convince me he was telling the truth, but I was angry with him. Maybe I was stubborn or selfish, but I'd earned that right.

Silence fell over us. Everyone stared at me. I wasn't old enough to make these choices. My only worry should have been my history grade and giving up my virginity. My eyes stung, but I refused to cry or let them bully me.

"So, what are we going to do now, drag her across the pit?" Luis had a gleam in his eyes as if that was precisely what he wanted.

Cato looked at me. "It wouldn't work. We'd all burn before we made it halfway."

Luis stomped his foot, sending soot into the air. "Damn it. You mean to tell me this decision hangs on a teenager who doesn't know what she wants?"

Willa stopped Luis from pacing by touching his shoulder. "Calm down. You aren't helping things by yelling." Willa's glance at me softened. There was warmth in her eyes that made me want to trust her.

Odessa came to stand beside me. She wrapped her arm around my shoulder and pulled me close. "I know you're mad at Cato. You have every right to be." She squeezed me. "What we dealing with here is bigger than you, bigger than me, bigger than any of us." She paused. "It stinks, but it's the situation we're in. So, take a breath, child. Close your eyes and tell me from the bottom of your heart if you can trust us and cross that pit. Be honest with us, but most of all, be honest with yourself."

"So, you trust him?" I stared into her eyes, hoping to see her truth. Odessa had always been upfront with me.

She looked at him. "I don't have no reason not to. But I think that's what this journey is all about. If we don't stay together—help each other, we may all perish."

"If you think I should, then I will." I kept my voice low so that the others couldn't hear us.

Odessa shook her head. "It don't work that way. You got to make a decision based on your heart." She patted my left breast.

I took a deep breath, closed my eyes, and tried to listen to what I had to say. There were so many voices in my head that I heard none of them. What I wanted was to be back at home in my bedroom. I wanted my purple blanket that I kept in the chair beside the bed. I wanted to hear my father's voice one more time. I wanted the anger in my soul to go away so I could be happy again. I wanted so many things, and none of them had anything to do with the Interruption. Finally, I opened my eyes and looked into the faces of the people standing with me. Their expectant expression gave me strength. "Okay. Let's do it."

There was an audible sigh of relief from both Willa and Luis.

"You're sure?" Cato directed his question at me and appeared to hold his breath. "You've got to really want to do this. We all do. No half-assing."

"I am." I sounded more confident than I felt.

Luis started toward the pit. "Then let's get the hell outta here."

The rest of us followed him. As we neared the pit, the temperature grew hotter, and the wails grew louder.

I pointed. "Are the bones from those who only made it halfway across?" I wanted Cato to answer.

"I don't know. The last time I crossed, we all made it." His face was grim.

"Then how do you know what will happen if we don't agree?" Willa stopped short.

Cato closed his eyes and inhaled. "Are we having the same conversation again? I'm telling you what we did, and it worked. It worked," he yelled. "No one has any better idea, do they?"

We were quiet.

"No more debating. We've got to keep moving to get to the next realm. We've wasted precious time already," Cato said. "Once we start, don't stop. Don't stop to swat a fly or rub your nose. Let's just keep moving and keep believing. Understood?"

Everyone nodded but me.

We stood at the pit's edge. I took Odessa's hand, and Cato held her arm above the stump, sandwiching her between us. Even Luis, with all his big talk, hadn't come closer than we had. But Odessa was in control. I could feel her energy coming through the palm of my hand.

She released Cato's hand. "Tell us what we need to do, and boy, you better get this right. We're all depending on you."

I knew Cato better than the others. With his shoulders hunched and his face pinched, he was nervous. He didn't like others depending on him. His free spirit was probably swimming in fear.

"Okay." He turned his back to the pit. Facing us, he talked with his hands. "Just like when you all wanted to do everything else, you've got to concentrate on crossing the pit—nothing else. We must hold hands, and whatever we do, don't let go, don't look down, and don't stop moving."

Willa pointed at the black tar-like substance. "We're going to walk on water? You're sure we'll stay on top if we do what you say?"

Cato tapped his forehead. "See, that's the thinking we don't need." He talked so loudly that Willa winced.

Odessa shook her head. "We all need to be sure, Cato. That's all." She looked at Willa and Luis. "Ain't that right?"

They nodded, but I saw some reluctance on their faces. I kept my head down to mask mine.

In the distance, the wailing started again. Louder than before. I craned my neck to see beyond us. Another swarm of flies headed our way. Behind them was another mass of skeletal people with flesh hanging on thin bones. Their advance was slow but steady.

"They're coming," I shouted.

Everyone turned. The fear showing on their faces spoke for them.

Luis moved closer to the pit. "We can't fight all of them off. We're not as strong as we were the first time."

Willa covered her ears as the screeching grew louder.

"Let's go," Cato called our attention back to our task. "I'll go first." He reached for my hand, and for the first time, I let him. I planned to take him with me if I was going down in a steaming tar pit.

Cato looked into my eyes. "Please, do what I say, and I'll take care of you."

His sincerity rang true. I had to believe him.

I held Cato's hand and Odessa's.

Willa held onto Odessa's stump, and Luis was at the end of our line.

The pit was only a few yards wide, but it might as well have been ten miles.

"Don't look down and don't stop." Cato stepped off the edge.

I focused my eyes on the back of Cato's head. One large curl touched the base of his neck. It was always there, and I'd imagined playing with his curly hair one day. That day never came.

I refocused on that lock of hair whenever I felt my gaze slide away. The curl that would occupy my fingers as Cato changed my life. Maybe if we ever got to the other side and were out of harm's way for more than a few minutes, I could still have that dream.

Cato tightened his hold on my hand, and I focused my attention on everything Cato said. Under my feet, something crunched, but I kept my head high. The stench stung my nose, and as much as I wanted to rub the itch, I closed my eyes and held on to Odessa and Cato.

I needed them and had to stay strong.

And they needed me.

Solid Ground

Odessa

I didn't let Ronita's hand go, and she continued to squeeze my fingers. Several times during our crossing, I thought she might waver, but I wouldn't let her.

I didn't look back until we all reached the other side of the pit.

I put my foot on solid ground and whispered a prayer that probably wouldn't reach anyone's ear. Only then did I release the breath I'd been holding. With the tar pit behind me, my heart slowed to a steady pounding instead of the irregular thunder that started when Cato told us we had to cross that pit.

The moment all five of us stepped on the other side, the rancid scent of burning flesh, rotting corpses, sewage, and every foul smell I could think of lessened. There were no flies on this side either. A gentle breeze evaporated the sweat on my forehead. "Hallelujah."

This side of the tar pit was as different as heaven and hell, like a curtain had dropped, eliminating the awful other side.

Over here, it reminded me of that first meadow. The birds sang high in the trees, and flowers blew in the gentle breeze, tickling my nose with their sweetness. The grass was cool under my feet. Yes, things were about to change.

"We made it." Cato sounded half surprised at our success. He threw his arms into the air.

Ronita's eyes shone with a new respect for him. She dropped her hands to her knees. Her breathing was heavy. "I was so scared. We did it." She fell to the grass and then heaved. We each had relieved expressions.

Cato placed a hand on her shoulder. "I told you we would."

She didn't pull away. Either she was too exhausted or just plain happy to have her friend back.

If the stench of rotting flesh hadn't clogged my memory, I could almost make myself believe everything that happened before had been a dream.

I turned around, taking in the surroundings, allowing my senses to absorb the beauty. "Why couldn't we see this beauty from the other side?"

"It was a test," Cato offered. "If you had known it would be this beautiful, you wouldn't have crossed over on faith. You would have done it for the wrong reasons."

"Then why didn't you tell us how nice it would be?" Willa placed her hands on her hips, and her face creased with anger.

With all eyes on him, waiting for an answer, Cato shrugged. "It doesn't work that way."

My old ear tuned in to that answer. Cato wasn't just a grumpy teenager. He was a moody teenager with Interruption knowledge. I filed that information away for later.

"Thank you, Cato." Willa stepped forward and pressed her palm to his chest. "I don't think we would have made it without you."

"That's why we need to adhere to Princess Kenyata's advice. She gave it to us for a reason, but we've ignored her." I waved my hands about like those blowups that advertised the sales at the used car lot.

"Well, that isn't so easy." Luis leveled a finger at me. "Telling us what to do is easy, but we could use more information."

"All I know is when we were in that beautiful park, if we had all sat on that bench and waited like we was told, none of this other stuff would have happened." I didn't hold back my resentment. "We couldn't have been given simpler instructions."

Willa held up her hand. "Let's not argue. Now we know better, we can do better." She paused. "I know I keep saying the same thing, but—"

I spun on her. "Here we go again. You gonna tell us you need us to do your thing, right? With your children, right?"

She shook her head like a bobblehead doll. "Yes. But this is different. It's crucial and different from the last time."

"Yeah, sure it is." I rolled my eyes toward the sky.

Ronita straightened and fisted her hands at her sides. "It's my turn." Her voice was stronger than I'd ever heard. "You all have done your thing." Her glare moved from Willa and Luis and paused at me. "You all need to stop being so selfish."

Cato watched Ronita like she was something good to eat. "She's right. Why don't we do her thing next?" He held his palms up like that might convince us to do what he said.

"We need to figure out how to get to the next realm." I directed my comment to Cato but meant for them all to hear.

"If we wait here long enough, Princess Kenyata will come to us." Cato spoke with confidence.

Ronita wrenched loose from him. "Are you sure?" Her voice rang with excitement. "Will she help us? I mean, like, really help us this time?"

His eyebrows rose. "I don't know. It's not like we can tell her what to do."

I'm sure he didn't care if she showed up or not. He was the only one not chasing or running from something.

"So, do we sit and wait?" Willa glanced at Luis like she wanted him to agree with her. The two of them shot looks at each other a lot. We all knew what the two of them did, but we continued to pretend we didn't.

"Can we at least put more space between us and that stuff that happened over there?" I motioned to what had disappeared. "I'm sure Princess Kenyata will find us even if we move." I started walking towards a field of wildflowers, not caring if they followed or not. A few moments alone would do me good. I needed time and space to hear my thoughts.

Ronita caught up to me. "I agree with you." She fell into step beside me, and sure 'nuff Cato ran like a faithful puppy to catch up to her. I kept breathing and moving, not caring about the others for the first time since the beginning.

A fresh breeze caressed my dry skin. The green grass tickled my bare feet, and the trees bloomed like a pleasant spring morning. I could make myself believe that I was moving forward, my final transition that could be moments away. If Princess Kenyata descended on her giant griffin, then this time, she might swoop me up and carry me with her.

I'd done the hard thing—rubbed the pin to bring us all back together, even though it put us in a worse situation. Now that's about as unselfish as I've been in a long time.

My breathing grew harder. I wanted to sit. I stopped short and glanced around. There was nowhere to rest. I feared if I settled in the grass, getting up again on my aching legs would be hard. I turned to Luis and Willa, who whispered to each other like someone might care what they said. "I need to sit a spell. Help me get down here, Ronita." I leaned against her, dropping to one knee.

Ronita braced my arm until I settled in the grass. "Are you okay?" Her eyes widened. "Are you running out of strength?" She sat beside me and placed her hand on mine.

"Child, I'm old. Of course, I'm running out of strength. Look, as much as we been through, I'm entitled to run out of steam, ain't I?"

"No." She slid closer and lowered her voice since the others were close behind us. "I mean … the Princess told us we'd run out of time and strength. I'm not talking regular tired. I mean, you know." She gave me a timid nod.

I tried to think if I could tell the difference in how I felt.

I hadn't thought of Princess Kenyata and didn't want to think about all the hazards that still tracked us. I'd have pushed her hand away, but I knew it would hurt her feelings. She was sensitive, but I didn't want to think about her question.

Luis and Willa sat in front of the three of us. We was one cozy group suddenly. I turned my attention to Luis. "So, who snatched you, Luis? You might as well tell us all about her while we wait."

He rubbed his hand across the jagged scar on his throat. "The same woman who killed me. She's here in the Interruption, too, and she's about as evil as they come." He crossed his legs and glanced over his shoulder as if he thought she might come up behind him. "I think I might be done with her now, but I can't be certain."

I rubbed my good hand over my stump. "Ain't that the truth? I'm still doing battle with the creature that took my hand. And I ain't sure it will be the last one."

Luis collapsed his hands. "One thing we need to know, during that brief time when we try to transform from one thing to another, we're vulnerable. That's how Janet got me." He nodded to each of us. "So, don't think moving all over the place is the panacea it sounds like."

I turned to Willa. "You got anything you want to share?"

She dropped her head, just like I expected her to do. "I don't want to say." She wrung her hand. "But my children are still in danger. More now than they used to be." She stroked a blade of grass.

I was tired of her trying to look innocent when she carried as much guilt as the rest of us. I leaned toward her. "How so? What kind of trouble?"

She stopped short of looking me in the eye. "I have a question for you and Cato, since you know so much about this place. Can we," she paused like she wanted to gather her thoughts or revise her question—"as dead people do anything to living people?"

I smacked my knee. "Yeah, we can." I swallowed. "I got revenge on my husband for the mean he did to me when I was living." I pointed to my bare feet. "He even buried me in my worst dress and no shoes." I snapped my chin up. "First chance I got, I took his heart right out his chest."

Ronita drew back like she was seeing me different.

"Oh, don't give me that look. He got what he deserved." I turned back to Willa. "Why you asking?"

"Because someone threatened to hurt or kill my children." Her voice hitched.

Tears filled her eyes.

I swear if she started that sniffling, I would smack her silly.

But she pulled herself together and continued.

"It's all my fault. My children shouldn't have to pay for what I did. They shouldn't." She wrung her hands so tight her large blue veins strained.

I lifted my hand to keep my promise to smack her, but Luis reached over and rubbed her shoulder, which calmed her.

"Maybe Princess Kenyata will tell us how we can protect your children. I know I have a question for her." Luis continued to rub Willa, and her tears dried up.

"What?" I shot back, trying to distract Willa cause she grated my nerves.

"Janet said I had a son."

I never seen him look more serious.

"She said it just before I took her pin. You whisked me away before I could learn more."

I could only nod. We were a bunch of thugs. We just looked different. I reckon Ronita was the saint among us unless she was hiding a big secret.

Everyone grew quiet. It felt good to sit in silence. I had imagined the Interruption as a calm place with good smells, gentle breezes, and beautiful colors because Grandma never mentioned the constant noise or movement. Instead, I glanced down at my stump that had hardened along the edges. Nobody ever talked about the bad or scary parts.

With my eyes closed, I took a deep breath, the way the doctors told me I needed to do, drawing in my stomach and easing the air out of my nose. I kept trying, but it would take more than breathing to settle me.

Sleep tried to overtake me, but the brightening skies drew my attention. The iridescence rainbow ushered in Princess Kenyata.

I got to my feet with no help. This had to be my time to move on.

A Child Shall Lead Them

Ronita

Odessa jumped up so fast I thought she might lose her balance. I scrambled to my feet and gazed at the sky with her. She acted as if she always had to bow down at the sight of Princess Kenyata, but I struggled to see what her arrival would change.

I'd seen her two times, and neither of her visits made me better off. I didn't feel like Ronita Miller anymore. I'd lost her somewhere at the bottom of that cliff, but I hadn't stepped into a new identity. Maybe I never would, and I'd given up hope that Princess Kenyata would help me.

So far, all she'd done was show up, say a few useless words, and vanish long before we got any of our questions answered. But I'd grown so attached to Odessa—she filled the space in my heart that my grandmother used to occupy— so I wanted her wishes to come true, even if it meant she might leave me on this journey. Wherever she thought she belonged, that's what I wanted for her.

Cato jumped to his feet too and, like always, stood so close to me that our shoulders touched. I reached for Odessa's hand because she couldn't stop shaking.

I leaned close to Odessa's ear. "I don't know why you get so excited every time she shows up," I whispered. Even though I wasn't enamored by the princess, I didn't want to offend her. I imagined she could turn me into a toad—or worse.

Odessa turned to Luis and Willa and motioned for them to stand. "It's the Princess." She said it like no one knew what was happening but her. Any minute, I expected she might curtsy.

Luis climbed to his feet, rubbing his eyes, not happy to be told what to do.

A calmness settled over me like a warm hug. Then, as Princess Kenyata descended in front of us, I turned to Cato, once again in awe of him. "How did you know she'd come?"

He grinned and winked as if he was happy I'd said more than a few words to him and hadn't snapped. The ice I held in my heart for him melted. Just like that, I was happy he stood beside me, but no way would I tell him. I'd never let him know how I felt. One thing I'd learned was that it wasn't necessary to let people know when they carried your heart in their hands because, sometimes, they got careless.

The griffin's clawed feet touched the ground. Its large wings flapped but stirred nothing. The princess climbed off in one graceful move. Even though she didn't impress me, I couldn't stop staring at her. I'd never seen anyone more beautiful. She moved like a butterfly and spoke like a choir. Her skin gleamed, reflecting the gold around her neck. I couldn't help but wonder what she did when she wasn't tending to us.

Sure Odessa was about to fall, I slipped my arm through Odessa's. She patted my hand but didn't turn her gaze away.

"Are you breathing?" I squeezed her.

"I don't know, baby." She nodded. "But that ain't impor-tant. Anytime the princess shows up is another chance for me. I can't help getting excited." She bounced on her toes.

Princess Kenyata walked toward us, her jewelry catching the light that arrived with her. "Gather around." She gestured for us to tighten around her. The smile she wore stretched across her face, touching her cheeks and eyes.

"I think this is it." Odessa's voice was barely audible. She took a giant step forward.

We stood in a straight line. Luis, Willa, Cato, me, and

Odessa at the end. Lined up for inspection. I shifted, worried about what this visit would bring.

"Well, well, well. The five of you are all together." She looked at each of us and nodded. "I was beginning to think it would never happen."

Odessa raised her stump. "I did that." She piped up like a toddler. "It was a hard decision, but I did it." She bounced, and her smile was brighter than the light Princess Kenyata came in on.

I hoped it worked out for Odessa. This side of her, I could do without. She'd rubbed the pin without asking us for our thoughts. It wasn't supposed to work that way.

"Odessa, I am aware of what you did." Princess Kenyata took a step closer.

Willa came forward, waving to get the attention of the princess. "I need your help. It's really important that I protect my children. Someone wants to harm them." The panic in her voice tore at my heart. But she was wasting her time. I don't know why she didn't know that by now.

Princess Kenyata sighed. "Willa." She tilted her head. "There is not one thing any of you have done or said that I am unaware of. Nevertheless, the Interruption has its limits and restraints, and you must abide by them."

Luis dropped his head. His hands held his interest.

"But as a mother—"

Princess Kenyata held up her hand. "Willa, enough." I'd never heard her so stern. "As much as you think your wants and needs come first, they don't. That is one reason you're here." She clasped her hand, letting her words sink in for all of us.

Willa whimpered.

I still hadn't figured out why I was here. Maybe I didn't want to know. At least I didn't have any dire circumstances like Willa. Of course, I'd like to see my mother to make sure she was okay, but she was tough. She'd be fine.

Princess Kenyata directed her attention to Luis. "Luis, you have something that doesn't belong to you."

He lifted his head but not his eyes. "Excuse me?" He sounded indignant.

She shook her head. "You know what." She snapped, then narrowed her gaze on him, making him step back. "You don't want to play with me, Luis. I am called *Princess* for a reason. I'm not one of you."

"Yes," he croaked. "I have Janet's pin." He reached into his pocket and pulled it out.

"You need to return it. That pin belongs to Janet. Each soul must keep their pin until they cross through to the final portal."

"Return it? I can't. I don't want to go near that woman. I don't want her to keep hounding me."

I couldn't tell if I saw fear or anger in his eyes.

"You have to, and you will. Janet hounds you because you mistreated her."

"She killed me. Doesn't that make us even? Shouldn't she apologize to me?"

Princess Kenyata gave Luis a knowing smile. "We're talking about your redemption. Not hers. Until Janet repents for what she's done, she may languish in the Interruption forever, but that's her journey. You must decide what your journey will be."

He nodded. "But how?" His voice quaked. "We have to stay together." He leaned forward and looked at Willa first, then turned to glance at the rest of us. I didn't give him my attention.

The princess continued. "It's a journey the five of you will have to make, together."

"What?" Odessa stepped out of line. "You done it again,

Luis." She clamped her hand into a fist. "Damn it! Damn it! Damn it!" Spit flew from her mouth. She shook her head. "I can't stay with this group, Princess Kenyata. They is the most selfish bunch of folks I ever met. I can't." The agony in her voice made my knees shake.

"Odessa, this is what you must do. You made your journey tougher than it had to be, so this is the price you pay." Princess Kenyata's voice held no incrimination. Instead, she talked as calmly as if she was telling us about the weather.

"Then why are you here? If you can't get us to the final destination, why are you here? Why are you here?" Odessa banged her fist against her thigh.

Her despair tore at my heart. She had been through so much. No one deserved a break more than her.

I intertwined my fingers and held them up. Maybe the Princess would think I was praying or begging, but I didn't care. "Can't you at least take Odessa and let the rest of us finish this journey? She's older, and she's been trying so hard."

Princess Kenyata turned her attention to Cato. "Cato." She walked to him and placed her hand on his shoulder. It was the first time she'd touched any of us. "You've done well. Your soul is redeemed."

I couldn't take my eyes off how her elegant fingers graced his shoulder. Her connection with him differed from how she connected with the rest of us. I drew away to see Cato and the princess better.

I should have kept my mouth shut, but the questions popped into my head faster than I could keep up. "What's going on? What do you mean, he's done well? What did he do?" The way she spoke to him set butterflies loose in my stomach.

She moved to stand in front of me. "My dear Ronita." She

reached for my hands and held them tight. Her hands were soft and warm and reminded me of my grandmother. "Cato has helped you to fulfill your destiny." She glanced at him with a glint that I didn't understand.

My heart pounded. Afraid to ask for more information, my tongue touched the roof of my mouth and stayed there.

Odessa appeared taken aback, with her good hand pressed to her chest. "What are you talking about? I done just as much as Cato, why are you praising him. He was just a bird. An annoying bird."

Princess Kenyata didn't reply to Odessa. Instead, she locked eyes with me and wouldn't release my gaze.

I wanted to pull away, but she held me in place with her hands and stared.

"Welcome, my child."

"Welcome to what? Fulfill my destiny. How?" I jerked my gaze to Cato, but he stared down,

and then I looked at Odessa. She appeared clueless for the first time since I met her. With my attention back on the princess, I blinked slowly, forcing my brain to pay attention. I couldn't fall off another cliff. It would be my luck to die again.

She held my hand even when I tried to pull away.

"Ronita." It sounded as if my name lingered on her tongue. "I know the Interruption is tough for you, but this journey has a purpose." She touched the crown of my head. Her hand lingering there until my skin tingled.

I closed my eyes, afraid of what might happen.

My ears rang, but I refused to open my eyes.

"What is going on?" Willa's voice rang over the noise in my ears and head.

No one responded to Willa. Then a hush fell over the field. The birds stopped singing. The breeze stopped blowing. With my eyes still closed, I thought everyone stood still. I only felt the electrical sensation pulsing between Princess Kenyata me.

"Open your eyes, Ronita." Princess Kenyata released my hands.

I did what she asked.

Odessa and Willa gasped. Luis's eyes were so large, I thought they'd stuck in place. And Cato stepped away from me. Their reactions made me feel like an alien.

Something heavy pressed around my neck. My hand went to my throat, touching the gold necklaces that felt cool. I looked down. The gown my mother had dressed me in for my funeral was gone. Instead, I wore attire like Princess Kenyata, with layers of dark colors that flowed to my sandal-clad feet.

Princess Kenyata bowed her head to me. "You are now Princess Ronita. Welcome to your position in the Interruption."

Unreal

Willa

I squeezed my eyes so tightly that color burst behind my lids. Even when I shook my head to get my brain to comprehend, I couldn't understand what Princess Kenyata had said or done. She'd transformed Ronita from a high school girl in sleepwear to what the princess called a *princess* and left the rest of us standing there like discarded rags.

At times like this, a swallow of vodka would have numbed my pain and silenced the worrying voice in my head. But I had nothing to grab onto now. Instead, I had to stand straight and absorb the torment.

"Wait, a minute. Wait, a minute." Ronita flapped her arms up and down. "What are you doing?" The look in her eyes said she wanted to flee.

Figuring I had nothing else to lose, I stepped out of formation and raised my hand. "I'd like to know what's going on?" My voice sounded shrill, but this situation had its foot on my neck, and I couldn't hold back.

Princess Kenyata directed her attention toward me. "Is there a problem?" Her tone gave nothing away, but her eyes drilled into me, letting me know I had no right to question her.

"Why does she get to be a princess? How did you decide to pick her and not one of us?" I pointed to myself and then to Odessa and Luis. "Aren't we all worthy?" I crossed my arms. My intent wasn't to offend Ronita, but no one here would stand up for me. I spun to face Luis. "Say something, Luis."

He shook his head. "I've got enough troubles. I will not make her angry."

I thumped his chest. "Don't you think this is unfair?"

He placed his hand over the spot I'd thumped as if I'd hurt him. Then he pressed his lips together leaving me alone in the argue.

The desire for a sip of vodka still lingered on my tongue. Too bad death hadn't taken away that longing. A long swallow would do me good, just like it used to before all this happened. I shook those thoughts away. They didn't serve me now and were the souce of all my trouble.

"My dear, Willa. I'm not the one making these decisions, but waving your hands around won't work to get you what you want here. The Interruption is about earning redemption." Princess Kenyata placed her braceleted hands on her waist. They jingled and glinted against the sun. "You have given a sincere apology to the ones you've hurt. You're making progress."

"Are my children safe?

"You can't worry about the actions of others. You're only required to be the best person you can be.".

Her answer didn't soothe me. "If I've done everything I could, then why was I still here?"

"Let's hear what you've done to earn the next portal?"

I wanted to rattle off a list as long as my arm, but nothing came to mind. Anger burned the back of my throat. "You haven't told us how to earn anything." My voice ratcheted up. "You didn't tell us we could be princesses. The only thing you've said is to stay together." I spat out those last words because they tasted foul in my mouth. If I couldn't help Ava or BJ, I had nothing else to lose, so fighting with Princess Kenyata satisfied me.

Princess Kenyata batted her long lashes. "Simple instructions, indeed. That was all I required of you. Stay together. I'd hoped you would do everything you could to help each other." She paused as if her words needed to sink in.

"I had to help my daughter." I threw my hands up. "None

of you can understand that because you don't have children. I did what every caring mother would have done." I talked so loudly that my throat scratched.

The birds nesting in the nearby tree took flight and, for a moment, quiet reigned. I felt foolish, but why couldn't they didn't see I had no choice?

Princess Kenyata shook her head as if I were a child she'd grown tired of trying to talk to. "Willa, my dear, you're still trying to follow the rules of the living. When will you understand the rules are different here?"

Ronita adjusted her stance. "Hold on, everybody. I'm the one who should ask questions." Then she looked to me. "Nothing has changed for you." Her sharp tone surprised me. She ran her hand down the front of her colorful gown. "But what does this mean for me?"

Odessa danced from one foot to the other. "Yeah. Shut up, Willa. Let's find out what's going on."

Princess Kenyata reached for Ronita's hands again. "You will lead this group to the next portal and their final destinations."

Ronita's eyes grew bigger. With panic on her face, she shook her head. "No." She stepped back. "I can't. I know nothing about this. Odessa should be the one."

"This is no mistake. I will help you like before, but you are the only one who has been unselfish."

"No. No. No." Ronita shook her head. "Odessa is the one. She sat on the bench, just like you said. She's helped us all in one way or another. She's the one." Ronita croaked like she was getting ready to release a flood of tears.

Princess Kenyata released Ronita's hands and backed away.

I had so much more I wanted to say, to turn this around, but the idea that Princess Kenyata thought I was selfish burned in my chest. Maybe she was right about me. I dropped my head. It hurt too much to look up.

"Please don't leave yet," Ronita begged.

I wanted to tell her not to bother because it wouldn't do any good. Somewhere, someone had decided our destination, and nothing we could do would change it.

"I've never left you." Princess Kenyata glanced at each of us. "I've left none of you." She clasped her hands. "We did not design the Interruption to coddle you. You need to deserve the next portal—earn it."

"But I've done nothing to deserve being here." Ronita threw her index finger in Cato's direction. This is all Cato's fault."

With his gaze on the ground, he puffed his cheeks out.

"No, Ronita. You didn't. But at birth, your destiny was set. Being a princess is an honor. Only a few get this gift." Princess Kenyata gave Ronita a warm smile. "You're going to make out just fine. You'll reap rewards well beyond anything you could have imagined."

Ronita crossed her arms in a huff. Her new bangles clanged together. "Will I get one of those?" She nodded her chin toward the griffin that Princess Kenyata flew in on. Only now did she show interest in her new role.

"That and so much more." Princess Kenyata took another step back. "Follow your instincts, Princess Ronita. They will lead you where you and this group need to go. And anytime you need me, whisper my name, and I'll be here for you. At the end of this journey, you'll be ready."

"What about my mother?" Ronita asked.

Princess Kenyata touched Ronita's shoulder. "You will be able to comfort your mother."

"Will I be able to tell her about all this?" She spread her arms to include all of us.

"Not in the sense you think. But there are ways to let her know you are fine."

Princess Kenyata's assurance made me feel better. Maybe there was a way for me to do the same thing with my family.

Then Princess Kenyata turned her attention to Cato. "You've done well. You've followed instructions. And for that, I've granted you the redemption you need. You and Ronita will do this together."

"What does that mean?" Cato inched closer to Ronita.

"It means just that," said Princess Kenyata. "Ronita is the Princess. You will help in any way she chooses."

"That's fine with me." Cato pressed up on his sneakered toes.

I waited to see if he would get new clothes and a crown, but nothing changed. I couldn't hold my tongue.

"What about the rest of us?" I pointed at the princess. "What do we get?"

No one acknowledged my question or even looked in my direction.

"What about me, Princess Kenyata? You done addressed everyone but me. Don't you have something to tell me?" Odessa's voice wobbled. I believed the mean, old woman was near tears.

Princess Kenyata gave Odessa more reverence than she gave me. "Odessa, just like Luis and Willa, you have some apologizing to do."

"How can I apologize to Daniel when I don't even know where he is? We both done bad to each other, but I suffered a lifetime with that evil man." She folded her arms under her chest.

Princess Kenyata kept her gaze on Odessa for what seemed like forever. Then the princess turned away.

Looking as skeptical as the rest of us, Ronita chewed on

her bottom lip as she stared at Princess Kenyata mounting her griffin.

If only Princess Kenyata had planted one of those reassuring gazes on me, then maybe I wouldn't feel so out of sorts all the time. Maybe it would help me cope with the terror of being away from my children. But I'd angered her in the process. So now, I only hoped to make amends with Ronita.

Now What?

Ronita

I stood perfectly still and watched Princess Kenyata climb on her griffin and disappear the same way she'd arrived. Questions popped in my brain like bubbles. I could not put them into words to ask them.

When the colorful surroundings returned to normal, everyone turned their attention to me, looking at me as if I had an explanation for what had happened.

All except Cato, who continued to study the ground.

I tapped him hard on the shoulder. Slowly he raised his head, and our eyes met the way they used to in school. He dipped his chin—it was his tell—and that was enough for me. He knew more than he had ever let on.

"Stay here," I spoke to Luis, Willa, and Odessa. Pointing my finger at each one, so there would be no misunderstanding. "No funny business from the three of you. Don't disappear. Don't raise your hands above your shoulders." I waited for them to acknowledge my command. I didn't know how long they would respect my power, so I had to use it well.

I grabbed Cato's hand and pulled him toward the grove of thick trees. The sun had already settled low in the sky, and I had no idea what darkness might bring to this new place. I didn't need to worry about it anymore, but now I had to look out for the others.

Cato allowed me to take him into the shadows, where I was sure the others couldn't see us. There I settled my hands on my hips and glared at him without saying a word.

He shoved his hands in his pocket and kept glancing at the ground, but I refused to speak first.

"Okay," he finally huffed. "I did not know about it. None

of it." He kept shuffling. "Not until I arrived in the Interruption."

"Why should I believe you?" My throat constricted around the words.

"Because I've never lied to you. I have no reason to lie to you." He reached for me but dropped his hands. "You know me, Ronita."

"I thought I knew you. But look at all this stuff." I motioned toward my new gown.

"You heard Princess Kenyata. This would happen no matter what I did or didn't do."

I closed my eyes and rubbed my face. He was right, but I liked things better when I had him to blame. I had so many questions. There was one that he could answer. "What happened that day, Cato—up on the ridge? Why did you do that?"

He looked down, hesitating for a moment. "This is how it happened," he paused as if waiting for me to pat him on the back for finally telling me.

"I jumped, Ronita, my life was a wreck. I'd hurt your mother's boyfriend, Jack Randolph, really bad. My grades were shit. That night, the police knocked on our door, asking questions about Jack. They hadn't even returned to the squad car before my father lit into me with both fists. This time, he said he'd either send me away or tell the police to put me in a juvie. All the fighting. It happened every night." He dropped his head, but not before I saw the pain in his eyes. "My father always came home drunk and ready to hit someone. If I was closer than my mother, then it was me. And as I grew older, I made sure I was always coser. You were the only thing that made me happy, and I knew I'd drag you down sooner or later. I didn't want to do that."

"Well, you did it anyway."

Cato shook his head like all the sadness filled him again. "I couldn't take it anymore, so I ..." He looked at me. "I didn't mean for any of that stuff to affect you. I don't even know why I took you there." He stepped toward me. "That's not true. I know exactly why. You're the only person who cared about me. So, I wanted to spend my last hours with you." He reached for my hand and squeezed it as Princess Kenyata had. "I should have done better at protecting you, but no matter what happened that day with me, you'd still be here." He gave a long glance up and down my fancy new clothes. "And still be a princess."

I took a deep breath and fingered the soft material of the gown. "Tell me about this part. How are you involved, and what do you know?"

He rocked back and forth and rubbed his hands together like always when nervous or anxious. He'd done the same thing on our last day together, but I was so set on what I wanted I paid little attention. "Because of what I did, jumping off the cliff. I didn't have a choice but to accept the proposition from Princess Kenyata or I would have become one of those creatures that attacked us over there." He pointed with his chin. "If you think the other side of that tar pit was bad, imagine it ten times worse. That would have been my eternity. *That* was in store for me. Princess Kenyatta offered me a way out. They wanted you." He dropped his head. "I made the only deal I could. I figured if I got the chance to be with you again, then I'd be lucky."

I kept my eyes on his face. Cato usually spoke little, but the way he kept going on and on had to be his way of distracting me, taking my mind off the change that had overcome me. The change he'd helped facilitate.

"Stop talking so much." I pushed my hands into my head and touched the tiara for the first time. I pressed my palms against the stones and tried to lift it, but it didn't budge. "Why won't this thing come off?" I flopped on the grass.

Cato shrugged, then sat beside me. "I don't know anything about that, and I sure can't tell you anything about your new duties. But I'm glad we're together."

Even though I didn't want to smile, I couldn't help it. If I had to be here, I was glad it was with him.

Maybe I'd never get beyond what Cato had done, but for sure, I couldn't go back. At least Princess Kenyata hadn't told me how. Yet.

Odessa stomped into the edge of the bushes with her stump resting on her hip. "How long ya'll gonna be over here?" Her sharp tone made Cato jump.

I met her eyes. "Odessa, we can talk when Cato and I finish." Even though I didn't need her permission, she deserved my respect.

"Yeah, but why can't we do it all together?"

Cato raised his brows, signaling me like he did in high school. I didn't need to hear the words to know he wanted more time alone with me.

Though I sat on the ground, I straightened my back. I wanted more time with Cato, too. Around him, I felt comfortable, like I'd found the spot where I was supposed to be. "I have a deal for you, Odessa." I pretended to give my idea more thought.

"What, child?"

"Give us some time together, and I'll give you your hand back."

She glanced at her stump, bringing it up to her face like she'd never seen it before. "You gonna give me my hand back if I walk back over there and give you time with Cato?"

"Yep."

"What? You planning to have sex?" Her disapproval rang in my ears.

"Maybe," I said, without wincing or backing down.

"Deal. Now give me my hand." She waved her stump at me.

I held up my finger. "Afterwards. Give Cato and me some privacy."

She narrowed her. "You young people." She shook her head and walked away, mumbling, about how she would never understand young folks and about me thinking I was the boss of her.

When we were alone again, Cato wouldn't meet my eyes. Instead, he pulled several blades of grass. "Did you mean that about, about us having sex?"

I moved my tongue around my mouth, imagining our first kiss, the feel of his mouth on mine. He'd taken me by surprise in the school hall. The way he'd grabbed my butt had excited me. And even though it hadn't happened, I still wish it had. "You do owe me."

He finally lifted his head. "You weren't ready back then. I know you think you were, but— " he shook his head—"but we were trying to fit in, and that wasn't a good enough reason. And that messed with my head, too."

"I made a decision. I was old enough to decide what was best for me, and you shouldn't have second-guessed it."

"Maybe not. But I was always looking out for you."

"Like now." I ran my hand over my flowing new dress.

"Yeah. Like now." He made it to his hands and knees, then crawled to me. He came so close I saw the permanent pimple on his chin.

He placed his palms on my face, pressed his lips to mine, and inserted his tongue into my mouth. My first reaction was to pull away, but I couldn't. I wanted this more than anything the Interruption could have provided.

My body relaxed into his, the way I imagined lovers would do. He smelled the way he always did—like wood and earth. Something solid I could depend on, like my father. I wanted to forget everything in our past and hoped we could stay in the meadow forever.

I wanted to embrace him but kept my hands in my lap.

Waiting.

Waiting.

But I had no idea for what.

Without releasing my tongue, Cato pressed me into the thick grass that cushioned me and my enormous dress. He stretched his body over mine, and his erection pressed through the fabric, sending my mind racing. My flesh warmed, especially between my legs. Could this happen?

I wasn't even sure it was what I wanted. Giving my virginity to Cato was important for the other Ronita, but Princess Ronita had more important things to do. With my eyes closed, a flash of a woman strapped to a bed stung my lids. I shook my head, only to have another flash of a man and a woman hunting a teenage girl.

I didn't want to, but I released Cato tongue. The images were so vivid. They shook me and made me pant.

He looked puzzled. "Why are you stopping me? I thought this was what you wanted."

I scrambled to my feet and smoothed the folds in my gown. The pressure of responsibility bore down on my shoulders. As much as I wanted to put myself first, now wasn't the time. Other priorities occupied my thoughts. "Not right now."

"Then when?" He came to his feet.

Cato had the sincerest expression he'd ever worn. His feelings for me were true. I'm not sure why I knew this. It was as if I'd looked inside his head and heart and seen his feelings myself.

"Are you still mad at me or something?" He tilted his chin slightly to show his disappointment.

I put my hand over his heart. "We'll know when it's right for both of us. The others are waiting. We have so much to do. It's overwhelming. We'll have our time."

What's Happening?

Luis

While Odessa and Willa sat rubbing their hands together like we were helpless, I circled around them. First, I walked one way, then spun around and walked the other.

Returning the pin to Janet troubled my stomach. I couldn't walk up to her and say sorry, then hand it over. The woman had slit my throat when she thought I hadn't treated her right. She'd probably consume me whole this time, then spit out my bones. And maybe that's what I deserved. I could have treated her better. I could have treated everyone better, but the bitterness in my heart kept everyone just far enough away they couldn't penetrate the shield that protected my vulnerability.

Princess Kenyata had made the demand as if it were a simple task. In the beginning, she should have told us she frowned on pin taking. In this place, we only learned after we made the mistakes.

I closed my eyes and pinched the bridge of my nose, trying to figure out how to accomplish this new task.

Since nothing was chasing us or trying to tear our limbs off right now, I had too much time to think. Too much time in my head. Janet said I had a son. But if that were true, wouldn't I already know him? I ran my index finger along the scar on my neck. Sure, I bounced from woman to woman, having fun, but any of those women would have come after me for money if they'd carried my child.

My child.

I stopped, shoved my hands into my pockets, and stared at the sky. I had no idea what to do. There was no use trying to find out about a son now that I was dead. What would I do? Stand across the street from his school and cry about the life I could have had.

I turned to Odessa and Willa. "Why are we waiting? What are those kids doing over there? Don't they know I got something to do?"

Odessa shielded her eyes and glared at me. "Where you in a hurry to get to? It didn't sound like you much liked the idea of returning that pin earlier."

I looked over to where Ronita was now standing in clear view with that boy. "Can we tell them two to hurry up?"

Odessa chuckled. "You can, but it won't do no good. They got lots of stuff to talk about."

I exhaled. "I don't know how you do it, Odessa. How do you find the fortitude to keep up this struggle? I'm ready for it to be over."

She nodded. "I'm with you there. I been ready." She glanced at Willa. "How about you, Willa? Ain't you tired?"

She hung her head. She looked defeated. "Yeah. I am. I thought I could still help my children—my daughter—but." She shook her head.

"Well, now we all feel the same way. Maybe we can work together and get out of here. I don't have any strength left to fight no more battles or run from no more goblins." She rubbed her knees. The woman I'd pinned against the tree and had sex with was long gone. This Willa looked as if the world had cast her aside.

Leaving the worry of a returning Janet and zombies behind sounded good to me. But, if I started searching for the son that Janet mentioned, I might get sucked into another realm with her. The thought warmed my neck.

If Janet was in the same place, I couldn't tell them how I got there. It wasn't as if the place had an address.

Willa touched her shoulder to her ear. "It's not worse than what we just went through, right?" Her voice wobbled.

I nodded. "Yes, it is. It was darker than anything I'd ever seen. The room had some dim light, but outside was the color of that tar pit. I don't know what was out there. It could have been the devil himself."

Odessa reached for my arm and stroked it. "Luis, I believe you're shaking."

"You're damn right I am." I rubbed the back of my neck. Handling Janet should be easy here. Her power was no more substantial than mine, but Janet wouldn't stop at anything. Unlike her, I had limits. Killing another person never crossed my mind.

"Look." Willa pointed across the field.

Ronita and the kid headed toward us.

Willa stood and shielded her eyes. Her anticipation showed in the way her body never stopped moving. She had a permanent twitch.

I helped Odessa to her feet.

"Willa ain't no use in getting all excited." Odessa brushed her dress, though no grass clung to the fabric. "We got to let Ronita feel her way in her new role. You can't dictate what she does."

I couldn't help but wonder if Odessa wanted to put Willa's wants on hold so Odessa could get her own. They saw nothing the same way. But this time, I kept my mouth shut, waiting to see what Ronita had planned. If going back to Janet to return the pin didn't come up, I would take my chances and never see her again.

As Ronita neared, her calm presence settled my jumpy nerves. Unlike before, when everything spooked us, now the air surrounding her was serene enough for two butterflies to follow her.

Odessa was the first to step forward. "So, what's next? Since you're the Princess, you can whisk us all to a better place." She rubbed her hands together as if she was getting ready to taste something good.

Willa opened her mouth.

Ronita held up her hands, halting all conversation.

"I know. I know. I know." She rested her arms at her sides. "You all have something you want to do, or somewhere you want to go, but it doesn't work that way." She pointed to me. "The first thing we're going to do is return that pin to Janet."

I dug my foot into the lush grass. "Do I have to untie her?"

Ronita's eyes narrowed. "Do you want to be stuck in the Interruption? Forever? Why don't you do all the right things so you can move on?"

I gave the question some thought. "If leaving Janet tied up is the only way to keep her away from me, the thought ain't so bad."

"She's not the worst thing you have to worry about." Ronita touched my arm. It was gentle.

Maybe there was another way to handle Janet.

I looked into Ronita's eyes. "I don't know why, but I trust you. If you think it's the right thing to do, then I will."

"We'll all be there with you." She turned her gaze to the rest of them. "We will stay together and support Luis on this journey. Agreed." It wasn't a question but the softest command anyone ever made of me.

Patience Is for The Birds

Odessa

I wasn't always selfish, and staying married to Daniel was proof. But I learned in life that the last don't always come first. And if the meek inherited the earth, that would never happen for me either.

Ronita and I done built a bond. I looked out for that child when the others dashed off to do whatever they wanted. But the way she marched toward us, I'd hoped it was because she was gonna give me what I wanted.

Besides, I was the one who told them to sit on that bench. We would have all been saved if they'd listened to me. So the way I'm thinking, Ronita owed me. Making us all help Luis first was like a slap across my face.

I put my good hand on my hip and kept my mangled stump behind my back. "Let me get this straight. Luis stole some woman's pin, and now we all got to venture into some unknown so he can replace it." I shook my head. "It don't seem fair. I been trying my best to get ya'll to do the right thing, and ain't nobody listening to me. I don't know how much more I have to do to get my chance."

Ronita turned her soft brown eyes on me like they might soothe my anger. I should have given her the same reverence I gave Princess Kenyata, but to me, she was still that young girl who ran toward the bushes instead of sitting beside me when I'd asked.

Ronita acknowledged me. "Like I said, we are going to return the pin first. That is critical."

Willa pretended to clear her throat 'cause I didn't hear no phlegm. "And how do you know this? You've only been a princess a few hours."

Ronita's chest rose and fell as if she was trying to expel the bad energy Willa and I generated.

"I have visions." Ronita stared into the sky as if she might get another one any minute.

"Visions?" The hard edge in Willa's voice made me step away from her. She might decide to hit someone based on her tone.

"Yes, Willa. Visions. That's the only way I can explain it. So, you all are going to have to trust me." She shrugged. "You don't have other options."

"Okay," said Luis. "So, how do we return the pin? I don't know where Janet was. It was one room with a bed and maybe a table." He drew his shoulders to his neck like the memory reminded him of torture.

"I know where Janet is." Ronita nodded with satisfaction. "But the four of you will have to hold your hands in the air, and Luis will have to focus on Janet. And only Janet."

I swatted my good hand. "Can't you just whisk us all there and get this over?"

"Yeah, because in transition, bad things can happen. We're vulnerable to all the stuff out there." Luis looked reluctant.

The more we talked, the more nervous he became. Any minute, I expected him to wither to the ground. I had no idea what drove that man, but fear was a good starting point. I've never seen nothing like him. He continually dodged the hard stuff. Imagine being afraid to confront a woman. I wished Daniel could've taken a page from that book.

Ronita's slow nod said she contemplated something. "Yes, I can whisk us all to any place. But we all have more to learn. During our time together here, we are supposed to learn something about and from each other. Help each other." Ronita pointed at Willa. "What can you tell me about Odessa? That has nothing to do with her grandparents because we all witnessed that."

Willa's mouth opened, then snapped shut. She looked over at me and studied me as if she expected to see something written on my face. Then she threw up her hands. "She was married. But why is that important?"

Ronita turned to Luis. "What do you know about Odessa?"

Her question hung in the soft breeze while Luis hunched his shoulders.

Ronita clasped her hands. "You see. We've been missing the point. It would have been better if we sat on that bench and talked. We didn't have to go through all this stuff." She glanced at Cato, who hadn't spoken in a long time. Maybe he was just happy she wasn't swiping at him.

I couldn't hold my tongue much more. When I couldn't hold back another moment, I said, "Well, it's too late for that kind of thinking now, and I'm missing my hand to prove it. You promised to give it back to me." I sounded crosse because I was.

Ronita directed her gaze at me, and I felt bad for snapping at her. She probably had enough on her mind. But she made me a promise, and I wanted to collect it.

"I kept my promise, Odessa. Pull your hand from behind your back."

Ronita had a new way about her. Unlike Princess Kenyata, Ronita was approachable. I didn't feel all tongue-tied when I talked to her or when she talked to me.

With a deep breath, I did as she requested. Like a child on Christmas morning, I couldn't wait to look, but I was afraid to. I held my hand in front of my face, flipping it back and forth like I'd never seen nothing more beautiful. I even had that nasty scar from when I burned my hand on the stove. Seeing my familiar fat fingers made me laugh. I pulled each one to make sure they wouldn't come off.

I met Ronita's eyes. "You did it!" I rushed toward her and

threw my arms around her neck. "Child, you made me whole. You the real thing." I squeezed her so tight she squirmed to get loose.

"If you can do that for Odessa, why can't you do something for me?" Willa whined.

Of course, she'd be the one to say something. Don't nothing sit right with that woman. She was born sour.

Ronita clapped her hand, making a sound that echoed. "Enough. Let's prepare to go." She turned to Luis. "Are you ready?"

He gave a slight nod, then stuck out his hands for someone to grab. I was the first to reach out because I believed what I was looking for was getting nearer.

I stood next to Cato, and Willa and Luis were on my other side. "Don't mess this up, Luis. Remember, you taking the three of us with you."

He squeezed his eyes, giving me a look that showed his displeasure.

"Ronita, are you coming with us?" Luis's voice held a plea.

"Don't worry." A glow appeared over Ronita's head. The light made the stones in her tiara sparkle, almost blinding me. "I will be with you all until we complete this journey. Even when you don't see me, I'll protect you."

Luis exhaled, and his chest deflated.

Cato had a confident expression, as if he knew how this would end, or maybe because he was still soaking up the pleasure of being in the bushes with Ronita.

"Let's get this over with." Luis looked at Willa and then me.

I closed my eyes and lifted my hands. I kept my thoughts free. Whenever they drifted—which comes easy when you get my age—I erased them.

Finally, I opened my eyes, and the four of us me, Cato, Willa and Luis stood shoulder to shoulder, but we were in a tight room that was hot as I imagined hell being. The place had little light, so it took time for my eyes to adjust.

"What is that smell?" Willa released my hand and used her forearm to cover her nose.

Cato bent at the waist.

His hacking drew my attention, but only for a moment, because a woman strapped to a bed started yelling. Janet. Her flawless face reminded me of a magazine model. I understood why Luis fell for her. Even in the darkened room, with her beauty, she could manipulate whoever she wanted.

With her hands tied above her head and her feet tied to the footboard post, she jerked about, her legs were splayed so wide, she couldn't hide a damn thing.

"I knew you'd come back, Luis." Janet's voice wasn't as pretty as her face. "I knew you would." She pulled at the ties holding her in place.

Luis looked stricken. "Not because I wanted to. I didn't have a choice."

"Finish this up, Luis, so that we can get outta here." I nudged him forward, but he'd didn't budge, almost like he'd grown roots.

He fished the pin out of his pocket and threw it on the bed.

"Can we go now?" Willa continued to cover her nose.

"Aren't you gonna untie me, Luis?" Janet's voice softened.

I knew that tone. I'd used it when I wanted Daniel to be nice or I wanted something from him.

I felt sorrow for the poor woman. I know what it feels like to want a man to love you but only getting disrespect. "Set her loose, Luis."

He looked at me like I'd lost my mind. "You can't be serious. I came here to give her the pin. I did. If I untie her, we're all doomed. This woman is pure evil."

"Don't you want to move on and get away from this place

forever?" I used my two good hands and motioned around the room. "Maybe we got to finish all our business before we get set free."

They stared at me like I was a crazy old woman, and maybe I was, but I was tired, and I don't mean the mopping floor kind of tired. This is the feeling that Princess Kenyata had warned us would happen.

Willa pulled Luis's sleeve. "Odessa might have a point." She rubbed her forehead. "I want to move on, too. I'm tired."

Cato straightened. "I agree."

"Listen to them, Luis." Janet tugged harder at her restraints.

Luis's chest rose and fell. His breathing was so labored I worried he might pass out. He was doing a lot of thinking. Finally, he moved closer to the bed and clasped his hands so tight his veins popped.

"Just do it," Janet shouted.

Luis's head snapped up. He inched forward. At the foot of the bed, he looked back at us. "Look, Janet, I could have treated you better. I was lousy to you, and I'm sorry. I should have let you go if I couldn't love you like you wanted or needed. It probably doesn't mean anything to you now, but I'm sorry." He placed his hand over his heart. "I mean it. I hope one day you'll believe me." He paused like he couldn't swallow. "I mean it. I'm sorry." He repeated with more sincerity.

His tone was so heart-felt I wanted to hug him.

Janet stopped kicking and pulling and looked at him like she was seeing somebody different. Even the anger that had marred her face disappeared. She kicked her legs in the air when he released her feet, not caring that she exposed her lady parts.

With a sigh, Luis freed one hand and reached across the

bed to release the other. Fear blazed in his eyes like fire. My heart went out to him. I'd been there.

With her legs and arms free, Janet sprouted fangs and lunged for Luis's neck. The forgiving expression she'd worn for a moment disappeared.

I gasped, my hand went to my throat, protecting it.

Then everything went black.

It's My Turn

Willa

Janet may have been a pretty woman, but those fangs and claws popped out and tore into Luis's flesh so fast that I felt she was going after me.

I screamed, and then we were ping-pong balls, bouncing to the next place with no will of our own and no say. I'd never get used to it, and maybe that was good.

I closed my eyes as tight as possible, praying we'd land somewhere that smelled better and held no danger.

Now that Luis had done his thing, maybe everyone wouldn't shoot daggers at me the next time I mentioned my children.

My feet touched a solid surface, and I let go of the breath I held. Opening my eyes took longer because fear thumped in my chest like a marching band. I squinted to see where the Interruption planted us this time.

"Oh, thank God." My shoulders relaxed when Ronita came into focus, surrounded by the same iridescent light that welcomed Princess Kenyata. She looked more like a princess than before, and I couldn't help but wonder how long it had taken us to return the pin. I'd imagine it was mere minutes, but it could have taken years.

"Are you okay, Luis?" I touched his arm. Blood trickled down his neck onto the collar of his shirt. For a man who valued his appearance, he had to be dismayed. His once pristine suit had collected dust, dirt, bloodstains, and sweat.

He cupped his neck where Janet had taken a hunk of flesh. "I'm glad that's over." He labored to breathe.

I turned my attention to Ronita just as the sky brightened. Rainbows surrounded us.

"She's coming." Odessa squealed. "Princess Kenyata is coming."

The griffin settled in the field behind Ronita. Every time I saw the griffin, I marveled at its beauty. I'd never seen an animal that was pure black.

Princess Kenyata climbed off and glided toward us.

I held my breath, hoping she'd see me differently this time. I kept my hands in front of me, pasted a pleasant expression on my face, and held back my tongue.

"Well done, Luis." Ronita nodded in his direction, then raised her hand and waved it from his head to his feet. "You did more than I required." She nodded approval.

"Well, I want to move on. I'm sorry Janet holds so much animosity." He released his hand from his neck. "I hope she leaves me alone."

"You are redeemed. You did the right thing." Ronita's voice had taken on a tone that sounded more regal, more befitting a princess. I couldn't look at her now and see the scared teenager that had run when we first arrived.

I glanced at Luis. Relief flooded his face. The gash in his neck disappeared. The man standing beside me had transformed. Gone were the ravages that had pounded him since we arrived in the Interruption. Even his clothes returned to their pristine quality.

I reminded myself to hold my tongue. All the complaining I'd done so far hadn't helped my cause, so it was time to switch tactics if I wanted the transformation that had happened to Luis.

Odessa put her hand on her hip. "Well, ain't that something? First Ronita, then Cato, and now Luis. They all got redemption. But they are still here. Why can't they move on now?"

"Because we all must stay together. Remember?" Ronita answered though Odessa had spoken to Princess Kenyata.

"So now what?" Odessa's tone sharpened.

The way her eyes narrowed, she was as cross as I was at how we were left hanging. I had promised myself to keep my mouth shut, but I couldn't hold back anymore.

"I keep asking for the same thing, and no one is listening to me."

Ronita directed her attention to me. "Willa, I've heard your request, and today it's your turn."

I wasn't sure I heard her correctly, but when Odessa nudged me, my heart swelled, filling with happiness. "You mean it? You're going to let me save my children?" I rubbed my hands with anticipation.

Ronita placed her thumb under her chin and stroked her cheek with her index finger. "I will allow you to see your children. I didn't say I would let you intervene in their lives. That should never happen between the living and the dead."

"But I couldn't get the words out fast enough. "Odessa helped her grandparents. She even did something to her husband. How come you let that happen?"

"You all have free will." Princess Kenyata spoke for the first time. "Some decisions you all have made have kept you stuck here."

I exhaled. "So, what are you saying?" I asked, even though I wanted to get on with seeing Ava and BJ.

"I said you were next, and you will see your children. But I won't allow you to interfere in their lives." Ronita's voice left little room for arguing.

"But they need me?" I held my palms together, praying I hadn't angered her, but my heart couldn't let this go.

"Do they?" Ronita raised her arms in the air.

A rush of wind roared in my ears, and I had the sense of flying. Just as quickly as the wind started, it stopped. The five of us were still in the same positions, but Princess Kenyata wasn't with us. Gone was the silence of the pasture, the lush trees and green grass. The sounds of a city replaced the quiet, and an older house in need of yard maintenance came into view. It was the house where I'd gone to looking for Ava in when I returned home. Only now, the shutters were no longer crooked, and there were no broken windows. A new entrance door painted a bright yellow had replaced the old one.

"Why are we here?" An overwhelming sense of dread filled me. If this was Ava's hangout, then she'd gotten worse. I tried to move closer to Ronita for comfort but couldn't. Maybe this was Ronita's way of ensuring I didn't go rogue again.

Ronita reached for my hand, squeezed it, and then she released it. "To see your children, as I promised."

I looked into Ronita's eyes. "Do you already know how they're doing?"

"Of course."

"Is it bad?" I bit my lip. Any minute, I expected my legs to give way. After all the trying and wishing, what I wanted was right in front of me.

She extended her hand toward the house. "See for yourself."

I followed the direction of her hand. She'd worked her magic, and the house walls vanished, allowing me to see inside.

A woman sat at the kitchen counter with a small boy at her side. Her blond hair hung to the middle of her back, and her smooth face placed her in her thirties. The frayed plaid shirt she wore over a white tank top matched the furnishings in the house. Even though the chair and sofa looked worn, the house was clean and neat. "Come on, William, you know the answer to this question. As soon as you get it right, we can all leave for Grandpa's house and see Ethel." She pointed at the book in front of them.

"Why are you showing me these people, Ronita?" I squinted at her as tears welled in my eyes. I'd had such high hopes this time.

"It's your daughter and her son." Ronita's voice was so low I wasn't sure I'd heard her.

"My daughter?" I stared at the scene in front of me. "My grandson? How can this be? I saw her a few days ago as a teenager. Is she a stepmother? And who is Ethel?"

Ronita put her hand on my arm, and her face softened. "Willa, thirteen years have passed in your daughter's life." She spoke slowly. "She's married and is now a mother." She pointed toward the house. "Look there's her husband."

I turned my focus back inside to see a tall, lean man with dark hair kiss Ava on the cheek. She looked up at him and smiled. Ava looked happy, and relief flooded my soul. "She's clean." My tears spilled over.

"She even named her son William in honor of you."

I shook my head. "But how..." I ran my finger through my hair. "There were people in the Interruption who said they were going to kill her." I leaned on Ronita's arm. "How can this be? And who is Ethel?" I asked again.

"How about we just watch her life for a while? You'll see."

I turned toward Odessa, who had stayed quiet. I had almost forgotten that Odessa, Luis, and Cato stood behind me. "What do you think?"

As if his redemption had rendered him mute, Luis didn't speak.

Odessa hunched one shoulder, already looking bored. "This is what you wanted. Right?"

I nodded.

Moments later, we followed Ava, William, and her husband as they walked toward the banged-up car parked on the decaying asphalt. I had so many questions but was afraid to ask them. I wanted the joy I felt to last forever. Seeing Ava this way is enough. My grandson reminded me of my son, BJ. He had the same sharp nose and thick black hair. I touched my heart when my eyes landed on his small, round face.

We watched Ava, and her husband pull away with William strapped in the back seat. Panic rose in my chest because they were leaving us.

I reached for Ronita. "Aren't we going with them?"

She smiled weakly and patted my hand as if I were a kid. "We will."

I released the air building in my lungs, wishing I could relax, but in the back of my mind, the name Ethel poked at me. But I couldn't figure out why.

I decided not to press Ronita about keeping up with her. I felt sure she'd take care of me.

In an instant, we stood in the living room of the place I used to call home. The gray tones from before hadn't changed, but this time, I was more interested in what was happening inside than how it looked.

I kept my hand in front of me to calm my nerves. Being this close to my daughter, I should have felt relief that she was doing well, but I couldn't help feeling left behind. I had missed so much.

I glanced over my shoulder to see if Odessa, Luis, and Cato were still with us. "Why are the others so quiet? Odessa has never gone so long and said so little."

"This is your journey. They are here to observe. There is nothing for them to do or for you to do. Just keep watching. Your time here is running out."

Never wanting this to end, I sucked in a big breath. I could have stayed here forever, even if it was on the fringe of my family's life.

My husband, Burt, walked out of the kitchen and returned my attention to my family. He carried a massive tray of sandwiches and set it on the table. He had grown more handsome, though he'd aged. He'd kept his firm physique, and his full head of gray hair only added to his appearance. I wasn't angry with him anymore. If Ava still loved him, then I could, too.

"Grandpa," William squealed and charged toward Burt.

Burt scooped up my grandson and held him tight. The bond between them was apparent. I noticed his reluctance to put William down on the floor.

BJ came out of the kitchen next—a younger replica of his father.

Ava embraced her father, then her brother.

I waited for Joan, Burt's new wife, to appear, but when they sat at the dining table, and she hadn't shown up, I exhaled.

My heart raced. I wondered how I stayed upright. Seeing them all together was more than I'd hoped.

Ava reached for a sandwich, cut a small piece, and placed it on a napkin before William. "Have you heard from Joan and Birdie? I guess she's heading to middle school now."

"Birdie will spend the summer with me again." Burt chewed around the food in his mouth, but I saw sadness behind his eyes. "Now that she's older, Joan and I don't have to talk as much, so there is much less arguing. She's happy, and I'm happier."

BJ remained quiet like always, but his periodic smiles and nods let me know he was content.

The doorbell rang, and Ava jumped up. "That must be Ethel."

I braced my knees as Ava opened the door, and a young woman entered the living room. She had to be in her early twenties, but nothing about her was familiar to me.

"You guys started without me." Ethel laughed.

William jumped out of his chair and ran to her, grabbing her legs.

"Hey, Will." She hugged him. "How's my little brother?"

He giggled and continued to hold on to her.

"You better come grab a sandwich before we eat them all." Burt waved her into the room and then embraced her.

I turned to Ronita. "Who is Ethel?"

"The girl whose parents you killed." There was no condemnation in Ronita's voice.

Then everything went black.

I'm Next

Odessa

Ronita snapped her finger or clapped her hand, or whatever a princess does, and we left Willa's house and landed back in the peaceful meadow. At least it had a bench where we all sat except Ronita.

It took me several minutes to catch my breath. All this going and doing tired me out. I only wanted to crawl under a soft blanket and nap.

Willa sat on the end of the bench, gripping the arm like she thought she might fly away. "Ronita, why did you take me away? I wanted to see more." She didn't hold back the tears, and after all we been through, she ain't run out of them yet.

"You don't make that call. I do." Ronita remained calm. "You wanted to know how your children, your family was doing, and now you do. That's what I promised."

Willa used the hem of her dress to wipe her tears. "Yeah, but … but … I wasn't ready to leave. Why was Ethel there? I don't understand."

I'm glad I had two good hands to place on my hips because I couldn't make the statement I wanted with only one. So, as hard as Willa tried, her secret finally came out. She wasn't better than me. I only killed one person. She'd killed two.

I crossed my ankles to get comfortable because the way Willa was sniffling, we were gonna spend more time talking about her. By now, she should have gotten thicker skin, but she hadn't changed a bit.

"Willa, you don't need to understand everything. But there are some things you have to accept. Your death is one of them." Ronita spoke as wisely as Princess Kenyata. I shifted my shoulders, feeling like I had a hand in her growth.

"Ethel brought your family back together. When Ava found out about the little girl who'd lost her parents, she became obsessed with trying to help Ethel get through the ordeal because Ava, too, was going through a difficult time. She'd lost you. Ethel is the reason Ava got clean and has stayed clean."

Willa rocked back and forth as if she had to absorb every word. Finally, she stopped rocking. Her tears dried up. "I couldn't save my daughter, but I'm glad someone could."

She didn't sound glad, but I never believed much that came out of Willa's mouth.

Ronita gave a slight smile. "Your family worked hard to make amends for the accident you caused. Be glad they did. Their work probably saved them from the harm you feared."

I popped off the bench like I had the energy of a toddler. "You mean to tell me I sat on that bench in that first park and tried to get the others to stay put, and now, every one of them got redemption except me?" I jerked my arms. "Ain't no way that's right. No way in the world!" I was yelling when I finished.

Ronita's facial expression didn't change. She held up her index finger, silencing me. "Odessa, we'll discuss your situation." She sounded much more confident now that she wore a tiara and with Cato standing at her side waiting to do her bidding.

I had a closet full of skeletons bursting to get out, and from the way Ronita looked at me, she saw them. I knew better than to kill Daniel, but I couldn't restrain my ability to beat him for once. And now, I reckon it was my time to pay for that sin.

Ronita had turned her body to face me. I'd shot off my

mouth, but now I wanted to take it all back. At least here, my ass wasn't roasting over flames all day and night. I didn't want to force Ronita to decide what was supposed to happen to me.

She studied me long enough to get me fidgeting. That's something I've done since I was a little girl. But I felt like I wasn't going to be happy with what she'd have to say.

"Odessa, it's redemption you think you deserve, right?" Ronita tapped her foot, already knowing how I'd answer.

"You know that's what I want. It's the only thing I've talked about since getting here."

"What have you done to earn it?" Ronita wouldn't meet my gaze. This had to be as uncomfortable for her as it was for me.

I opened my mouth, then shut it. Sitting in church every Sunday, I thought I was building a solid foundation for when this question came. But now, I didn't feel so certain, which scared me more than anything.

In my head, a clock ticked loud enough to drown out my roaring heartbeat. They all stared at me, waiting on me to give some big speech. I felt ashamed. My behavior was worse than theirs. I knew better than to do the things I did. There was no way out for me.

"Are you going to answer me, Odessa?" Ronita's tone didn't change.

I sighed. "I lived a good life, always doing the right thing. Pushing down my anger, being nice when I didn't want to, and when folks certainly didn't deserve it. And what I got to show for being so good?" My voice grew softer. "I ain't got nothing. Absolutely nothing. I was even buried in this old house dress instead of the good one I'd saved in my closet." I stopped long enough to expel the pressure building in my chest. "What do I get for all the years I did everything right?

They've gotta be worth something." I did everything but get down on my old knees and beg.

Willa and Luis had backed away from me like they were avoiding a lightning strike.

"Oh, what?" I spat at them. "You think you better than me now?"

Ronita turned back to Luis and Willa. "Your time on this level of the Interruption is over. Your journeys continue separately but on much easier paths."

"I'm moving on?" Willa squealed like she done won the lottery.

That woman never looked happier. I should have had that feeling instead of the burning sensation that grew hotter, and ran through my veins like lava.

I envied nobody until then. Why couldn't I be wearing her shoes?

Luis nodded but kept his regal nose high as if he expected no less.

Ronita motioned for them to stand, then quickly embraced them. Afterward, she waved her arms, and they were gone.

Just like that.

Without a nod my way.

Without a word.

I would have sworn I heard angels singing. The meadow brightened as if heaven had opened the doors for their arrival. The place where they had stood continued to glow moments after they disappeared. I had expected to see angels lead them away, but nothing fancy like that happened. And as quickly as the sky had glistened for them, dark blue clouds sealed them off and hovered over my head. I expected a pitchfork to pierce my butt. Fear made me gasp for air. This moment had to be the darkest I ever faced because I wouldn't receive the promise I'd lived for.

Ronita stepped to me and placed her hand on my shoulder. "Calm down, Odessa. I only asked you what you'd done for redemption."

"I'm not worthy?"

"I never said that. I know you have a good heart. Or at least you used to." Her face went blank. "But you can't complete this journey until you make amends to Daniel."

Her words were like a drum in my head, pounding out what remained of me. "Daniel." I shook my head. "We ain't never got along. When we were living, he dominated me. In death, I extracted as much revenge as I could. The pieces of Daniel that remained wasn't in a position to hear an apology. And even if he was, ain't no way he'd want to hear one from me."

"He doesn't have to accept it or hear it. You only have to make it from your heart."

I dropped my head. "I don't know if I can. I can say the words, but I'm not sure I'll mean them. What's going to happen to me?" Bewilderment left me numb. "You can make this right. You have the power."

I stared into Ronita's eyes, willing her to see my desperation.

"Don't give me that weak smile. You know it's true. Snap your fingers and send me on my way like you did for Willa and Luis."

Cato hadn't said a word in my favor since we arrived, so I narrowed my gaze on him. "Tell her, Cato. I spoke up for you. Ain't you got a good word for me?"

He shook his head. "Ronita doesn't need my advice. That's not the reason I'm here."

"Well, she doesn't need you standing in her armpit either, but you keep doing that."

I always vented my anger on anyone close enough to receive it, except when it came to Daniel. And Cato made a good target. "Now what, then? The others are gone, and it's just us three. Are you going to leave me here alone?"

"Well." Ronita didn't hurry to respond. She probably had the answer but knew I wouldn't like it.

She sighed. "Odessa." My name hung in the crisp air.

She'd seen me battle that wolf creature, and it damn near took me out. I'd done things the wrong way, but I hoped she understood my reasoning.

"You have to go back, Odessa."

I shook my head, afraid of what she suggested. "Go back where?" Fear spread through me.

Ronita's chest rose and fell. "Daniel followed you into the Interruption because you left him no choice. Now you have to make it right with him."

"He took off my hand. Don't he owe me something, too?"

Her expression said what words couldn't. I knew how things worked. Ronita was here to help me. Daniel wasn't my problem.

I dropped my head into my palm and rubbed my forehead. "I can't. That man is evil. Why can't whoever is pulling my strings see that? Ain't I suffered enough? I can't do that, Ronita." I lifted my head and backed away as if I could escape my fate.

"You have to. It's the only way." She reached for me but dropped her hand. Keeping our distance was best for both of us.

"I'll go with her." Cato moved beside me and touched my arm.

My shoulders relaxed but not enough to ease the tension in the air.

"Yeah." I stood a little taller. Hope filled me. "We all went with Luis and Willa. Why is this time different?"

"She's right, Ronita." Cato nodded. "She shouldn't have to do this alone. Why can't we help her too?"

"Princess Kenyata told me I'd know everything I needed to help everyone reach their final destination." Ronita paused and reached for my hand. Her eyes softened, and I saw that high school girl again. "I hope she's right."

It's Never That Easy

Ronita

I do not break the rules. Even when unsure, I always errored on the side that I thought would please my mother. In the Interruption, I barely knew what was required of me, and I'd never crossed the lines like the others. But the desperate expression on Odessa's face gave me pause. I had the power to help her—to give her what she wanted.

"Okay, Odessa, are you ready?"

She nodded like speaking words was difficult.

Without me doing a thing, everything turned black.

A moment later, we were back on that first bench. It had stood still in time. I didn't enjoy the beauty when I was here before, but this time, I appreciated the magnificence.

Odessa looked both ways. "I have to start from the beginning?" Disappointment drew her face down.

We hadn't been there long when an iridescent glow signaled Princess Kenyata arrival. I wondered if I would get the same treatment or if she'd approach me differently since I was now a princess.

I was the first to stand, and Cato jumped up, too. Unlike all the other times, Odessa remained seated.

I turned back to her. "Aren't you going to stand?"

"What's the use? Whatever happens, happens." She dismissed me with a wave of her hand. "I've been kowtowing to her since the beginning. I'm exhausted."

Princess Kenyata dismounted and made her way toward us.

"Well, this is an unhappy group." She directed her comment to Odessa, who remained quiet.

"Princess Ronita, I know you want to guide Odessa on this unfinished journey, but that's not possible."

Odessa jumped up. "What do you mean?"

"Just like I couldn't help you the first time, Ronita can't help you this time. Odessa, you must make the right choices, or you'll be stuck here until you do."

Odessa dropped her head and shook it. "I don't have the strength. I just don't care anymore."

Princess Kenyata pressed her palm on Odessa's heart and held it there for several moments. Odessa's body jerked upright as if a jolt had passed through her. "You now have the strength. And you do care. You wouldn't be standing before me now if you didn't.

They held eyes briefly like Odessa had to piece together the statement.

"What happens next?" I asked.

"There are others that need your attention, and you must take your seat as a princess." The glow on Princess Kenyata's face erased any fears I may have had.

"And Cato?" I reached for his hand. Under no circumstances was I letting him go.

"Yes, of course, Cato comes with you. The two of you are now a team."

My body warmed at the thought of him being by my side forever. I wanted to ask if sex was allowed in the Interruption, but I knew we'd find a way. Maybe my next venture wasn't going to be so bad.

"And what am I supposed to do? Just sit on this bench and wait?" Odessa didn't hold her anger.

"Yes." Stay on the bench with the others until Princess Ronita comes to tell you and the others what you need to do to make it to the next level. It's simple."

Odessa huffed, crossed her arms, and plopped down. "If it was so easy, we could have done it the first time."

Princess Kenyata returned to her griffin and motioned

for Cato and me to follow. We climbed on its back, and instead of flying through the sky as I'd imagined, one moment, we were in the field with Odessa, the next we weren't.

More Waiting

Odessa

I flopped back on the hard bench with a huff. With my arms crossed tight under my breasts, I rocked. I knew this was a game I didn't stand a chance at winning. Of course, this wasn't a new way of being. I ain't never been good at learning lessons, and I had a whole life of unhappiness to prove it.

"I released my arms and ran my hand down my face. "I can't do this again," I moaned.

"Do what?"

I damned near jumped off that bench. I turned to see a young man beside me. He had to be in his early twenties. Based on his dress, he was one of those young men the church wanted to pull inside and help him find the Lord. His pants were too big and sat on his thighs, not his hips. He didn't even wear a shirt, only an undershirt, with untied high-top sneakers.

"Where the hell you come from?" I inched away from him. "If I wasn't already dead, I would be now." My heart knocked against my chest.

"So we're dead? I didn't make it, huh?" He nodded like this wasn't a surprise. "I should have known something like this was going to happen. My moms told me to stay in the house. She said if I got in trouble one more time, she would snitch on me, turn me in." He dropped his head and pulled at his thick hair.

"Yeah, you should've listened to your mama 'cause this place may look pretty, but all kinds of awful things can happen here. Don't be fooled by the shiny surface. What did you do to end up here?"

"I had some beef with some guys. I was set up and shot

five times. My boys kept telling me to hold on, to keep my eyes open. I tried. But …"

I was determined to do a better job this time. To ask questions. To listen. I would do right by this young person even if I had to grab hold of him to keep him in place.

"People call me Pookie." He didn't look up.

"Pookie? What kinda name is that? What your mama name you?"

He glanced at me. Fear was the only thing I saw in his eyes. "My mother named me Paul."

"Paul, how old are you?" While I was living, I didn't know many young people who died, but now I've come across three. Young folks shouldn't have to come through the Interruption. They should get a free pass.

"I'm, I'm twenty-one. Just turned twenty-one." He pointed to a fresh tattoo of a dagger that covered the length of his forearm. "I got this for my birthday."

"Maybe you should have gotten something else." I wrinkled my nose. If he knew what I knew, he wouldn't need to mark his body because he would have plenty of scars by the time he got to my age.

"Where are we? If we're dead, what is this place?"

"Son, you're in the Interruption. Just sit tight, and this might begin to make sense."

"Listen to the old woman." Another male voice coming from the opposite side, shocked me.

I turned to my right. "What the hell?" When I saw who it was I jumped off that bench and backed away as fast as I could. "Daniel, what are you doing? I don't want any trouble from you. I told you to leave me alone." I held up my hands, ready for him to come at me.

Daniel kept his hands in his lap. I ain't never seen him look so docile. "I'm not here to hurt you, Odessa. We've done enough harm to each other." He waved me back over.

I'm not stupid enough to fall for that again.

"No. I think I'll stay right here."

"You two know each other?" Paul looked at me for the answer. "Is he dead, too?"

"We're all dead. And he used to be my husband," I said. "The Interruption is just a place that you land when you die. You are probably here because you need to handle some unfinished business.

Paul stood. "Of course, I have unfinished business. I'm only twenty-one. There were a whole lot of things I had to do. This place can't be real. Dead people are just dead. Put in the ground and turned to dust. I must be dreaming." His hands were back in his hair. It's a wonder he wasn't bald, the way he kept pulling his strands.

"You're not dreaming. She's telling you the truth." Daniel looked up at me. "How do you know so much about this place, Odessa? And why didn't you ever tell me about it?"

This Daniel, I didn't know. My Daniel usually barked at me and demanded what he wanted. This man almost made me believe Daniel had changed. But I wouldn't get close enough for him to gouge out my eyes like I did. "You never listened to me, so there wasn't no use in talking to you."

He nodded several times and even looked a little hurt.

"So. what are we doing here?" Paul directed his question to me.

"We're waiting," I said.

"For how long and for what?" Paul's voice trembled. Either he was getting ready to cry or flee. He didn't look much like a crier, so I had to keep him in this place.

I inched toward him without taking my attention away from Daniel. Keeping Paul here was more important than worrying about Daniel.

I put my hand on Paul's arm. "Listen to me, child. If you sit right here and be patient, everything will be fine. Trust me. We didn't follow instructions my first time, and many awful things happened." I glanced down at my hand, which used to be a stump.

"She's right." Daniel nodded his head with certainty.

I've never heard him say that about me, even when the truth looked him in the face. Could he have learned his lessons?

"The last time I didn't listen to someone, I ended up dead." Paul lifted his head and glared at me. "But why should I trust you? Or anyone?" His tone was harsh.

I understood how he felt. I sure didn't trust Daniel, but to leave this damnable place behind, I needed to forgive him. That thought alone left a bitter coating in my mouth. But if this boy had thoughts of running, I had every intention of digging my nails into his shoulder and holding him still.

"Paul." I softened my voice. "Right now, I'm your only friend in the Interruption."

"Come on and sit back down on the bench, Odessa. I'm not going to harm you." Daniel patted the open space between him and Paul.

I had to bite my tongue. My typical reply would have been snappy. But I searched my heart, looking for the new Odessa I needed to be in order to move on. I shoved Paul. "Scoot down, will you? I'll sit on the end."

Paul moved, and I flopped down. Happy to rest for a moment.

Daniel said, "Odessa, I want you to sit beside me because I need to say something to you."

"I can hear you just fine from here." I leaned forward so he could see my face.

He rubbed his hands together. "Have it your way."

And I held my breath.

I'm Okay

Ronita

I blinked, and within an instant, Cato and I were inside of a home. I still hadn't gotten used to traveling from one place to another without the help of transportation as I knew it.

"Where are we?" Cato spun around with his arms outstretched, balancing on one foot.

It took me a moment to take it in. "It's my bedroom." I tried to rub away the goosebumps on my arms while my feet stayed planted, unable to move. "It's my bedroom," I said again, still not believing it. Finally, Princess Kenyata gave me what I wanted most, and I could only stare at the pink wall before me. Nothing had changed. It looked like I'd left it before going to school, with the bed half made, the clothes on the floor, and my stuffed animals pushed in the corner.

"What's this?" Cato picked up a piece of paper from my desk and waved it at me.

Without moving, maybe because I couldn't, I glanced at the paper in his hand. In my best script, I'd written *Cato & Ronita* repeatedly until I'd filled the page. "Don't get a swelled head. I was bored."

"Yeah, sure." His smile said he didn't believe me. "So what do you want to do?" He glanced around the room. I hoped there was no more incriminating stuff for him to find.

I unstuck my feet, picked up the small pink elephant, and went to the door. "I need to find my mother."

Halfway down the stairs, the sound of my mother sobbing shook me. The familiar din took me back to the day my father died. I hadn't heard her cry since that night. I eased my way into the living room to find her curled into a ball on the sofa and several of her friends staring helplessly at her.

Her friend Paula stood over my mother, rubbing her back.

"I can't believe she's gone. Why would Ronita jump after that boy? That morning, she didn't say anything about going somewhere with him. I don't think I'll ever understand this."

Paula rubbed my mother's back. "Maybe she didn't jump. The ladies say they think she slipped. It was all an accident." I'd never heard Paula talk so calmly. She was my mother's loudest friend.

"But that boy jumped. Maybe they had some kind of pact." My mother continued to cry.

Paula closed her eyes as if she needed to draw patience.

I turned to Cato. "She thinks I did this on purpose." The pain I'd caused ate at my heart. "How can I fix this?" I grabbed Cato's arm as if I could force his answer.

He inhaled and exhaled slowly. "You can't make yourself visible." He looked around the room. "Put the elephant somewhere that will let her know you did it and that you came back to bring her comfort."

My mother banged her fist against the sofa. "I want my baby back. I want her."

I turned to Cato, who stood at my side. "Look what I've done." I hadn't cried since all this happened, but tears stung my eyes. "Do you think this elephant will be enough?"

He shrugged.

I jerked my head up. " I know what I can do." I caught his hand and dragged him into the kitchen. From the pantry, I removed a box of brownie mix.

"You can't cook. Remember, that would be interfering."

"I don't need to cook them. If I put the box on the table alongside the elephant, she'll know it's a sign. She made brownies for me when my father died. That night, I thought everything would be okay." I held the happy memory, allowing it to play across my mind, and relishing the comfort it brought me. "She'll know. My mother will get the gesture. She sees signs where nobody else does."

Cato blinked his eyes and shrugged. "If you say so."

I touched his arm. "Someone's coming. You just wait and see."

My mother followed Paula into the kitchen.

"Try to eat something, Elaine. You'll look like a skeleton if you lose any more weight."

"Do you think I care about that?"

Paula pointed at the brownie mix. "You want me to make them for you?"

"I didn't put that there." My mother picked up the elephant and the box, one in each hand and studied them like they were foreign to her.

Cato nudged me. "I told you."

I kept my lips sealed. It might take her a moment or a month, but she'd get it. Nobody knew her better than I did.

"Paula," she slowly turned the elephant over. "Are you sure you didn't put this stuff here?"

Paula turned to my mother. "Elaine, you saw me walk in the house. I never left the living room. You know that." She settled her hands on her hips and glanced at my mother like she thought she had lost her ability to reason.

My mom continued to study the items, looking at them as if they were foreign objects from a different planet.

"I told you she wouldn't get it. It makes no sense," Cato sighed.

"She has to get it. I don't know what else to do." I touched her shoulder, even though she probably couldn't feel it.

"It's from Ronita." The sadness in her eyes lifted. "Ronita left this for me. She had to."

Paula nodded with skepticism. "And why would she do that? And how could she do that? She's been gone over a week."

"This box of brownies and her pink elephant weren't here last night when I went to bed, or this morning when I made coffee. Nobody's been here but you and me. If you didn't do it, and I didn't put it here, then who? It had to be my baby."

"Okay. If that's true, then what does it mean?"

"I don't know exactly. But it's something good. I can feel it in my bones, in my heart. Maybe Ronita is communicating with me."

"And saying what? That's she's hungry for a sweet snack."

My mom looked up at her friend with what almost looked like a smile. "Make fun of me if you want. But I know. Maybe she'll leave another." My mother glanced around the room as if she expected to see me.

I stepped forward and kissed her cheek. A moment later, she placed her hand over the spot.

"Yes, Paula. She was here. I know she was, and she's okay."

Princess Kenyata materialized beside me. "It's time for you to move on, Princess Ronita. You have duties to perform."

I faced her. "I'm ready."

Who Goes First?

Odessa

Maybe it was how Daniel craned his neck to look around Paul or the menacing glint from his eyes, but I let him hold my attention. Usually, when he started to speak, I let my thoughts drift away.

He cleared his throat. "I owe you an apology." He stopped as if those five words could erase a lifetime of cruelty.

I snapped my fingers. "If you think that's an apology, you're dead wrong. You said you owed me one. So where is it?" I fussed, but seeing him struggle to do the right thing had my heart singing.

"I know, woman. Let me finish." He looked down at his hands, then back at me. "You were a good wife. All that stuff you did for me in the beginning, and all I did was take you for granted. You deserved better. You deserved better than me. I'm sorry. I'm sorry for the way I treated you. I mean that, Odessa. I really do."

I thought he might shed a tear for a moment, but then I remembered it was Daniel, and that was a far-reach. The man had never cried in all our years together.

The hunk of ice that had coated my soul all those years started to melt. I thought I had so much hatred for Daniel that nothing would ever change my feelings. But maybe that wasn't true, or maybe there wasn't any room left for me to hate him. The time I'd spent in the Interruption had opened my eyes to things beyond me. I didn't sit in the middle of the universe. There was a lot of other people dealing with stuff worse than me.

I nodded. "Daniel, I'm sorry, too. You was one mean man, but I should have left you be. From what I know now, the Interruption would give you what you deserved. I wasted time, and it wasn't necessary. I hope you can accept my apology."

Paul started to get up. "I can move if you two want to hug or something."

I pushed him back in place. "Naw. I don't think we're going that far."

"Why won't you let me move, lady?" Paul sounded like a pot getting ready to boil over. "Every time I shift, you pull me back."

"Paul." I swallowed. "Like I said, you gonna have to trust me. Maybe you're here with me to save you from additional aches. You been through enough. But you got to figure out what business you left undone."

He sat forward and his voice choked out the words. "Somebody is serving a bid that I should be doing."

"You mean bid, like gambling?" I tried to see his eyes.

"No. Like serving time. I pulled a smash-and-grab at a jewelry store, but I blamed one of my hood boys. His little brother was the one who set me up in the alley."

I let go of the breath I was holding. "Well, that ain't good."

"No shit." Paul kept his gaze on his hands, which he kept rubbing together.

"What do we have to do, Odessa?" Daniel never asked my opinion, and for a moment, I wasn't even sure he was talking to me.

"Let me think for a minute." I closed my eyes. All I could imagine was that we needed to help Paul find his way out of this mess, and then my journey would have the happy ending I wanted. I kept my eyes closed because I wasn't ready to tell Daniel and Paul my theory. I hoped I didn't have to go with Paul to fix the mess he'd left behind.

"Paul," I started slowly. "You gotta tell the truth about your buddy in jail. You got to think of a way to get him out."

Paul jumped off the bench this time before I could grab

him. "How am I supposed to do that? According to you, I'm dead." He ran his hand down the front of his t-shirt like the idea of him being dead wasn't possible.

"Please sit, Paul." I reached for his belt loop and dragged him back. "If we sit still for a moment longer, this might make some sense."

I almost didn't get the sentence out of my mouth when the sky brightened, and the rainbow appeared.

"What's happening?" Paul stared straight ahead, his eyes wider than his mouth.

"You'll see, kid. Just you wait." Daniel patted Paul's knee.

I kept my eyes on the skies, waiting to see Princess Kenyata. I'd apologized to Daniel and meant it so I could move on now.

A golden griffin came through the wispy clouds. I wasn't sure if I was seeing things or in some alternate realm, but then I spotted Ronita seated on the griffin, dressed in the best finery I'd ever seen. I was off that bench like lightning struck my butt.

I didn't think it was possible, but that gal held her head up high as if she'd been a princess forever. The gold around her neck and her tiara caught the sparkle from the sunlight. "Princess Ronita." The rest of what I wanted to say wouldn't come out.

Paul came up behind me. "What is going on? How do you know her name?" He stepped behind me like he wanted to use me as a shield. After being shot, I guess I can't blame him.

"She's the one who's going to help us." I turned my head toward him and noticed Daniel coming over, too. Instead of the vocal man I married, this Daniel was quieter and more introspective. He didn't need to be the one doing all the talking and giving directions.

"I would say gather around, but the three of you already have." Princess Ronita held her hands at her side.

"It's good to see you, Princess Ronita. I've done what I needed and am ready to end my journey." The words came out so fast I wasn't sure she'd understand what I said.

"Yeah, me, too," Daniel spoke louder than I'd heard him all day.

Princess Ronita tilted her head to one side. "Odessa and Daniel, you know the rules. You all have to stay together."

"And we have." I looped my arms through Paul's and Daniel's. I even bounced up on my toes, excited to get it right this time.

"Would you two leave Paul alone? You two know how it works. You must help Paul through this journey."

My hopes dropped lower than my shoulders. "I'm not finished yet?"

Princess Ronita touched my hand. "Almost, Odessa. And this last task is an easy one. All you have to do is help Paul make amends, and then you're done."

"But how?" I released Paul's and Daniel's arms.

"You'll figure a way." She smiled, then stepped back. I would have felt proud of Princess Ronita if I weren't so sad. She looked more content than I'd ever seen her. She mounted her griffin and disappeared before I even had a chance to ask about Cato.

One More Time

Odessa

If I were a woman who lived by curse words, I would have released every single one I knew. Whenever I thought I was getting close to the promise for being a good Christian, something else popped up to push me back. I stood at square one once again.

Paul looked at Daniel and then at me. "You two know what she's talking about. Amends?"

I sighed. "It means we got to figure out how to save that innocent kid in jail."

Paul stepped away from me. "What about his brother, the one who shot me? I figure we're about even."

Daniel put his hand on Paul's shoulders and appeared quite fatherly. I couldn't help wondering if he would have been different if we had had children. "See, Paul, it doesn't work that way. That boy who shot you will end up here and have to face his destiny. In the Interruption, everyone has to stand on what they've done or not done." He directed his attention to me. "If I'd known that, I wouldn't have tried to attack Odessa when I arrived. She would have paid for what she did, and I could have moved on."

"But where were you heading, Daniel, to hell?" I wanted to know. "The way I figure it you had a one-way ticket."

"Maybe I do, maybe I don't." He shrugged as if he didn't care about his final destination.

Paul held his palms up to us. "Okay. Enough about you two since you have it all figured out. What's next?"

"We can't break him out of jail, but somehow, you've got to let someone know he doesn't belong there." I made sure I didn't look at Daniel. I forgave him for all he'd done, but we'd never be the best of friends.

"Can we talk to people who are still alive? If so, I can tell the detectives that came to our place that I'd did all that stuff and give them the jewelry back."

"Well." Daniel shook his head. "Talking to the living is frowned upon."

"I have an idea," I said. "You said your mother planned to turn you in if you got in trouble again. Maybe you could put the jewelry where she could find it. If you're sure she wouldn't decide to keep it." I didn't know much about his family, but if his mother kept the loot, that boy would stay in jail, and we'd have to devise another way.

"No. My moms is a goody-two-shoes. That's why we never got along. She'd probably go running to the police station. "I have all the loot in my bedroom, so that should be easy." Paul looked like he just found the way to world peace. "How do we get there?" His eyes glowed.

"That's the hardest part. I can get us all there, but we must be of one mind. Whenever we transition, we put ourselves in danger. So we all have to concentrate on being at your house. We have to think of that and only that, or we could end up in a worse place. And believe me, there are some places we don't want to go near. Do you think we can all think of your bedroom, Paul, and nothing, nothing, nothing else?"

"You scaring me, Miss Odessa."

"It's that important, that's all."

"I can do it then." Paul nodded with certainty.

"Me, too," Daniel added.

"Okay, then let's get this done. Let's hold hands, close our eyes, and think of nothing but Paul's bedroom. Then we'll raise our hands to the sky. Gotta it."

"Yeah," they answered in unison.

We all did what I said. When I opened my eyes, we were in a junky, smelly room that could only belong to Paul. I sighed with relief that they had at least followed my instructions.

"Hey, it worked." Paul looked around with surprise. He patted Daniel on the back as if he'd done the work.

"I don't know why you're so excited, Paul." I shot him a lean look. "We here for a purpose, and the minute we accomplish that goal, we're right back where we started. You can't stay here."

"Don't lecture the boy, Odessa."

"I don't mean to lecture, but that glint in his eyes says he's got other plans."

"Why can't I stay?" Paul flopped on the bed. "I'm young. I got lots of things I want to do. I got a girlfriend I want to see."

I sat beside him. "Honey, they all know you're dead. The living don't want to hang out with dead people. Besides, the longer you hang around, the weaker you'll get, and soon the dead will start hunting you."

He shivered, and the hope I'd seen on his face faded. He remained still for several seconds. Long enough for me to start worrying. Young people were unpredictable.

Finally, he said, "The stuff is in the bottom of my closet. I'll get it."

Daniel and I waited while Paul threw out shoes, boxes, and dirty socks from inside his closet. Finally, he removed a duffle bag and carried it to the bed.

Paul unzipped the bag, peered inside and exhaled in relief. "It's still here."

"Where do you need to put it so that your mother will find it?" I stood.

He nodded toward the door. "Her bedroom. That's where she spends all her time."

"Let's do it so we can keep moving." Daniel opened the bedroom door.

Paul led the way. "Her bedroom is downstairs."

Unlike his bedroom, the rest of the tiny house was immaculate. His mother took pride in her place, and it sparkled to prove it.

His mother sat in a recliner in front a giant screen televisions that looked out of place in the small home. A large bowl of popcorn sat in her lap. She didn't appear to be mourning her son.

In the bedroom, Paul placed the loot in the center of the well-made bed. "I guess my mother took my tablet." He turned it on. The date was the first thing to pop up. Paul scratched his head. "This can't be right." He lowered his head closer to the screen, picked it up, and waved it at Daniel and me.

"Paul, the time in the Interruption is different."

He slammed the tablet on the bed. "But I just got in the Interruption. This tablet says five years have passed. How can that be?" With his hand in his hair, he spun around and looked like he was fighting back tears. "Five years? Five f-ing years?"

I wish I could have made this easier for him, but there wasn't nothing I could do. "Our work is done here, Paul."

He jerked away from me. "No. No. No." Tears spilled from his eyes. "I'm not going back. I don't want to."

His mother walked in. "What the hell is this doing on my bed?" She opened the duffle and peered inside. Slowly, she pulled out several gold chains, then several watches—the expensive ones. The pile on the bed grew larger.

She snatched open the closet door as if she expected someone to jump out. Then she dropped to her knees and looked under the bed. "What the hell?" She made her way through the house, opening and closing doors and looking under every piece of furniture. This went on for what seemed like hours, her looking in places she'd already checked. She even made sure the locks were still secure on the front door.

"That boy." She looked around like she expected to see Paul. "I knew he was up to something bad." She shook her head, then pulled her cell from her leggings pocket. Paul watched over her shoulder while she punched in numbers.

"I told you she'd call the detectives. She just dialed 911."

Then everything went black.

Her Turn

Ronita

I settled my golden griffin in the meadow and dismounted. Cato climbed off behind me. He had insisted he wanted to see Odessa get her wings. She was different from all the others. We had been on a journey together, so I understood his need.

The moment Odessa saw us, she charged forward. She'd never worn a bigger grin.

"I did it, Princess Ronita. I did it." She swung her arm wide. "I kept us all together. Paul made his amends." She turned around and waved Daniel and Paul to her.

"Well done, Odessa. I knew you could. I never doubted you." I reached for her hands and squeezed them.

"I'm so happy for you." Cato threw his arms around her. "I had to be here to see this moment."

"You mean," Odessa started, then stopped to swallow. "You mean my journey is over?"

"It is. You've done a fine job."

Daniel waved his hand. "And how about us? Is our journey finished, too?"

"Yes, it is." I nodded. I touched Daniel's shoulder and he was on his way. Then I touched Paul's. "Well done, Paul." Then he was on his way.

Alone in the meadow with Cato and Odessa, I faced her. "This has got to be the hardest one, I'll ever do."

"Will we ever see each other again?" Odessa asked.

"No, Odessa. You're leaving the Interruption now. The place you're going is more beautiful than anything you could have imagined. That's what you deserved." I kissed her cheek, and then she was gone.

ABOUT THE AUTHOR

Jacki Kelly has written dozens of short stories and several books. She lives in the North East with her husband. When she's not writing, she's painting or planning. She loves hearing from her readers so please contact her and follow her on social media.

Connect with her online:
https://jackikelly.com
https://facebook.com/jackikellyauthor
https://facebook.com/jacki'sjoint
Instagram – jackikellybooks
TicTok - Jackikellybooks

And don't forget to sign up for the Jacki Kelly newsletter at - https://jackikelly.com

If you enjoyed reading The Interruption, please tell everyone you know. Please post a review for other readers on your favorite reading forum.

www.ingramcontent.com/pod-product-compliance
Lightning Source LLC
Chambersburg PA
CBHW040519170726

48295CB00012B/259